An Uncertain Ceremony

AN ARABELLA STEWART HISTORICAL MYSTERY-BOOK 8

D.S. LANG

D.S. LANG

Ebook ISBN: 979-8-9867318-6-5

Paperback ISBN: 979-8-9867318-7-2

Cover Designer: Karen Phillips

Editor: Alyssa Colton

Chapter One

As her best friend, Ida Byington, pulled the Buick roadster on to the main highway, Arabella Stewart leaned back in the passenger seat. Usually, a Monday morning in mid-March was nothing special, but this one was exceptional. While the weather was typical for early spring, chilly and damp, Bella felt as if she was floating on a cloud in the bluest of skies. "I can hardly believe we're going for the final fittings on our wedding gowns."

"Neither can I," Ida agreed, "or that we'll be wearing them in five days for the ceremony."

"Two ceremonies, really," Bella added.

Ida grinned, but kept her attention on the road. "I'm so glad we're having a double wedding. Preparing has been twice the fun."

"It's been wonderful, and things are almost set. We only need to decorate at the end of the week. Your parents are kind to provide fresh flowers. At this time of year, they aren't easy to get in Ohio," Bella said.

"They'll drive to Cleveland on Friday morning to pick them up at a greenhouse. Mother wants us to have the freshest, prettiest blooms for decorations and our bouquets, so she'll look them over carefully. When they get back, we can finish everything."

"Jax and Griff will pitch in with last-minute preparations."

"Both of them have done a lot already," Ida said. "Of course, Griff won't be busy until the season starts at the resort, and Jax has spent all of his free time pitching in."

"They've been willing to do whatever we need," Bella agreed. Their intendeds were as enthusiastic as the two young women themselves. Although fewer than fifty people would attend the celebration, both Ida and Bella wanted everything to be perfect. Since some guests were coming from a distance, preparing rooms and planning menus for the long weekend were crucial. So was providing activities on the days before and after the weddings. The resort staff pitched in whenever and wherever necessary. Bella's heart lifted when she thought about all the extra effort the employees had made. They were like family to her, and each was excited about the big day.

One was the most enthusiastic. Ida's betrothed, Griff Biggins, was the golf professional at Ballantyne, the resort owned by Bella and her business partner, Mac MacLendon, who was also a pro. More than that, Mac was her honorary grandfather, and someone she had known her entire life. Although Bella's fiancé, Jax Hastings, had been a fixture at the resort during their growing-up years, he had become the local constable after the Great War. Being a golf pro had been his dream, a dream that had perished in the trenches of France. Her brother Matt, Jax's best friend, had died there, too. For a time, the once close bond between Bella and Jax had seemed to slip away. During their last meeting overseas, he had acted like a stranger. His demeanor had slowly warmed, and finally, the pair had started courting. Now, they were about to wed.

After returning from her service as an Army Signal Corps operator in December 1919, Bella had helped Jax with seven homicide investigations, the last of which had seen him wrongly charged with murder. In the end, the killer was found, and Jax had returned to his job as Moreley constable. Over the last two-and-a-half months, peace had reigned. With only five days left before they wed, Bella felt increasingly relaxed. As time passed, the likelihood of a serious crime taking place diminished. Inwardly, she chastised herself for fretting. Past complications and concerns should not affect her now. She released a pent-up breath.

"You sound like an enormous weight has been lifted off your shoulders." Ida shot Bella a sidelong glance. "Last year was hectic for you and Jax, but there's been a lull in the chaos since Christmas."

"Thank heavens." Bella shifted to study her friend's profile. "You were involved in several of those cases."

"But not nearly as much as you were," Ida replied, "and I wasn't around for the one in September at all." A shudder rippled through her. "Frankly, I'm glad I didn't know until the case ended that both you and Jax went undercover. He always says you're intrepid, and I agree, but I hope your last investigation is behind you."

For a long moment, Bella pondered the observation. Although she didn't want anyone to die, Bella enjoyed searching for clues and piecing them together. Most of all, she loved working with Jax. Warmth spread through her. No, most of all, she *loved* Jax. And he loved her.

Ida's voice broke into Bella's reverie. "Since you didn't answer right off, I'm guessing you'd like to keep playing amateur sleuth.

You're certainly good at it. Not that you don't have enough to do at the resort." Ida expressed a valid point.

"I like detective work," Bella admitted, "but you're right about Ballantyne keeping me busy. Married life will, too."

A giggle escaped Ida. "Of course, and it's about time."

Bella moved her focus to the passing scenery. "I can't argue with that sentiment." Jax had been her brother's best friend, her childhood buddy, her girlhood crush, and her sometimes college escort, before the war and misunderstanding had put a wedge between them. Last spring, they had cleared up their differences, gotten on a solid path, and started courting later in the year. She touched the sparkling ring on her left hand. Soon, a gold band would join it. Her pulse raced at the thought.

Ida turned off the road into a long drive leading to a three-story Victorian house. After pulling to a stop under the portico, she surveyed the structure. "This place seems big for one person. Every time we come out here, I wonder why anyone would live in it alone."

"It is an enormous home. Mrs. Lackner grew up here but left before I was born. I know she had a brother and sister. And parents, too, of course, so it was filled back then. Both of her siblings died in childhood from scarlet fever. Their father, who was the town doctor back then, evidently brought the disease home. He had a heart attack not long after their deaths. Possibly related to being sick himself. I'm not sure. My mother and grandmother said that was when Mrs. Lackner started sewing to help her mother pay the bills." Bella paused briefly. "I sound like one of the town gossips, but my grandmother was acquainted with the family and always found it sad that three of them died within one year."

"It is," Ida agreed, "but you're hardly gossipy. It seems funny, Mrs. Lackner stayed away for years, but she's so reserved that I haven't asked why she went away or returned." Ida chuckled. "I haven't pried since she chastised me for being snoopy."

Bella couldn't repress a grin. Her chatty friend had run into a stone wall with Mrs. Lackner.

"She's a private person. Townsfolk who knew her years back thought she left to get married, but no one seems to know much about how she met the man, who he is, or where they lived. Her return has evoked gossip because folks wonder why she waited to return, since her mother died of Spanish flu in 1919." A slight chill rippled through Bella. Both of her parents had also succumbed to the terrible disease, which had hit the area hard. With effort, she brushed off the painful memory.

"You mentioned the house being empty for two years, when we came for our first fittings," Ida observed.

"It was. No one knows why Mrs. Lackner waited to return or why she didn't sell the house. Moreley is in better shape than when I first got home. Only a couple of houses are empty now, and they'll likely sell soon." Bella opened the car door and slid out. "We better go to the front door and ring. She's making another wedding gown and said the bride is coming today, too, so we don't want to be late."

Ida jumped out and joined Bella at the base of the porch steps. "I can't wait to see the dresses and try mine on again." A light flush rose in her cheeks, while her hazel eyes sparkled. "It's exactly what I wanted."

Bella's anticipation matched her friend's zest. "Me, too." Although she had originally planned to wear her mother's gown, Bella had been swayed by Ida's desire to don more modern attire. The young women mounted the stairs and rang the bell. When no one answered, she shrugged and tried again. After a few moments passed, she turned to Ida. "The housekeeper is off today, but Mrs. Lackner expects us, and she made a point of telling me about keeping to a tight schedule."

"Maybe she's still upstairs puttering with our gowns."

"Maybe so." Bella shifted from one foot to the other. "It isn't at all like her to keep us waiting."

"It certainly isn't. The woman is punctual, and she expects her customers to be."

Bella tried the doorknob. Finding it unlocked, she said, "Let's step into the foyer and call out for her."

After nodding, Ida followed Bella into the house. The spacious entry held a round oak table with a Tiffany lamp. Every time she walked inside the lovely home, Bella admired the light fixture. Even now, in mid-morning, it was lit. The warm, colorful glow enchanted her. Her friend's voice broke into her reverie.

"Someone tracked mud inside." Ida gestured toward the back hall and the wide, winding staircase. "And even up to the second floor."

"How strange." Bella looked around. "The mess goes toward the kitchen. Mrs. Lackner is fussy, and so is the housekeeper. I can't believe either one would allow this."

"Mrs. Lackner mentioned getting new materials. Maybe the deliveryman hauled them to her workroom."

"Possibly," Bella agreed, "but she won't like him tracking mud all over, especially when Mrs. Marren is off until tomorrow." The housekeeper always took Sunday through Tuesday morning as her *relief*, as she termed it. As persnickety as Mrs. Lackner was, Bella understood why. She would need a respite from the demanding employer, too. Keeping up the sprawling house had to be arduous work, but the mahogany stair rail always shone, as did the woodwork at ceiling and floor. Although she had only been in the front parlor once, Bella never noted a speck of dust any place, and the windows sparkled. Mrs. Marren deserved two days off, in Bella's opinion. But how the woman got everything done was a mystery.

Ida glanced around the area. "If Mrs. Lackner has seen the mud, she's already given him what-for."

"I'm sure you're right. Should we call out or go up?" Bella asked.

"Let's let her know we're here. Otherwise, that will upset her, too."

Bella nodded before loudly announcing their presence. After no response came, she glanced back at Ida. "This feels strange Like something is wrong."

Ida pursed her lips. "I wouldn't enjoy living alone beyond the edge of town in this big house, but your imagination is working overtime. Likely because you've investigated a bunch of crimes."

Bella bit her lower lip to keep from saying that gut feelings were important in detective work because sometimes her imagination got the better of her. That was most likely the case now. "You're right. Let's go up. Mrs. Lackner is expecting us." The dressmaker had converted a second-floor sitting room and the adjoining bedroom into a showroom with a work space behind it.

"True, and I don't want to be chastised for running late."

When Bella got to the landing, she frowned. "The door to her showroom is closed. If she's in the back working, it's no wonder she didn't hear the chime or us calling to her." She moved forward and knocked. Again, no response. "We might as well go in. If the machine is whirring, it'll block out other noise." Bella figured they had tried to announce their presence in enough ways, so she stepped inside. And froze in place. Bits of fabric and lace littered the floor. The pieces, shreds really, were too small to be put on gowns. The silk, satin, and lace resembled costly confetti. When her gaze moved on, a gasp escaped Bella. Three of the dress forms held wedding gowns, gowns that had been slashed to ribbons. Gowns with tiny red spots splattered across them. After a shocked gasp left Ida, Bella turned to her friend, whose already fair complexion had gone stark white. Ida's hazel eyes looked enormous as she stared at the mannequins. Bella must be ashen herself, since she felt as if blood had drained from her head.

"Why would someone ruin these beautiful dresses?" Ida looked from one to another before repeating the process. She gestured around the room. "And the materials aren't salvageable. The same person must've cut them up. Shredded them. But who? And why?"

"I don't know." Bella took a deep breath and struggled to focus. "This is ghastly." She moved closer to the gowns but didn't touch any of them. "These red specks have to be blood."

Ida didn't move. "Are you sure?" The question came out in a hoarse whisper.

"Pretty sure," Bella replied as she continued to look around the room. "Where is Mrs. Lackner?" Apprehension knotted her stomach. Had the woman gone out? "She knew we were coming."

"She might've had an emergency."

Bella did not miss the hopeful note in her friend's voice. "She has no family in the area, or any close friends who might be called to help. Mrs. Marren's Packard is gone, so she's at her sister's house, as usual."

"Mrs. Lackner might've gotten sick and went to see Doc Smedlay," Ida suggested.

"That's possible. Someone might've seen her in town and come out to rob the house while it was vacant." The Tiffany lamp, one of the most expensive items, was in its usual place. Were there other valuables on site? If so, how would someone know? Mrs. Lackner never entertained, and she showed little of her home to customers. Perhaps, deliverymen saw more rooms. And she had hired help to redo the dressmaking suite.

"You don't look or sound convinced," Ida said.

Bella turned toward her friend. "Maybe working on murder cases has made me suspicious, but this all seems very odd."

"It does, but I remember the housekeeper saying one bride was upset when Mrs. Lackner couldn't make her gown. The girl was evidently furious."

"Right. Mrs. Lackner didn't have enough time to make more dresses, and Mrs. Marren didn't want to say who was angry and I've heard no town talk." Bella looked around the room again. "Some shreds are colors, so they must be from attendants' gowns."

Ida pointed to the rack in the corner. "You're right. The bridesmaids' dresses are ruined, too."

Bella struggled to make sense of the scene. "Most folks know Mrs. Marren is gone on Mondays. If Mrs. Lackner was seen in town, especially at Doc's office, someone could've come out and robbed the place. But that doesn't explain why the gowns are destroyed."

"No, it doesn't." With a shrug, Ida stepped toward the door at the far end of the showroom. "Let's look at the work area. Maybe there's a safe in there that we never noticed."

Bella went into the adjacent room before halting in her tracks. A gasp escaped her, and she put both hands to her mouth. Mrs. Lackner was on the floor with a veil wrapped around her neck. Bella's veil. Queasiness assailed her. "Oh, no." Her voice was a thready whisper. She felt, more than saw, Ida come to a stop beside her.

For several seconds, Ida simply stared at the body. "Do you think she's dead?" Her friend's voice was as hushed as Bella's had been.

"I can't be sure." After a long inhalation, Bella tiptoed toward the dressmaker. She stopped a few feet away. Closer inspection increased her horror. The dressmaker was not breathing, and her lips were blue. "She's gone."

"How can you be certain?"

Again, Bella breathed deeply to gain control. "My veil is tied around her neck, and one end is shoved in her mouth. She doesn't appear to be breathing, and her color is odd."

"What?" Ida's question resonated with shock and revulsion.

When Ida started forward, Bella put out her arm. "We don't want to disturb fingerprints or other evidence. We need to get out of here and call Jax."

"All right." Ida's attention remained on Mrs. Lackner.

Bella felt as shaken as her friend looked. With a trembling hand, she grasped Ida's elbow. "Let's go."

When they got to the foyer, Ida turned to Bella. "Maybe we shouldn't touch the telephone with our bare hands."

On trembling legs, Bella led the way to the wall instrument hanging near the kitchen. Before calling, she extracted two linen handkerchiefs from her pocketbook before putting one on the earpiece and another on the crank. Her palms were sweaty as she made the call. Within moments, the operator came on the line. After Bella told her how to direct the call, Jillian Quentin, the clerk in the constable's office, answered. When the girl asked about the wedding, Bella redirected the conversation. "I need to talk to Jax. Or Nolen or Newton, if he's not there. It's really important. Please hurry." Urgency underscored her words.

"Jax is available. I'll get him," Jillian replied in a rush.

Less than a minute passed before his reassuring baritone came over the line. "Are you all right? Jillian said you sounded upset."

Relief flooded Bella when she heard his voice. Nolen Rogers and Newton Grawley were capable deputies, but she wanted to speak with Jax. She wanted him to come to the scene. Bella had seen other dead people, even murder victims, but this death struck too close for comfort. The image of her lovely veil used as a weapon rose like a wraith in her mind's eye, and Bella blinked hastily to focus on her surroundings. "Ida and I are fine." Physically, they were. One glance at her friend showed Bella that neither of them had recovered emotionally. How could they? "We had an appointment to see Mrs. Lackner for our final fittings. But no one answered the door, so we went in and upstairs. The showroom is wrecked, and she's dead." Her words came out in such a rush that Bella had to gasp for air when she finished.

"Mrs. Lackner died. How? A fall? She seems young for a heart attack or such."

The confusion in Jax's deep voice led Bella to take another breath and try again to explain. "All the gowns are completely ruined, shredded with blood spatter on them, and Mrs. Lackner is dead. Murdered, most likely, since my veil is around her neck and in her mouth." As dizziness assailed her, Bella leaned against the wall.

"You're in the house?" he asked.

"Yes, but we can wait on the porch. We touched nothing in the rooms or around her body."

"I didn't think you would," Jax replied. "Nolen is here, so we'll both be out in a few minutes. You and Ida might want to sit in the car until we arrive. You'll be warmer and safer."

"I'm sure the killer is gone," she said.

"I'll feel better if you're out of the house."

"All right," she agreed. "Please hurry, Jax."

"I'm on my way, Bella."

The simple statement alleviated her distress. Jax was coming.

When Jax pulled into the driveway, he saw Bella scramble out of the Buick roadster, and the tension eased from him. Since getting her call, he had been a bundle of frayed nerves. Despite her assertion that the murderer was not on the premises, there was no way to be sure. When he reached her side, he lightly clasped her slender shoulders. "Are you really all right?" He searched her lovely features for some sign. The glow was gone from her complexion, leaving her cheeks pale. Although Bella was courageous, finding a murder victim was a shock to anyone. But had the dressmaker been killed? Or could her death be an accident? Bella was an experienced amateur sleuth, but even the most skilled detectives could be wrong at first glance. Maybe the woman had accidentally tangled herself in the veil and fallen. He hoped so. Starting a murder investigation five days before their wedding was an ugly, unwanted complication.

Bella nodded. "We're fine. I think the killer was long gone when we arrived."

"We didn't hear or see anyone," Ida put in. "No vehicle, either."

By then, Nolen Rogers, a camera in his hands, joined the group. After exchanging greetings with the two women, he turned to Jax. "Are we going in now? Do you want me to take pictures of the house's exterior or just the interior?"

Jax let his hands drop to his sides. Despite the grim situation, he smiled. His deputy had been studying and practicing how to use their newest equipment since the camera's arrival last month. Now, unfortunately, Nolen could employ his new skills in a case. "Some exterior shots would be great. But let's all go inside first."

"What about getting fingerprints?" Nolen tapped the bag slung over his shoulder. "I brought our kit."

"You can check for those, too. In the meantime, we all need to be careful about touching things." Jax turned back to Bella. "Will you show us the way?"

"Of course. Her workroom and display area are at the top of the stairs." Bella glanced at her best friend. "Do you want to wait in the car or in the foyer?"

"I'll wait right here, and I won't disturb anything." Ida wrapped her arms around her slender waist.

Jax glanced from his fiancé to her friend, who looked paler than Bella. "I called Griff, and he'll be here shortly. You can ride back to Ballantyne with him. Bella and I will bring your roadster later, if that's good with you. Then, Nolen can use my Chummy."

"That's fine." Ida shivered as she spoke.

"Will you be all right here for a few minutes?" Jax asked with concern.

As Ida nodded, her wavy auburn hair, cut in a fashionable bob similar to Bella's, flipped back and forth around her still ashen face. "Seeing Mrs. Lackner and the dresses...it shook me up."

"It did me, too. Terrible sights." Bella laid a hand on her friend's arm. "We won't be upstairs for long."

A faint smile touched Ida's lips. "I'll be good here."

Bella led the way to the second floor and past a door standing ajar. When they entered the area, Jax understood why his betrothed and her friend were shocked. The display room was in shambles. Dress forms laid on the floor, while several gowns were shredded and soiled. Lace and fabric remnants littered every surface. For long moments, he stared at the muddle.

"What a horrible mess." Nolen's voice was a murmur.

"That it is," Jax said.

Bella gestured with one hand. "Look over there. I didn't notice before, but there's a piece of paper stuck to one of the design boards."

"The two of you stay here, and I'll see if I can read it without disturbing anything." Jax carefully wended his way through the debris. The note wasn't folded, so reading the contents was easy. *Cancel the wedding or regret it.* Fresh alarm clanged in his head.

"What does it say?" Bella asked.

Jax swiveled to face her and Nolen before repeating the note.

"Does it say which wedding?" The color had again fled Bella's face, and her dark eyes were wide with dismay.

"It doesn't." He aimed to sound confident and reassuring, but the note shook him to the core. As a lawman, he might be the target of the missive. Because Bella had worked with him on several cases, she could be, too. That put their wedding in the bullseye. Or someone else might be targeted. But who? Jax picked his way back to her side. "I see several bridal gowns. Do you know who else is getting married soon?"

"Vera Placette's wedding is Friday evening," she murmured. "Her gown should be finished, and she has an appointment today. Other ceremonies are scheduled over the next few weeks, but Mrs. Lackner wasn't ready to start more projects until after this coming weekend, from what she told us. She does all the work herself."

"I see," Jax said.

"Why would someone kill Mrs. Lackner and create all this havoc? Why leave a threatening note?" Bella asked.

"I wish I had some idea, but I'd like to see the body." Jax pointed to the door on the right side of the room. "Is she in there?" Perhaps, an examination of the crime scene would point them in a particular direction and move the case forward.

"Yes," Bella replied. "I'll show you."

Jax and Nolen followed her into the adjoining space. When Bella stepped aside, the crumpled body was clearly visible. Jax crossed to where the victim laid and dropped to one knee. Nolen came to stand behind him. "The veil is tied around her neck with the end stuffed into her mouth," Jax observed.

"That's what I told you on the telephone," Bella said.

He glanced at her. "I remember, but we need to make notes."

"I brought a pad and pencil." Nolen retrieved the items from his jacket pocket, but his attention remained on the dead woman. "She must've been strangled."

"Look at the palms of her hands," Bella said. "There's blood. And the red specks on her clothes could be from those wounds. I didn't notice before."

Jax followed Bella's gaze. Slight cuts were visible on the dressmaker's palms, while some tiny scarlet spots soiled her otherwise pristine white shirtwaist. "You're right. Maybe she caught her killer destroying the dresses and materials in the other room, and they fought." As he spoke, Jax tried to put the few pieces together. Every investigation was a puzzle needing to be filled in. This one, like most, had a lot of sections to flesh out.

"That seems likely, since there are always a couple pairs of shears in the display area, and another pair in here. Mrs. Lackner might've tried to get them away from the attacker, and a fight ensued," Bella said.

"Why not stab her?" Nolen asked. "Why use a bridal veil?"

Jax shook his head. "I don't know. Both strangling and stabbing are personal crimes. Both require force from the perpetrator."

"Probably a man," Nolen suggested.

"Probably, but a strong woman might've done it." Jax turned to Bella. When he addressed her, he softened his tone. "You're sure it's yours?"

"Very sure. Ida and I both chose trendy veils, ones that drape from the top of the head down the front, like a flowing scarf. Mine is edged in satin. All the others have lace trim." Her face remained pasty pale, making her brown eyes appear even darker than usual.

Anxiety gnawed at him, but Jax schooled his features. Bella was naturally upset. She didn't need to know how worried he was about the situation. "It probably isn't significant. The killer most likely grabbed the nearest one." He tried to inject certitude into the statement, but his apprehension escalated. Using Bella's veil and leaving a threatening note might be crucial clues. If so, who wanted to ruin a wedding and why? Would the person stop with one murder? Jax planned to ensure he or she did, no matter whose ceremony was targeted.

Bella pointed to the body. "I was thinking. Mrs. Lackner always wore a ruby pin, either on her jacket or at the neck of her top. It's gone."

Both men followed her gesture. "She was never without it?" Jax asked.

"Never," Bella replied. "When Ida admired it, Mrs. Lackner said her father gave it to her mother as a birthday gift the year that he died. From the way she responded, the pin had sentimental value. It was the only personal information she ever offered. Plus, it was expensive."

"It could be a robbery gone wrong," Nolen suggested.

"That's a possibility." Jax turned to Bella. "Do you see anything else missing?"

She shook her head. "No, but it was the only piece of jewelry I ever saw her wear."

"All right," he replied. "We'll be on the lookout for other signs of theft."

Although Bella looked skeptical, she nodded. "I suppose you need to call Doc Smedlay, so you can tell him what happened, and he can examine the body."

"We do," Jax replied. Although stricken by the discovery, Bella wasn't so distracted that she wasn't ready to work on the case. Her detective skills had evidently kicked in. Not surprising. "It appears you were right about her being dead for a while. I'd guess a couple of hours, but Doc will have a better estimate."

"Do you want me to telephone him?" Nolen asked.

"Please do. You know to check for fingerprints on the telephone first," Jax replied. "It's unlikely the killer used it, but Bella was careful. We will be, too."

"Yep," his deputy said.

"Tell him what happened, and ask him to contact Mr. Forrester at the mortuary. You and I need to search the scene carefully, so we'll be here a while." Because Jax knew better than to suggest Bella go home, he made an additional comment. "Bella will stay, as well."

A smile lifted her lips. "I'm happy to help."

"You always are." Jax winked at her, and her grin intensified. "And I'm always happy you do."

Bella pursed her lips, but her gaze glittered with amusement. "Not always."

Nolen cleared his throat. "I'll make that call."

"Ida can show you where the telephone is," Bella told him.

Once Nolen was gone, Jax couldn't repress a chuckle. "It's been a long time since I objected to you assisting with a case."

"But a short time since you warned me to be careful."

He crossed the distance between them and lifted her left hand to his lips. After pressing a soft kiss to the palm, Jax released her "I'll most likely be advising you to be cautious until my dying day because I can't bear to have you hurt, and you've come too close for comfort a couple of times. The last one was only three months ago. It's not something I'll forget."

She lightly clasped his jaw. "You're the one who was knocked unconscious during a case, not to mention when you got shot, or the time you were drugged and kidnapped."

He gently wound his fingers around her wrist. "Which is why you warn me to take care, and it's a two-way street." For a moment, Jax scanned her face. "I admit I didn't want you involved in the first couple of cases, but I've welcomed you—

assistance since then. Especially in the past two investigations, when you came to my rescue both times."

She bit her lower lip. "I wish you didn't have such a dangerous job. I was hoping your surgery would fix your arm."

Jax let his hand fall away as he stepped back. The operation, to repair damage to his bicep from war wounds, had gone well. "It's better than it was. Turns out the damage wasn't as bad as the docs in France figured."

"I'm glad." After a long sigh, Bella glanced at Mrs. Lackner's body. "Do you think the note referred to our wedding? I know you said using my veil isn't necessarily important."

"How would the killer know it was yours?" Jax harbored a fear the culprit might have, but he didn't want to upset Bella. He'd bear that burden alone.

A shrug moved her slender shoulders. "I suppose he or she wouldn't."

When Bella looked back at the body, Jax followed her gaze. "It looks beautiful. I know it must be tough to see it used as a weapon." He slid his arm around her shoulders, and she relaxed against him.

"Ida talked me into wearing a fashionable gown, instead of my mother's dress. It was stunning and modern." She put one hand to her mouth.

"I'm sorry."

Bella swiveled to look up at him. "It's unnerving, but Mrs. Lackner being killed has to be our focus. I hope we can find her murderer quickly."

Her obvious attempt to overcome shock and dismay didn't surprise Jax. Bella was one of the strongest people he had ever known, but he wished she hadn't come upon this crime scene. He wished the crime hadn't happened. "We'll work hard to solve the case. Let's see if we can find any other evidence in this room." Jax reluctantly released her and searched for more clues.

A quick survey of the workroom and the adjoining closet turned up nothing else of interest, so they returned to the display area. Bella went to where the note remained on the board. "We need to contact the other bride. When Ida and I scheduled our fittings for today, Mrs. Lackner mentioned Vera Placette having an appointment this afternoon."

"So, you said. We don't want her to see this mess. I wish you and Ida hadn't." Jax again scanned the damaged gowns. "I won't ask which one was yours, but it doesn't look like any of them can be salvaged."

"They can't. I feel sorry for Vera, who's young. This will probably unnerve her."

"You and Ida are hardly old," Jax commented.

Bella's expression softened. "No, but we both served as operators during the war. We've had more arduous experiences than she has and more experience with death."

His heart seized as he recalled his worry for Bella during those months when they had both been in France. While, Bella had not been in the trenches as he had, she'd been close to the front as an Army Signal Corps operator. Too close for his comfort. More than once, word had reached him about enemy mortar shells striking close to her station. His only question had always been about the safety of the operators, because Bella was one of them. Those dangerous days were behind them, so Jax shook off the past and focused on the present. Nothing gets you down for long. A lot of ladies would be inconsolable." Jax made the observation with pride and love. Bella was an amazing woman and he was beyond lucky she'd agreed to marry him.

"Getting upset doesn't help, although I'm terribly disappointed, and so is Ida. Mrs. Lackner's death is a much bigger issue in the scheme of things." A slight smile played across her lips. "Besides, we'll still get married on Saturday."

"We definitely will, and nothing can change that." After all their ups-and-downs, Jax would move heaven and earth to ensure their marriage went forward, as planned.

"What if the killer isn't caught by the weekend?" Bella's gaze met his. Fringed by ebony lashes, her deep brown eyes were one of her most striking features.

"I hope he is, but we're still getting married. I may need to go back to work afterward, if the case remains open." Dismay filled Jax, but he had to be honest. "We might end up spending our honeymoon in one of Ballantyne's cottages instead of at Niagara Falls. We can take a trip in the future."

"I suppose, but we can solve this murder within a few days. I'm sure of it."

Bella's confidence lifted his spirits. They could, but would they? Pressure built as Jax considered what lay ahead with the investigation. "Then, we better finish searching the crime scene because we have a lot more to do."

Chapter Two

B ella surveyed one side of the room while Jax took the other. "There's a veil back in the far corner. I can get there without disturbing other evidence."

"Go ahead," Jax replied.

After picking her way through the mess, Bella went to the headpiece. "It's slashed and soiled. There are partial muddy shoe prints on it, like someone wiped his feet off." Disgust roiled her stomach as she studied the tulle veil.

"Since there's mud in the foyer and on the stairs, probably the killer did it. The tracks looked like they went toward the back of the house. I'll check it out. I assume there's a door near the kitchen."

"There is. It's the service entrance. Mrs. Lackner expected a delivery of materials today. She told us because Ida is interested in some new clothes for the summer." Bella went behind the corner desk. "A couple of boxes are here, so it's possible the mailman who brought them tracked mud in, although she's persnickety. She would've made him wipe his feet."

Jax turned to face Bella. "Mailmen rarely carry boxes inside and upstairs."

"No, they don't, but Mrs. Lackner is demanding. I can see her convincing him to do it. Hounding him into it is more likely."

Jax shrugged. "I'll check at the post office later to see exactly when he was here, and if he carried packages up. It's a long shot, but he might've seen someone on the road." Since Jax knew everyone who worked at the Moreley post office, he doubted one of those men was the killer. But he didn't discard the possibility. He once again studied the mannequins. "A lot of work went into these gowns. Someone had to be furious to destroy such beautiful creations."

A shudder of distaste rippled through her. "I don't understand why anyone would make a horrible mess, and to use one veil like a doormat and another as a murder weapon. It's awful and strange."

"It sure is. I'm going to have Nolen catalog all the evidence here. If you call the other bride and arrange a time for us to talk, that'd be great. What about a run-in with someone? Or her fiancé or parents could have. It's a shot in the dark, but any information would be helpful."

"I'll set a time up for today," Bella said.

"What about Mrs. Lackner? I don't know her too well, since she's only been back for a few months. I vaguely recall my mother going to the shop in town years ago. Any enemies?"

"I don't know of any. That store belonged to Mrs. Lackner's mother. They both worked there for a time. I'm not sure why Mrs. Lackner left town, and she cut off all conversation about the past, like it doesn't exist. I've heard town gossip about her taking off to marry, but no one mentions details. When Ida and I came for fittings, the woman was all business. She is a skilled dressmaker, though. To see all her beautiful work in tatters and her murdered..." A lump rose in Bella's throat, and she blinked hard to hold back tears.

He reached out to briefly clasp her hand. "Take a last look around and see if anything else stands out to you. Then, we'll leave."

Bella went to the desk where Mrs. Lackner kept her appointment book, along with a few office supplies. Alarm filled her as she poked around. "There's always a datebook right out in plain sight." She opened each of the drawers. "It's not here."

"Maybe it's in the workroom," Jax suggested.

"She never had it there, but we can check."

Bella and Jax carefully searched that area. "I don't see it," he said.

"Neither do I, and it's too large not to be visible." She put her hands on her hips. "Why would the killer take it?"

"No good reason, as far as I can see. Newton went out to make the usual rounds before you called. When he's back in the office, I'll have him come out and help Nolen search the entire house. It could turn up."

Although Bella didn't think so, she nodded. Briefly, her attention went to the dressmaker's body, and a shudder went through her. This murder hit deep in her soul. What if someone was targeting her and Jax, and Mrs. Lackner had died as peripheral damage? The idea was appalling.

Jax crossed the distance between them and held his hand out. "Let's get out of here."

Bella, emotion threatening to destroy her composure, allowed Jax to lead her downstairs. In order to focus on the case, she had to regain her equilibrium.

When the pair reached the foyer, they found Griff Biggins. Tall and muscular, the golf pro's usually cheerful countenance was set in grim lines, while his silver-gray gaze was clouded with worry. He had one arm loosely draped around his fiancé's shoulders, as if to ward off any threats.

Everyone exchanged greetings before Jax directed his deputy to list the clues upstairs, photograph the rooms, and dust for fingerprints. "Go through the entire house and see if you find any evidence of robbery." Jax looked from Ida to Bella. "Did she keep much cash on hand?"

Both women shook their heads before Bella responded. "We gave her checks for materials and deposits, since that was her preference. If she has money in the house, I don't know where or how much."

"We'll check and see if there's a safe or some cubby hole," Jax said. "Since Doc will be here soon, I'll bring him up before we head out to talk with the other bride. I'd like to do that before she hears about the murder. I'll call the office and get Newton to come and assist you, if he's back. Otherwise, he'll be out as soon as possible. It's a big house, so searching will be time-consuming."

Nolen nodded and disappeared up the wide staircase.

"I suppose you want to interview me before I leave," Ida, who had regained most of her natural coloring, made the observation.

"I'd like to, if you don't mind," Jax replied.

"Of course not."

"And I'll take notes for you," Bella added.

Jax turned a concerned gaze on her. "Are you sure? If you want more time to regroup, it's understandable."

"I don't. We need to catch the killer as soon as we can, and I want to help." Getting Mrs. Lackner's murderer behind bars was crucial. The woman deserved justice, and three brides, including herself, warranted peace of mind.

"You said the housekeeper is off on Mondays. Do you have any idea where she goes?" Jax asked.

"She has a sister in Boxwood. The two of them often go to a nearby town for lunch and shopping," Ida replied. "Sometimes, they visit friends."

"Mrs. Marren, that's the housekeeper, usually leaves Sunday afternoon and returns Tuesday morning," Bella added.

"Do you know her sister's name?" Jax asked.

Bella shook her head. "Not her last name, but her given name is Heloise. Someone in Boxwood will know her and where she lives, although she's relatively new to the area. They both are."

"Newton might know her, since he worked over there for years," Jax said.

"The two sisters didn't come to the area until August, and Newton moved to Moreley in April," Bella replied.

Jax shrugged. "Then, it's best if he comes out here for a while. We can stop at the office and ask Jillian to call some businesses over there. She was concerned after your call. She's really looking forward to being in our wedding." Jax glanced at Ida and Griff. "Make that weddings." The other couple grinned at one another, while Jax winked at Bella.

His gesture lifted Bella's mood. The solemnity that had marked his demeanor after her brother's death was gone, and Jax was once again the fun-loving boy of their childhood.

"Two weddings and one ceremony with Jillian and Nolen as our attendants. I'm guessing your clerk and your deputy will be next to walk down the aisle," Griff observed.

"It looks that way," Bella agreed. Both she and Jax hoped the young couple, who had been stepping out for several months, would wed soon. As she thought more about the clerk's presence in the bridal party, Bella felt another stab of dismay. "Mrs. Lackner was making Jillian's bridesmaid's dress. I'm not sure when the last fitting is scheduled. The material is rose silk. I didn't see it on any of the dress forms or hangers."

"I didn't, either." Ida's forehead wrinkled. "And I don't recall seeing scraps that color."

"There weren't any. The bits were white, shades of green, and shades of blue." Jax glanced from Ida to Bella. "Does Mrs. Lackner keep gowns elsewhere?"

"Not that I know of," Bella replied and Ida agreed. "We can ask Jillian where it might be stored."

"It's a minor point, but I'd like to know." The sound of footsteps on the front porch interceded before Jax could say more. After a knock, two men stepped inside. "Doc, I'm glad you got here quickly."

The shorter, gray-haired man nodded. "I called Mr. Forrester, and we came in his Autohearse."

The tall, gaunt fellow beside the physician gave a slight bow. "Such sad news. I knew Elsie when she was a girl and was glad when she came back to town, although she's mostly kept to herself out here." His gaze went to Jax. "I hope you find her killer quickly."

"That's our goal," Jax replied. "I'll show you two upstairs. Nolen is gathering evidence, and Newton will be here soon. Bella and I plan to follow other leads, but I'll check back with you later today, Doc."

Smedlay nodded. "I should have a preliminary report by four or five. I already made house calls and only have a few office visits early this afternoon."

"I'll be down in a minute," Jax said to Bella before escorting Smedlay and Forrester upstairs.

"Are you sure about helping with this case?" Ida asked her friend when the trio of men ascended the steps. "I know you've worked on other investigations, but seeing Mrs. Lackner and the awful mess and knowing how much you need to do before Saturday..." Her voice trailed off.

Griff lightly squeezed Ida's shoulders. "When he called me, Jax said the gowns were destroyed."

"They are," Ida agreed. "I'm not sure what we'll do."

The best friends exchanged a long glance. "We'll figure it out," Bella said, although she wasn't sure how.

"You must be traumatized. But you want to go ahead with the ceremony, don't you?" Griff focused on Ida as he spoke.

The slight anxiety in the golf pro's voice didn't come as a shock to Bella. Her friend had been betrothed before the war to a man who perished in France. Although in retrospect Ida insisted she had not experienced genuine love until meeting Griff, he sometimes felt dwarfed by the war hero who had put the first engagement ring on Ida's finger.

"Yes, of course, I do." Ida turned to Bella. "What do you think? It wouldn't be disrespectful, would it?"

"Jax and I discussed it briefly, and we plan to get married this weekend, as scheduled." Bella patted her friend's hand. "We aren't being disrespectful. As sorry as I am about the murder, we don't know the dressmaker very well."

"We don't," Ida agreed. "She's a skilled seamstress but not a friendly sort. From our first meeting with her, she made it clear we ought not to ask personal questions."

"Including where she lived after leaving home," Bella added.

Griff looked askance. "Really? Not friendly, was she?"

"Not at all," Bella replied. She and Ida hadn't discussed the dressmaker's personality with their fiancés, but they had been confounded by Mrs. Lackner's taciturn manner. "Going back to our ceremony, no one will think us callous if we keep to our plans. We only expect fifty guests, including the resort staff and family. Even so, changing everything so close to the date isn't practical."

"I agree. There's no reason to hold up the weddings, especially when a few folks have already planned to travel here. Some may be on their way." Ida chewed on her lower lip. "But what will we wear? There's not another fine dressmaker for miles."

"Even if there was, making two bridal gowns in five days would be a Herculean task." Bella leaned against the curved mahogany handrail and considered their options. One quickly came to her. "When I was growing up, I thought about wearing my mother's dress when I married. It's still in the closet and in beautiful condition." Bella looked at Ida. "I know you wanted the latest fashion."

"I did, but things have changed," her friend said.

"Does your mother have hers?" Bella asked. "They might be similar in style, since the two of them must've married within a few years of each other."

Ida's expression brightened. "It's one thing she kept when my parents sold the house and moved. The last I saw the dress, it was in pristine condition. I'll call Mother and ask about it as soon as I get back to the resort. She may know someone who can make alterations for us."

"Let's go now," Griff said. "We can't help here, and I have some chores at our house."

When Ida beamed at her fiancé, Bella smiled. Her friend deserved happiness. A new husband and a new home. Bella would have the first, but maybe not the latter. Some of her joy floundered as she bid farewell to the couple. Bella and Jax hadn't decided where they would set down roots. In the short-term, they had opted for his family home in town. Bella had not wanted him to part with the last tie to his own parents. Over time, being at a distance—even a minor one—from Ballantyne might be difficult for Bella, especially during the height of the resort season. How would she manage? After suffering two wounds to his right arm during the war, Jax had given up his career as a golf pro to take the job as town constable. Bella had hoped, more for him than for herself, the surgery would fix the major problem. Then, he could work at Ballantyne as a co-professional with Griff.

As far as she was concerned, Jax could have taken the job two years ago. But he'd resisted the idea because, to his way of thinking, a golf pro needed to play well. And he had hardly played the game after returning from France. Mostly due to his injuries. Since having surgery last fall, he could write more legibly, and she hadn't noticed him favoring his arm. Maybe there was hope.

Jax's return cut off her wayward thoughts. "Ready to go?" he asked. "We can call the other bride from my office."

"Fine," she replied before leading the way to Ida's roadster.

Once they were on the road, Jax shifted in the passenger seat so he was facing Bella. "After a cursory survey, Doc thinks Mrs. Lackner died several hours ago, likely from strangulation, which isn't a surprise. The blood spots are probably from her struggling over the scissors, since her palms have shallow cuts."

"The killer must've taken the scissors back to the front room to slash more gowns and material unless they struggled there and in the workroom."

"It's hard to say, but I'm inclined to think he used the scissors to create more havoc. Since we didn't find even one pair, he must've taken the shears with him."

"Too bad because Nolen could've checked for fingerprints." The killer knew how to cover up for himself, which was an additional concern. "But why destroy gowns of other women, and why stop the wedding of a customer? The note indicates that was a goal."

Jax's brow furrowed. "That puzzles me, as well. Maybe he wanted to ruin her business, but that doesn't explain his threat completely. The words make it sound like canceling the wedding will remove the risk of trouble. But which wedding and trouble for who? A bride, a groom, or the dressmaker? She's dead now, so intimidating her would be futile. Did he write the note before finding and killing her? I wish I knew."

"Maybe he didn't realize she was home. Her vehicle is always in the old carriage house. He could've knocked and gotten no response. The sewing machine is noisy, so she might not have heard him. Besides, a fair number of folks know Mrs. Marren is away on Mondays."

He nodded. "Then, the guy came inside and headed upstairs. Or he looked around downstairs to see where she had her display and workroom. Unless he'd been to the house before, he wouldn't have known."

"True, although she told us she hired a couple of fellows to convert the rooms into her business," Bella said. "The showroom had been a small parlor, and she wanted built-in shelves and part of the floor raised. That's where the mannequins are. She also had the men build a couple of screens, so customers could change in private."

"Did local fellows do the work?" Jax asked.

Bella shook her head. "Mrs. Marren mentioned running across the men at a restaurant near Marion. It sounded like they were itinerant workers, not real carpenters and not local. The renovations weren't done until January. Before that, she made do with the rooms as they were."

"So, the housekeeper should know who has come and gone, including the workers. We'll locate her today, I hope. That could lead to a major break. So could talking with the other bride. It's possible the killer only intended to destroy gowns and ruin a wedding," Jax suggested. "But it could be a robbery gone wrong, and there might've been other valuables in the house."

"Which is what we need to figure out. The lamp in the foyer is genuine Tiffany, but it wasn't taken. Mrs. Marren commented to Ida and me about how expensive replacing it would be."

"Interesting, but a glass lamp is fragile. The killer might've been in a hurry after the fact. We don't know that anything is missing, besides the pin and datebook. Rubies are valuable, but not the book." Jax slumped back in the passenger seat. "Until we figure out who's responsible, I'd rather none of the brides is alone."

Bella shot him a sidelong glance. "Including me."

"Yep, including you." His voice was firm.

Suddenly, Jax's actions became clear. "You asked Griff to pick up Ida more out of worry than because of transportation issues. When Newton gets to the house, he could drive Nolen back to town."

"Exactly. I can't dismiss the chance our wedding is the killer's target or that you might be in his sights as a victim. Or Ida. Or Vera."

Although Bella wanted to argue, Jax's contentions were sensible. "I agree to always be with someone. Probably mostly with you, since we're working on the case."

A grin kicked up one corner of his mouth. "I don't mind us being in each other's company most of the time. We will be after we're married, so it's good practice."

The hint of amusement in his tone made Bella smile. She didn't mind that kind of practice, either.

Since returning to his job as constable on January first, Jax hadn't been with Bella as much as he liked. For the immediate future, solving the current case had to be his number one priority. Number two, because Bella would always come first.

Fresh apprehension coursed through him. Could she be the killer's target? But why would someone want to stop their marriage? The two of them had solved several cases together, and all those criminals were behind bars or dead. Was the family member of one seeking revenge? Or could it be a bootlegger that Jax had arrested while he was a Prohibition agent? His heart hammered hard as that possibility rose like a flood tide threatening to swamp him. During his five-month tenure with the Bureau, he had primarily worked one case, while also being in several raids. His identity was known to various bootleggers, some of whom were still free. Jax would call his old partner for information. Even though that scenario seemed less likely than others, one rumrunner had threatened Jax. The man had been tried, convicted, and imprisoned. Had he gotten out? Escaped?

"You're quiet. Are you thinking about the case?" Bella asked.

"I am." Mostly true. Jax shoved the revenge issue to the back of his mind for the moment. "Didn't Mrs. Lackner become any friendlier as time went on?"

"Not at all. She didn't want to discuss where she lived after leaving Moreley, her marriage to Mr. Lackner, why she left here in the first place, why she came back, or anything remotely along those lines," Bella replied. "You know how Ida loves to chat. Mrs. Lackner flat out said she didn't engage in idle talk, but she was aware how small-town folks usually have nothing better to do. Ida was insulted."

Low laughter emanated from Jax. "Ida is from Cleveland. She's only lived in Moreley since the end of last semester." Until then, Bella's best friend had taught and resided at a nearby boarding school. For the past few weeks, Ida had been ensconced in a suite at Ballantyne.

Bella nodded. "Which is what I told the lady. She simply tsk-tsked and asked us both to be less chatty. People in villages and towns have plenty to keep them busy, and you'd think Mrs. Lackner would know as much, since she was raised here."

"True, but if her father was the town doctor, she might've undergone more scrutiny than the average person. That can be hard for a child."

Bella shot Jax a quick glance. "Like being the constable's son?"

He shifted toward her. "I definitely felt like I needed to be on my best behavior at all times. My dad never pressured me, but with him being a lawman and my mother being a teacher, people watched what I did."

"And you did the right things."

"Mostly," he agreed. "You and Matt were, too."

"We also got more than our fair share of attention, yet none of we three felt a need to leave town or judge folks for idle chatter. None of us were ever as aloof as Mrs. Lackner, either." Bella tapped one forefinger on the steering wheel. "Jillian revealed getting the same treatment from the woman."

"Interesting," Jax said. "We'll have to talk with people who knew her years ago."

"Mr. Forrester mentioned knowing her back then."

"He's somewhat older, but he probably saw the town doctor."

"Someone at the school could remember her. The principal is new, but some teachers have been there for thirty or more years," Bella said.

Jax pulled his notepad and pencil out. "That can go on our list for now. Before we see the other bride, we can get more details from Jillian. And there's the housekeeper. Plenty to keep us busy for a while." After tucking his materials away, Jax shifted toward Bella. "What about the wedding plans? Do you need to get back to the resort early?"

"Almost everything, except our gowns, is set. Today, I only planned to go for my fitting. We won't put up the decorations until late on Friday."

He laid one hand over hers where it rested on the gearshift. "I am so sorry your lovely dress was destroyed."

She gave him a quick glance. "How do you know it was lovely?"

A grin lifted his lips. "You make all clothes beautiful, but you told me how much you loved it, and I've heard brides put great stock in their wedding attire."

"Jackson Hastings, I didn't know you were such a flatterer. I make everything look beautiful. Nicely said," Bella replied with a chuckle. "I never realized you were so knowledgeable about bridal gowns, either."

He gently squeezed her hand before letting go. "I've listened to you and Ida, and I've heard Jillian exclaim over the latest fashions for brides. She didn't give me any clues about yours. Was it flapper style?"

"Not at all, but Ida guided me, so we had similar designs in a modern mode. With luck, we still will have stunning gowns."

"If you have to go to a new dressmaker, you'll need to find one soon, won't you?"

"We don't need one, since we now plan to wear our mothers' gowns. Hopefully, they will look good together, so we'll have a similar theme." A moment of silence preceded her next comment. "When I was a little girl, I loved looking at my mom's dress. It's so pretty. I dreamed of wearing it myself until Ida got excited about having the modish ones made. Now, I will wear Mom's attire, and I'll be happy doing it."

"Your mother would be pleased."

"I'm sure she would." A soft sigh escaped Bella. "I wish she and Dad and Matt could be with us."

"As do I." Jax didn't hide his sorrow. He and Matt Stewart had grown up together, played in golf tournaments together, and gone to war together. But only Jax had come home. Pain lanced his heart. Until a year ago, guilt had warred with grief when he thought about his best friend. Jax had found facing Bella difficult while he felt responsible for her brother's death. Last April, he had finally revealed the entire story, and Bella had not blamed him. In fact, she had helped him realize his repentance was misplaced.

In Fall 1918, still recuperating from grievous wounds, Jax had planned to return to his platoon. When Matt had visited his friend in a field hospital, he volunteered to take his buddy's place on the line. Something their commanding officer, and the doctors, had recommended. Looking back, Jax realized he wouldn't have lasted long in the trenches, because he'd been weak and hurting.

And Matt had died. Despite what others believed, Jax had assumed the mantle of blame. For over two years, every thought of Matt Stewart rekindled Jax's guilt. Many nights, he had lain awake in his bed, stared into the darkness, thought of his best friend at rest in foreign soil, and felt he should be there—not Matt. Bella's touch on his arm broke into Jax's mental meandering.

"You look far away. As far away as France."

"You read me very well. I wish your brother was here." His friend should be with them, sharing in their joy. "He always said he was going to be my best man."

"I know." Emotion roughened her voice but, when she continued, a lightness replaced it. "He'd be happy we're finally getting together."

Jax relaxed. "He definitely would." His buddy would be ecstatic, almost as ecstatic as Jax was. That should be his focus, not grief and loss. Matt would not be beside him on his wedding day but his friend was always in his heart...and Matt was in Bella's heart, too. "We haven't talked about a family, but if we have children...if we have a son." He cleared his throat. "We could name him Matthew."

Several seconds of silence ticked away before Bella answered. "I love that idea," she said in a hoarse whisper. "Matthew Stewart Hastings?"

"Perfect." He gently brushed a lock of her glossy brunette hair off her cheek. Cut in a stylish bob, the locks framed her face. While Jax sometimes missed her childhood braids, Bella looked like the lovely, modern young woman she was.

Neither spoke for the rest of the drive. When Bella turned into a parking spot in front of the constable's office, Jax jumped out and went around to hold the driver's door for her before helping her out and following her inside the constable's station.

Jillian, who was at the front desk, looked up with a grim expression on her face. "Do you know who attacked Mrs. Lackner?"

After crossing to stand by the counter, Bella shook her head. "We don't have any solid suspects yet."

"It's so awful," the young clerk said. "I was there Saturday to pick up my bridesmaid's dress, and she seemed the same as usual."

That explained why no trace of the clerk's apparel had been found. Jax pulled his notepad out and handed it to Bella. "We'd like to talk with you and get your impression of the dressmaker and her housekeeper. And anything else that might help us solve the murder. Why don't we step into my office? We can hear if someone comes in or if the telephone rings."

Jillian nodded. "Sure."

Jax let the two women proceed him and indicated they should sit at the big, battered table in the corner. Before Bella took a seat, he helped her with her coat and removed his own before sitting down himself. "You've been out to Mrs. Lackner's house a few times, right?"

"A half-dozen. First, I went with Bella and Ida, so they could help me choose materials and a pattern." Jillian folded her hands on the table. "I was glad to get good advice."

Bella smiled. "Ida is the one with the fashion sensibilities. I only agreed with her."

Although traces of anxiety still clouded Jillian's gaze, she smiled. "I'm so happy with my gown. It's beautiful. I can't wait for Nolen to see me in it." As soon as the last statement was out, color bloomed in her cheeks, and she put one hand to her mouth.

"You'll wow him, no matter what you wear," Bella assured her.

Jillian's blush deepened.

Privately, Jax figured his deputy would propose after the double wedding ceremony, which was another incentive to solve the murder. "I'm sure you'll be lovely in your gown, but what I'd like to know is if you saw anyone visit while you had your fittings, or if Mrs. Lackner mentioned someone bothering her."

"She isn't talkative. In fact, she was all business, wanting me to try on my dress as soon as I arrived. Then, she put in pins and such." Jillian chewed on her lower lip. "But one day, she was flustered by some incident. When I got there, she was hanging up the telephone. The housekeeper was in the hallway, and Mrs. Lackner was telling her not to accept more calls from *that man* again. She planned to tell the local operator not to put him through, too. When they noticed me, they stopped talking. After a moment, Mrs. Lackner said I should go upstairs. Neither spoke until I was out of sight. Even then, they whispered, so I couldn't make out their words."

While Jillian relayed the story, Bella scribbled as fast as possible and mulled over the implications. "How did Mrs. Lackner act when she joined you? Did she still seem upset?"

"Not exactly. She wasn't like herself. You know how she's always reserved, almost stiff, and detached." Jillian focused on Bella.

"I certainly do," Bella replied. "How was she different that time?"

Jillian clasped her hands together and put them to her chin. "She jabbered. Babbled, really. She gushed over how pretty I looked in the dress. Before, she simply commented on the garment, not me in it."

"What about the housekeeper? Did you see her after you arrived?" Jax asked.

"Mrs. Lackner escorted me out, which was also unusual," Jillian replied, "but she still seemed off-kilter. Mrs. Marren was bringing in the mail when I left. She's usually the friendly one, and she was nice but seemed nervous, too. When I went to leave, I saw a man in another vehicle at the end of the driveway. He careened on to the main road and was out of sight in a moment. I should've told Nolen or you all this before now..." Her voice trailed off.

Jax shook his head. "The telephone call may have nothing to do with her murder. Just to cover all the bases, I'll check with our local operator. She'll know where the call originated. What day was it?"

Jillian's brow furrowed. "Two weeks ago, on Saturday."

"That'll help." He paused briefly. "Was the vehicle for mail delivery?"

"No, I'd recognize that right off. This was an old, black sedan," Jillian replied.

"What about the man? Did he look familiar?" Bella asked.

Jillian shook her head. "I didn't have a good view because he was too far away. But he wore a hat."

"Did you notice which way he turned at the end of the drive?" Jax inquired.

"Away from Moreley," Jillian said.

"There aren't any houses for a ways in that direction," Bella commented.

"Which means we probably can't get any confirmation," Jax said.

"Even so, it's another detail that could help. As for the call, if the man was at a distance, he would've needed several operators to make connections," Bella pointed out.

A rueful smile tugged at one corner of Jax's mouth. "Again, your expertise is important. We can stop at the operator's house yet today, and you can ask the questions."

"I'm happy to do so." Bella grinned at Jax before shifting toward Jillian. "I agree with Jax. It's unlikely the caller is the killer. Even if he is, you couldn't possibly have known."

A soft sigh left Jillian. "I hope he isn't."

The bell over the main door chimed. "I don't have other questions," Jax said, "so I'll see who's here. If you have any, Bella, you and Jillian can go over them." He got to his feet and left the room. In the outer office, he saw his other deputy, Newton Grawley. "I'm glad you're here."

"When I was making the rounds, I ran into Mr. Forrester. He told me about the dressmaker," the deputy replied. Although a decade older than Jax and with more experience as a lawman, the man fit into the constable's office well. If he felt the slightest regret about his old jurisdiction being combined with Moreley, and being bypassed for the top job, Newton never let it show.

"Sadly, it's true." Jax leaned against the counter and folded his arms across his chest. "Bella and Ida found Mrs. Lackner dead when they went for their bridal gown fittings." He filled in the details before ending with, "I'd like you to go out and help Nolen. There's a lot more to do there. He can give you details. Bella and I are talking to Jillian, who was at the house a few times. We're going to interview one other woman who had an appointment this afternoon. Then, we'll see where things go."

"I'll head out there now," Newton said. "When Nolen and I get done, do you want me to complete the rounds?"

Jax shook his head. "Our top priority is catching the killer. Bella and I may be back before the two of you. If so, we can all discuss our findings and decide how to proceed." Before leaving again, his deputy agreed. For a moment, Jax considered the array of details. As usual, they did not fit neatly into one frame. Not yet. Maybe soon.

Before heading back to his office, Jax placed a call to his former Bureau partner, Mick O'Donnelly. Much to his surprise, the connections went through quickly. After revealing his concerns, Jax felt better. If the rumrunner who wanted revenge was out of prison, Mick hadn't heard about it. But he vowed to find out for sure.

Chapter Three

A few minutes later, Jax and Bella were on the road again. While in the constable's office, she had called the other bride to set up a meeting and to reveal what had happened. "Vera Placette was terribly upset. Her mother wasn't home, and the girl broke down sobbing. I didn't even give any details about the ghastly mess."

"Just as well, if she's already in tears. I've never seen such wanton destruction," he said.

Her fingers tightened on the steering wheel. "That, along with the note, makes it seem very personal. But does the killer have a score to settle with Mrs. Lackner, or was she in the way of him taking revenge on one bride? Or could it be a robbery gone awry?" Although Bella didn't want to use names, particularly her own, she wondered how Jax felt about their wedding, possibly being the one threatened. He had seemed anxious at the house, had even admitted his concern. But how deep did it go? Was he hiding some hunch? Bella felt too close to the situation for her intuition to function well. "My veil was most likely chosen at random." He'd already indicated that. Did he believe it, or was Jax attempting to ease her mind?

Jax cleared his throat. "Probably so, since who else would know it was yours?"

Bella recognized his words as a question. "Only Ida, Mrs. Lackner, and Mrs. Marren knew. At least, to my knowledge. Perhaps Jillian, too. Mrs. Lackner might've shown it to her." Anxiety prickled along her nerve ends, and she decided not to withhold other possibilities. In order to catch the killer, every puzzle piece needed to be on the table. "Vera could've guessed it belonged to Ida or me. As far as other customers, as Jillian mentioned, Mrs. Lackner is usually all business, so it's unlikely she would've shared details. Someone might've asked, though. But she took only a few clients at a time."

"We can find out from Vera, without giving too much away. You never know who she might have told, if she knew. You can handle most of the questions since you already said she's terribly upset. I'm sure her groom will be, too."

His tone and words further intensified Bella's certainty that Jax was more concerned about their wedding being the target than he had yet admitted. After a long, reassuring breath, Bella brought the issue into the open. "You're upset that we could be the ones under threat."

Before answering, Jax laid his warm hand over hers, which rested on the gearshift knob. "I'm concerned. You and I have investigated more than a half-dozen cases. All the criminals are dead or jailed, so they wouldn't be directly responsible. But a relative or friend could want to get even." A sharp exhalation left him. "Or someone from my days as a Prohibition agent may want revenge. It's a long shot, but I called Mick before we left the station. Miraculously, the call went through immediately. He also thinks that angle isn't likely, but he'll do some digging. I'll feel better if he can't turn up a connection."

The last revelation emphasized the depth of Jax's concern. His tone when he mentioned his friend and fellow agent, Mick O'Donnelly, telegraphed tension. Bella understood why. Mick had saved Jax's life during the war and, when Mick's wife had been murdered by a bootlegger, Jax had repaid his buddy by joining the Prohibition Bureau and tracking down her killer. While justice had been served, Mick was left with guilt, regret, and two small children to raise alone. "Mick is still an agent?" Bella asked. "I thought he'd quit, so he wasn't away from his family."

"He has an office job. No field work, so he's with his children every night. He'll move heaven and earth to find out if anyone is targeting us due to my time with the Bureau. He doesn't want me to suffer his fate." Jax's fingers tightened on Bella's hand. "Losing the love of his life nearly killed him, too."

Bella's heart constricted as she thought about Mick O'Donnelly and his little ones. "You won't lose me," she murmured.

"I plan to do everything to ensure I don't, but I'll admit the note shook me up. Although it could be a decoy to throw us off, I'm not taking any chances." He rubbed his forehead with the heel of his hand. "One man involved in the death of Mick's wife threatened me. The guy was sent to prison, but Mick will make sure he's still there."

"Surely, the man wouldn't be released." Alarm formed a lump in her throat.

"No, but escape isn't out of the question," Jax replied. "It's hard to picture him coming here, ruining dresses, and killing Mrs. Lackner. But some criminals like to toy with their victims."

"We'll find the perpetrator," Bella said. "And in short order." She certainly hoped so.

Jax nodded. "I hope Mrs. Placette is home when we get to the house."

Since he was clearly trying to put thoughts of an escaped convict aside, Bella followed suit. "I do, too. Vera was beside herself."

"I remember the girl from before I left for the army. She and her fiancé have been at school in Toledo, haven't they?" Jax asked.

"Both have been studying at Toledo University. Vera isn't in school this term because of the wedding."

"I wonder why she didn't get a dress in the city."

"Mrs. Placette and Mrs. Lackner went to school together, so that may be the reason."

"Probably," Jax replied.

Bella drove past the business district and turned on to a street with increasingly larger homes and bigger lawns. When she got to a two-story Colonial, she pulled into the driveway and stopped near the sprawling front porch. By the time she retrieved her pocketbook from the back seat, Jax was holding the driver's door open for her.

The pair went to the entrance, where Jax rang the bell. Within moments, an older woman sporting an apron and mobcap, answered. "Come in, come in. Miss Vera is waiting for you in the front parlor. Her mother has been out all morning, so the girl is fit to be tied and carrying on something awful. I hope you can ease the young miss's mind." As she spoke, the woman led the way. She gestured to the open French doors. "Go on in."

"Thank you," Bella replied before stepping into the room. Her first impression was that Vera had been weeping nonstop. The young blonde's eyes were red and swollen, while her face was splotchy and wet. Her heart went out to the girl, and she was a girl—only nineteen. "I'm glad you agreed to see us. You remember Jax Hastings."

Vera turned her attention to Jax. "I've mostly been away, since you took over the constable's job. But I saw both of you at

Ballantyne before the war." She wiped at her eyes with a lace hanky.

Bella vaguely recalled Vera coming with her parents. Although the young woman was only a few years younger than Bella and Jax, a sizeable gap loomed between them—mostly due to them serving in France when the girl would have been completing high school. This was apt to be Vera's first experience with sudden, violent death. Bella kept that in mind when she spoke again. "May we sit down and ask you a few questions?"

"This is all so distressing. Knowing my beautiful gown has been destroyed..." Vera's voice trailed off as she wiped her eyes with her already wet hanky. "It's horrible. To ruin my dress...?" Her voice broke.

On the telephone, Bella had informed Vera about the murder. Surely the dress did not take precedence over Mrs. Lackner's death. A quick glance at Jax revealed he looked as perplexed as Bella felt. To clarify Vera's reaction, Bella posed a question. "We're very sorry about the damage, but the murder is our first concern."

For several moments, Vera stared at Bella as if she could not comprehend the words. Finally, she gave a slight nod. "The killer must be the hooligan who destroyed my gown." Once again, tears spilled down her face.

When Bella looked at Jax, he rolled his eyes in disgust. Although she felt the same way, Bella maintained her composure. "We believe so. As I said on the telephone, we want to ask some questions in the hope you know something useful."

"I bet it was Ophelia Upchurch." Vera wiped away the tears and lifted her chin. "She wanted Mrs. Lackner to make her gown, and ones for her bridesmaids—six of them. And the mother of the bride's dress, too. Can you imagine? I also have several attendants, and Mother needs something to blend with us. So does my future mother-in-law."

The revelations surprised Bella but resonated with the house-keeper's observation about an angry bride. Now, Bella knew who it was. "If Ophelia didn't ask Mrs. Lackner before the rest of us did, why would she want to exact revenge? Surely, she understood a dressmaker can only take on a certain number of projects." The dressmaker had been clear about that fact. Although willing to make Jillian's dress, Mrs. Lackner balked at creating a gown for Ida's mother.

Vera chewed on her lower lip. "I don't know. Ophelia can be difficult and demanding."

Bella gripped the pencil more tightly as she struggled to control her dismay. Clearly, Vera was fixated on herself. "Since three gowns were ruined, along with the other dresses, we're wondering if the killer wanted to harm Mrs. Lackner's business, or if the person had a grudge against one of us brides."

"I already told you Ophelia is probably behind the crime," Vera said in a petulant tone.

"What?"

The voice came from the hall, and Bella swiveled to see Mrs. Placette standing there. As petite as Vera, the woman was elegantly clad in a burgundy silk chemise outfit and t-strap shoes. A wristwatch, the newest fad, peeked out beneath one of the dress's wide sleeves. She hurried to her daughter's side and settled on the settee next to Vera. The older woman slid an arm around her grown child's shoulders but focused on Bella. "I heard about the murder from Mrs. Downing at the mercantile. It's awful to think someone would kill Elsie, but why would Ophelia be responsible?"

"We don't know the motive, ma'am," Jax put in. "We're gathering information right now."

"I see." Mrs. Placette narrowed her gaze on her daughter. For several moments, she studied Vera's face. "Did you know Ophelia wanted Elsie to make gowns for her wedding when you asked me to call? As I remember, you insisted I telephone right away, even though it was after eight o'clock in the evening."

The younger woman folded her hands in her lap and bowed her head. "You'd already said Mrs. Lackner was talented. You thought we should go to her."

"And you wanted to have dresses made in the city, even though it would've added a lot of travel time and more expense. Before that evening, you wouldn't hear of having our apparel made here." Mrs. Placette maintained a stiff expression. "Then, suddenly, you had to have Elsie make the dresses. I thought you'd realized that it would be easier for me and most of the others in your bridal party to avoid long drives. Now, I have to wonder."

Silence echoed in the parlor as Vera continued to stare at her hands.

"Vera, you were with some friends that afternoon. Was Ophelia one of them?" her mother asked.

The girl shrugged. "Ophelia and I aren't really friends. She was at the café with her attendants."

A heavy breath escaped Mrs. Placette. "Is that why you wanted to get an appointment scheduled with Elsie right away? Because you aren't friends, and you wanted to make sure Ophelia couldn't have her gown made there." When her daughter didn't immediately answer, she continued. "Tell me the truth right now."

When Vera's head came up, her face was flushed and her eyes glittered. "Being the mayor's niece, Ophelia thinks she's so special. She was bragging about how her wedding would be the most impressive of the year, what with getting married in her aunt and uncle's big house, hiring Mr. Push from the café to make the food, ordering her cake from the town bakery, and having the gowns sewn by Mrs. Lackner. She went on and on about how important it is to support Moreley businesses. That was after I told everyone about going to the city for our dresses. The other girls were taken with my idea until Ophelia started blathering about keeping money in Moreley. I'm sure that all came from Mayor and Mrs. Cawlings."

Mrs. Placette's fine features hardened. "So, you hurried to make sure she couldn't get dresses locally."

Pink splotches bloomed in Vera's cheeks. "She shouldn't have tried to steal all the attention."

"Perhaps not, but you shouldn't have one-upped her, especially not when you involved me." The mother's tone held a sharp edge.

Fresh tears filled Vera's eyes. "I'm sorry, but Ophelia got really mad, and she planned to get even." The girl's attention moved to Bella and Jax. "You should talk to her."

The comment made Bella shake her head. "I don't know Ophelia well, but I hardly think she'd vandalize dresses, steal jewelry, and kill Mrs. Lackner."

"She wouldn't lower herself to actually do those things," Vera hurried to say, "but she's close with Cherry Ammers, whose brother Charley is a ruffian. Ophelia could've paid him and one of his buddies to go out there. She brags about having lots of money. I'm sure she could afford to hire boys to do her dirty work."

"Did anyone else hear Ophelia threaten to get even?" Jax asked.

"Yes, my maid of honor," Vera replied. "She lives in Toledo, but her family has a telephone, so you can contact her. She'll verify my story."

"I'll want her full name," Jax said, "because I'll definitely do that."

"I'll write it down," Vera said. All traces of tears were gone. "Then, you'll know I'm right."

Jax didn't comment on the assertion. "When did Ophelia talk about getting even?"

"A few weeks ago," Vera replied. "She was mad right off and she snubbed me for a while. Then, I was eating at the café with my maid of honor, who was in town for a fitting. Ophelia overheard us chatting about the dresses and stopped by our table on her way out. She said I shouldn't plan on wearing my gown, because something could happen to it."

Alarm filled Bella as she continued to take notes. As soon as she and Jax were alone, Bella wanted to get his perspective on Vera's assertions. For her part, Bella found them both unnerving and compelling. "When did you order dresses?"

"Over the holidays," Mrs. Placette replied. "Elsie had to send away for the materials, so Vera went back to school and finished the semester. We had pictures of dresses from magazines when we went out at the end of January. At the time, Elsie was having the two upstairs rooms renovated, so we only discussed designs and materials. After the first of February, we set up fittings."

"Did you see the men doing the work?" Jax asked.

Mrs. Placette shook her head. "No, we didn't."

"We heard them, though. They made a lot of noise." Vera wrinkled her snub nose, as if in distaste.

"Did you see a vehicle?" Jax asked, ignoring Vera's comments.

"An old black sedan was parked around the corner of the house," Mrs. Placette replied. "I hadn't seen it before, so I'm guessing it belonged to the workers."

"Could you identify the make?" Jax asked.

"I pay little attention to kinds of automobiles, Constable."

"What about the men? Did Mrs. Lackner say how she found them?" Jax asked.

"Elsie told me that her housekeeper recommended them. Both were down on their luck," Mrs. Placette replied.

Bella jotted a few notes before addressing the woman. "You and Mrs. Lackner were schoolmates, weren't you?"

Mrs. Placette clasped her hands in her lap. "We were. She was Elsie Walling back then. Her father was the town doctor. We must've been in fifth or sixth grade when he died. After that, Mrs. Walling had to find work. She was always a talented seamstress, so she opened a shop in town. Elsie helped summers and after school, which she didn't like. I'm sure it wasn't easy, but they kept the house and lived well enough. Not as well as when Dr. Walling was alive, of course. At least not until Mrs. Walling remarried."

The words tumbled out so fast that Bella had a hard time getting the main points down. "Mrs. Lackner left after she turned twenty-one, didn't she?" Bella simply posed a question and hoped Mrs. Placette continued to be chatty.

The woman nodded. "She would've left sooner, but her mother wouldn't hear of it. I was sad, since we were friends, but we grew apart after her father died."

"Wasn't that soon after the other children passed?" Bella recalled hearing tales of the Walling family. *Those poor folks* was how her grandparents had identified them.

Mrs. Placette offered a weak smile. "It was. Scarlet fever was going around the area. Many of us suffered with it. Dr. Walling made many house calls, so it's impossible to say where he got the ailment. Mrs. Walling blamed him for bringing the disease home. Everything changed for them after that. The children, including Elsie, were always beautifully dressed, and so was Mrs. Walling. The best of everything, until Doc died."

"Small town physicians are usually comfortable but not wealthy," Jax put in.

"True," the older woman replied. "More than once, I overheard my mother say Mrs. Walling bought at the shops in town on credit. When her husband passed, proprietors wanted to be paid. Owing money was the reason for her going to work."

"I see," Bella murmured. That was news to her. "I'm sure Mrs. Lackner was terribly upset over losing her siblings and father."

"She was devastated. A few others in the area died, but no family was hit as hard as the Wallings." Mrs. Placette shook her head.

"Did Mrs. Walling and Mrs. Lackner get sick?" Bella asked.

"Only Elsie, who fell ill before her brother and sister. I always thought Mrs. Walling blamed her as much as she did Doc, although she never said so. Once Elsie was well, she was expected to help nurse the other two children and, from what she told me, Elsie shouldered most of her father's care. Unfortunately, the illness taxed his heart, which is evidently what killed him. Their housekeeper helped, but she had her hands full caring for that big house and cooking all the meals." Mrs. Placette worried her lower lip. "Elsie was close to her dad. Sometimes, she went with him on calls. She hoped to be a physician, and her father encouraged her even though very few girls went to medical school when we were young. Not that many attend now, either."

"No, they don't." Once again, Bella felt a mix of emotions. Although she had spoken with the dressmaker many times, Bella had never gotten the slightest hint the woman had entertained lofty goals as a girl. How sad. "Is that part of the reason Mrs. Lackner originally left Moreley?"

Mrs. Placette clasped and unclasped her hands. "Not exactly. More issues arose when her mother remarried a few years after Doc died. The stepfather, Major Birtinger, was a retired army officer. He tried to be fatherly in his way, but he was a strict disciplinarian—nothing like Doc. Elsie wanted no part of him.

He belittled her goal of becoming a physician, which upset her. Nor was he willing to send her to college."

"Her mother and stepfather didn't want her going to a university, either?" Bella asked.

"No, they didn't support her dreams at all. When she wasn't working at the dress shop, Elsie had lots of chores at home," Mrs. Placette replied. "It's such a big house. When Doc was alive, they had a hired couple, and Mrs. Walling often got extra help—especially for their parties."

"I've wondered how Mrs. Marren keeps everything up by herself," Bella said.

The older woman shrugged. "She had a couple of local boys who helped for a time, when needed. I didn't see them, and Elsie didn't give names. After they stole from her, she fired them. There were the two men who remodeled the rooms. They stayed for a while, doing odd work for room and board."

"I saw no boys or men there," Bella said.

"I didn't see any of them, either. As I told you, we heard the workers at first, and saw the vehicle."

"And Mrs. Marren somehow found and recommended them?" Jax's voice held a note of disbelief.

"One was a childhood friend of the housekeeper. Supposedly, the two of them got jobs elsewhere now and then, since Elsie didn't want to pay for more full-time employees. Giving them a place to stay and food to eat kept her expenses down. And they worked intermittently." Mrs. Placette's words expanded on her earlier revelations.

"The pair do odd jobs other places?" Bella made the inquiry.

"Mrs. Marren told me they did. But she gave little information. I wasn't sure if she didn't know or she didn't want to tell me." Mrs. Placette shrugged.

"We need to speak with the housekeeper, so we'll ask her about them," Jax replied.

Bella wondered if the men could be key in the investigation. "Do you know of anyone else who came to the house?"

"Delivery men, occasionally. A couple of local boys, Charley Ammers and Abner Crater, worked for a time. Other clients, of course. Like you, your friend, and your bridesmaid." Mrs. Placette scowled at her daughter. "Elsie couldn't take on anyone else because she worked alone."

Vera avoided her mother's gaze and made no response.

Because Bella did not want the interview to get off-track, she posed another question. "What about why Mrs. Lackner left originally and where she went?"

"She moved out on her twenty-first birthday. Packed two bags and took the train to Toledo." Mrs. Placette pursed her lips. "Although we hadn't been close those last few years, another friend and I saw her off at the station."

"Did you stay in touch?" Bella asked.

Mrs. Placette turned to focus on Vera, who was still wiping her eyes, although no more tears fell. "Elsie wanted to cut ties with Moreley. Last summer was the first she'd been home since leaving."

Jax slid to the edge of his chair. "She didn't come for her mother's services?"

Neither Bella nor Jax had been home when Mrs. Walling passed.

"No, she didn't, but there was no service. Her stepfather died a few years before her mother. I don't know of any other family," Mrs. Placette said.

"Did you talk much with Mrs. Lackner since she got back?" Bella asked.

Mrs. Placette toyed with her watch. "She came here from Columbus but said she'd only been there for a few years. Talking about the past seemed to trouble Elsie, and I didn't want to upset her."

53

The statements didn't quite answer Bella's question. Was Mrs. Placette distracted by the destruction of her daughter's gown? Or by the girl's machinations? Either was possible. "What about her husband? Did she mention him?"

"Only to say marriage wasn't for her," Mrs. Placette replied.

An interesting observation, Bella thought. Was it significant?

"And she said it when I was trying on my bridal gown. Can you imagine?" Vera, no longer crying, pursed her lips as she turned to her mother. "We need to get another dress for me right away. The wedding is Friday, and the one that friend of yours made isn't fit to wear, according to these people."

Bella looked over at Jax, whose expression had not changed although his green gaze glittered. With annoyance? Most likely. Dismissing a constable as part of *these people* would offend many lawmen.

"Vera, we'll find a dress," her mother said. "Right now, we're answering questions in a murder investigation, which takes precedence over your attire."

Vera looked discombobulated. "I don't want just anything. It has to be made, and that takes time. A lot of time for a lovely dress. We should call grandmother and have her schedule an appointment with her dressmaker, and the woman needs to make my gown her top priority. We could be in Toledo by this evening, if we hurry."

The utter selfishness appalled Bella. Vera was a self-entitled crybaby. Not only had she chosen Mrs. Lackner to thwart another girl, she seemed completely unconcerned about the crime. Except to finger Ophelia Upchurch. Just as bad, Vera interrupted the flow of the interview.

"We can call, but her modiste is apt to have regular customers who need dresses and such. Besides, going back and forth to Toledo is time-consuming. There are several seamstresses in

Sandusky. We should probably see about having my gown altered for you," Mrs. Placette said.

"Oh, Mother. I wanted the latest style." Vera sounded horrified. "I can't wear yours. It's old."

Mrs. Placette's hands clenched into twin fists. "We will discuss this after Constable Hastings and Miss Stewart leave." When Vera opened her mouth, her mother put one hand up. "Enough. I said we will talk about it later."

"You and your friend are ruining my wedding," Vera shouted before jumping up and running from the room.

Mrs. Placette briefly closed her eyes before looking back at Bella and Jax. "I'm terribly sorry. Vera is spoiled, mostly by my husband, who has always given in to her every whim. Perhaps being a wife and mother will change her attitude, although I have my doubts."

Bella did, too. People as self-absorbed as Vera Placette rarely changed. Instead, they continued to make those around them miserable with their petty demands and selfish attitudes. "Getting back to the case, you don't know if Mrs. Lackner was divorced or widowed?"

The older woman stiffened and glanced away. A long moment passed before she responded. "For all I know, she could've still been married."

Her voice was so soft, Bella had to strain to hear. Amazement held Bella momentarily mute. "What makes you think so?"

As Mrs. Placette shifted on the settee, her attention went to her lap. "I don't know. Elsie was always rather quiet, but since she's been home...it's hard to explain. She was evasive about where she went from here. I heard Toledo, but she wouldn't confirm it. What did she do for years? I don't know." She pulled a hanky out of her skirt pocket and wiped her eyes. "I'm so sorry she was killed. I didn't like the housekeeper being away from Sunday evening until Tuesday morning. Not that two women alone aren't targets for vagabonds and crooks. Being out there without a man would've bothered me. She kept the doors locked, but someone could've slipped in through a window, I suppose." She glanced from Bella to Jax. "Is that what happened?"

"We aren't sure," Jax replied.

Because they never gave away details before a case was solved, Bella agreed. "We have a lot to investigate."

Anxiety darkened the older woman's gaze. "Do you think the killer is still in the area? We usually lock our doors, but it's a concern."

Again, Bella felt like Mrs. Placette was fishing for information. Was she simply curious? Or did something else evoke her question? The woman's manner bothered Bella, although she couldn't pinpoint why. Since she and Mrs. Lackner had been childhood friends, Mrs. Placette had to be upset, which could explain her words and actions.

"We can't be sure. Keeping your doors locked is always a good idea." Jax paused before going on. "If you'd write the name of your daughter's friend on a slip of paper, I'll call her today."

"Of course, but I never heard anything about Ophelia threatening to ruin Vera's gown," Mrs. Placette said. "My daughter mentioned Ophelia being jealous because she had to go out of town for her wedding party's dresses. Now that I know what happened, I'm sure that's true. But it's hardly a cause for such havoc."

"We'll check every angle," Jax replied.

A glance at Jax revealed his tension, which did not surprise Bella. Considering his history with their mayor, he would be circumspect but thorough.

"Good. Her wedding is next week, and I'd hate it spoiled. Especially after my daughter's antics."

Jax nodded. "Just to cover every possibility, you or your husband haven't been at odds with anyone in town?"

Something akin to shock widened the older woman's gaze. "No, we haven't. We both grew up here and have many friends. We've helped more than a few folks who were down on their luck. My husband kept all his workers on, even when the town went through the long downturn."

"That was good of him," Jax said, "and I know people appreciated it. But I don't want to miss a potential troublemaker."

"We've had no trouble with anyone," Mrs. Placette replied. "Of course, I'll tell him what happened this morning. If he knows of some problem, he'll call you immediately."

"Thank you, ma'am," Jax said.

A shudder rippled through Mrs. Placette. "I hope you catch the killer soon."

"We'll find the person," Jax assured her. "It's only a matter of time."

How much time? Bella wished she knew. Her assertion about a fast resolution was more optimism than certainty.

"Is there anything else you can tell us about Mrs. Lackner's friends in the area or other connections?" Jax asked. "You mentioned Charley and Abner working out there."

"I don't have details about those two. Elsie mentioned them in passing." Mrs. Placette again folded her hands, with the hanky in them, in her lap. "Most of our schoolmates have moved away. Sadly, a few died. Sam Push, the café owner, was two years ahead of us. He was friends with Elsie's brother. Not sure he'd know anything of use now. Elsie was close with two other girls in our class. Ruth Baggeley and Sadie Duckson. Closest with Ruth, and I know the two of them got together since Elsie came back."

Bella jotted the names down.

"Weren't there other customers? Women who purchased dresses for special occasions?" Jax asked.

"Both Mrs. Geneve and Mrs. Cooper had dresses made for the Christmas dance. Elsie did all the work herself, so she limited the number of clients. She kept a notebook with their names and dates of the appointments. It was always on the desk in the front room, where the dress forms were," Mrs. Placette said.

"I saw it when Ida and I went for fittings, but it wasn't out today. Did she ever put it elsewhere?" Bella asked.

"Not that I'm aware of," the older woman replied. "I'm sorry. I don't know more."

"What about Vera's fiancé? Do you know if anyone would want to target the wedding because of some grudge with him or his family."

The older woman shook her head. "Vera met him at college. He's visited with us here, but he doesn't know others in the area, and neither do his parents."

"Thank you. We appreciate your time." Jax stood up. "We won't keep you any longer. If something important comes to mind, please call my office."

"Of course." Mrs. Placette also rose to her feet.

After tucking away her pad and pencil, Bella thanked their hostess. "We can see ourselves out."

When she and Jax were once again in the roadster, Bella turned to him. "We got some information. What did you think overall?"

He shook his head. "We learned a lot. No thanks to Vera, who is a spoiled brat. She was completely callous about the murder. I understand being upset over her gown, but it was her only concern."

"I agree, and her conniving is appalling." Bella paused for a moment. "Ophelia Upchurch is snooty, too. She wanted to have her engagement party at Ballantyne, but we couldn't accommodate the date. She got very upset."

"You never told me that."

"It was before Christmas, when you were under arrest. I didn't know about it myself until later. Griff and Mac handled the issue."

Jax laid his hand on her arm. "Because you were busy proving my innocence."

"That was far more important, and they both knew it. Anyhow, Ophelia can pitch a fit, although she didn't threaten the resort or any of us." Bella chewed on her lower lip. "What if we find information about her getting Charley Ammers to vandalize the place? Maybe they thought Mrs. Lackner would be away this morning. If she caught Charley, he might've fought with her."

"The same scenario could've played out with anyone, but let's not jump to conclusions. First, we have to talk with his mother about the calls, since she's the operator. We'll find out more there, I'm sure. Did you ever see Charley or Abner out there?

"Never," Bella replied.

"It may not be significant, but I want to learn more." Jax released Bella's arm and leaned back in his seat. "I've crossed paths with Ophelia a few times, and she is stuck-up. Since Mrs Lackner sometimes went out on Mondays, it's possible someone thought it'd be a good time to go into the house and make mischief."

"Mrs. Placette knew a little that might help us. Her comment about the datebook increased my concern about where it is What if Mrs. Lackner had another appointment before Ida and I were scheduled, and the killer took the book to avoid being implicated?"

"It's certainly something we have to pursue. With a little luck, Nolen and Newton may unearth fresh facts while they're logging evidence."

"Maybe so." She put the automobile into gear and headed out of the driveway. "What about the other two friends? Miss Duckson teaches second grade, so she's at school. We might chat with Mrs. Baggeley, though."

"Since she's the one who evidently met with Mrs. Lackner most often, we should put her at the top of our list."

"What about Mrs. Placette's reactions? Did you find any of them interesting?" Bella found several issues of importance, but she wanted Jax's unvarnished opinion.

Jax shifted toward her. "Obviously, you did." Amusement lightened his tone. "You always have great insight, so tell me what you think."

"She dropped some odd comments. And she never answered my question about how often they spoke. Instead, she said her friend didn't want to talk about the past."

"I noticed the evasion, too, but why wouldn't she give a direct answer? I didn't want to press her, but it seems like she may know more. Or maybe suspects more."

"I felt the same way. Why wouldn't she tell us outright? That puzzles me," Bella said. "And the mention of hiring and firing local boys before getting two men. I really want to talk with Mrs. Marren about them. Neither Ida nor I ever heard about any extra help, except for the renovations."

"She clearly wanted to know how the killer got in. Was that out of curiosity or because she fears being a target herself? We may end up talking to her again, if we don't turn up something worthwhile elsewhere. I feel like she didn't tell us everything."

"Could Vera really suspect Ophelia Upchurch? Her mother seemed less certain."

"Mr. Placette's business does work for the city. Maybe his wife doesn't want to accuse the mayor's niece unless she's absolutely certain."

"That makes sense, and she could be worried about Vera's wedding being spoiled, since we have no idea whose ceremony was referenced in the note." Bella tapped her forefingers on the steering wheel. "Or the note could be meant to mislead us."

"I haven't dismissed that possibility." Jax slumped back in the seat. "It's early days...hours, really. We may get a key clue yet today."

"Talking to Mrs. Geneve and Mrs. Cooper may prove useful. They're a little older than Mrs. Lackner, but both lived in Moreley when she left, so they could have some insights. Mrs. Cooper always has town news, since she and her husband own the hotel."

"Mrs. Geneve may get tidbits from her husband. As railroad stationmaster, he sees all the comings and goings on the trains," Jax said. "After we speak with Kamalie Ammers about the calls, we can go back to the office and call them."

"Mrs. Ammers seems proficient as an operator, so she should have detailed records," Bella put in. "That's a good place for our next stop."

He nodded. "With luck, Jillian reached Mrs. Marren. Then, we can speak with her, as well." Jax shifted to look at Bella. "You don't have to go with me on all the interviews. I know you need to get your mother's gown out and have it altered. You're about her same size, aren't you?"

"I am, and not much work will need to be done. The flounce at the top was coming loose. That has to be fixed. Ida has to talk with her mother and get the dress. We won't get to altering them until tomorrow." Solving a crime quickly was always important, but this one weighed heavily on Bella's heart and soul. She didn't want to pressure Jax, so she continued with care. "I'll be able to help a few hours each day, at least. You, Nolen, and Newton will have your hands full."

"We will, but solving the case is important. Very important." He released a long, low sigh. "I don't want you worrying about a pall being cast over our ceremony. If I have to work twenty-hour days to get the killer, I will."

His tone telegraphed determination. Bella was grateful because the last thing she wanted on her wedding day was a murderer on the loose. A murderer who had left a threatening note that could be aimed at Jax.

Chapter Four

J ax gazed outside as Bella drove to the Ammers' house. The two of them were finally headed to the altar, and a murder now endangered the joyous occasion. Added to that was the note. Maybe it was a diversion. Maybe not. He didn't know for sure, which added to his apprehension. Until they caught the killer, Jax planned to ensure Bella was safe. Although he couldn't be with her every hour of every day, he could tell his concerns to Griff and Mac, who would watch out for both her and Ida. But her safety would never leave his mind.

The issue with Ophelia Upchurch bothered him. While the girl probably wouldn't wreck the place herself, she might pay for someone to do it. With luck, they could confirm Charley's whereabouts for the morning, which might eliminate one suspected vandal. But would the boy kill? When Bella stopped in front of a neat two-story home, Jax brushed back his worries.

"Here we are," she said.

As Jax hurried to help Bella out of the roadster, he nodded. "Do you want to ask her about the calls? You know more about the process than I do. It'll take her some time to contact the other operator or operators. Won't it?"

She grinned. "You know it will."

A chuckle rumbled out of him. "And I learned it all from you. That's part of why you're a brilliant partner. But only a small part of why."

"Thank you. You're a fine partner, too."

Within a few minutes, they were in the tiny front hall of the Ammers' home, which was situated close to Main Street. Kamalie Ammers, who answered the door, gestured toward the small parlor off to one side. "Cherry will take the calls while we talk. I'm lucky she's old enough to help. It takes a load off with many more connections to make nowadays." She led the way and took a chair across from the settee, where Bella and Jax sat down. "I figured you'd be here, eventually." With one hand, she smoothed back the errant locks of dark hair escaping her chignon.

Although the telephone operator was only in her late thirties, the fine lines around her eyes and mouth made her appear older. So did the dark circles under her eyes. Raising two children alone, one of whom was an energetic adolescent boy, couldn't be easy. "We won't keep you long," he said.

"I'll try to help. I could start a fire. We don't spend time here during the day, so we usually wait until evening."

"Don't bother," Jax replied.

Bella pulled her writing supplies out and laid them in her lap. She offered a smile before speaking. "You've already figured out we might come to ask about the calls made to Mrs. Lackner? Calls she didn't want put through again."

"As soon as I heard about her murder, I wondered about those. She was terribly upset. I keep a log, so I already looked back." Mrs. Ammers leaned forward and put her elbows on her knees. "It was the same man on several occasions, but the first call came through Columbus and the last one was directed from Mansfield to Karston before I got it. I'm not sure about the origin of the others, since Cherry handled them. I can contact the operators and find out what they know."

"That could be very helpful," Jax said.

"I'll do it as soon as we finish," Mrs. Ammers replied.

"Did the man telephone after Mrs. Lackner told you never to put him through again?" he asked.

She folded her thin hands in her lap. "He did. One time, she rang back and told Cherry not to connect him again. Unfortunately, my daughter didn't tell me, and I put him through a few days later. Mrs. Lackner was upset and informed me know within minutes. I don't know if the call lasted that long, because I never listen in." Mrs. Ammers cleared her throat.

"Most operators don't, despite what some people think," Bella put in, but her attention was on Jax.

He couldn't withhold a grin. "Just for the record, I'm not one of them. I know operators respect privacy."

"I should hope so," Bella replied with a smidge of superiority. Operators eavesdropping was an old, and now humorous, bone of contention with them since, in an earlier investigation, he had made the mistake of saying they needed to take care in what they discussed on the telephone for fear of being overheard. Bella had, based on her experiences in France, vehemently objected.

Mrs. Ammers put one hand to her mouth. "I've warned my daughter not to listen, and I hope she's heeding the admonition. I also told her not to put calls from any unknown man through to Mrs. Lackner, and she hasn't since then, as far as I know. But I don't think he's called back."

"I'm sure she doesn't listen, but we'd like to speak with her, if that's all right with you," Bella said.

"Of course. We want to help in any way we can," the operator assured them.

"Tracing all calls back to where they originated will be the most useful information," Jax said. "And the dates of the calls."

"Do you want me to get Cherry?" Mrs. Ammers asked. "I can contact the other operators while you talk to her. I may not get all the details right off. In bigger towns, more than one operator is hired, and they take turns working various shifts. In small places, they all keep their own records like I do."

"We understand," Jax said. "You don't have to give us all the information now. If you jot the details down, I'll send one of my deputies to pick up the notes later."

The operator nodded before scurrying out of the room. When she was gone, Jax turned to Bella. "I have a hunch Cherry might've listened, and I'm not criticizing operators. She's a young girl and could let curiosity overcome high professional standards, despite her mother's admonition."

"I agree." A slight smile played across Bella's lips. Neither said more because Cherry appeared in the doorway.

"Ma says you want to see me." The girl hovered at the edge of the room, shifting from one foot to the other. Her gaze, round with something akin to fear, skittered from Bella to Jax and back. She had the same dark hair as her mother, but it was cut in a modern bob.

"We only want to ask a few questions," Bella replied. "Why don't you sit down?"

The girl's response was to take the chair her mother had used. Cherry perched on the edge, folded her hands in her lap, and stared down at them. "I know I should've told Ma what Mrs. Lackner said, but I forgot. Mrs. Lackner was plenty mad, said I shouldn't be given so much responsibility, since I couldn't handle it." When her head came up, tears glistened in her gaze. "Ma needs the job. She was lucky to get it when the other lady left town. It didn't used to be so busy. Now, it is, and she can't be tending to the telephone all day and all night. I want to help, and I'll do better."

Jax felt a lump rise in his throat. Mr. Ammers had died of Spanish flu, which had cut a wide swath through the area, leaving his wife and two children to fend for themselves. Kamalie Ammers getting the operator job had been a boon, since she could do it from home and make a decent living. "Understandable," he said.

Bella nodded. "We all make mistakes," she said in a kindly voice, "and it's easy to forget when you're busy, which I'm sure you are. People use the telephone a lot these days."

Some of the tension ebbed from Cherry's expression. "I was real busy that day, and I forgot because I hadn't gotten a break for over three hours. Ma had gone to a Ladies' Aid meeting, so she couldn't spell me. That's what we do when it's hectic."

"A sound strategy," Bella said.

Cherry shifted to look at her. "You were an operator during the war, over in France."

"I was," Bella replied.

"That must've been scary," the young girl observed. "And hard."

A smile curved Bella's lips. "Sometimes, it was both."

Jax felt a surge of remembered anxiety. He had not liked her being in danger. Whenever he brought it up, as he had in the past, Bella pointed out he'd been in more hazardous places. Since he couldn't argue, he had stopped commenting. But he hadn't stopped feeling uneasy because Bella would always be fearless. And he would always fret about her safety.

Cherry nodded. "I don't know if I could do that, but I'd like to go to the city and work at a switchboard. After my little brother is out of school, I can. Right now, Ma needs me."

"It's good of you to help her first." Once again, Bella put pencil to paper. "Now, you can answer a few questions for Jax."

"Sure." The young woman slid a glance toward him.

"We need to know if you got any information about the man. Your mother will contact the other operators, but did anything stand out to you? For example, did you hear his name?" Jax asked.

The young girl's attention again went to her clasped hands. "Operators don't always say who's calling."

"No, but sometimes we can catch a few words at the start of a call," Bella observed.

For a long moment, Cherry seemed to mull over the statement. "That's true, and I caught a nickname, I think. Mrs. Lackner berated him right off. He called her *dear heart* before I could disconnect myself. Never heard her use his name."

Was *dear heart* a clue? Mrs. Lackner often took a drive on Mondays. Had she been meeting a man? Stepping out with someone special? Finding out could be important. "That's very helpful," Jax said. "I don't suppose they said anything else in the short time you overheard them."

Cherry shook her head. "No, sir. Nothing else, but the call didn't disconnect last Friday for a few minutes. I can tell without listening. I know I made a mistake not telling Ma about Mrs. Lackner wanting the calls to stop. Really, I forgot. I hope we don't get fired."

"I'm sure you won't," Bella said. "It was one minor mistake. But how long did they talk on Friday?"

"Ten minutes or so. I had several calls while they were on the line," Cherry replied. "The week before, Mrs. Lackner said she'd call and report on us." Cherry folded her hands in her lap. "She was real mad. When my brother found out, he threatened to go out there and tell her off."

"Where is Charley now? At school?" Jax asked the questions in quick succession.

"He should be," Cherry said. "But he doesn't always stay all day. Ma gets real mad, if she finds out."

"But he was home before going to school?" Since the murder could have happened in early morning, Jax needed to know when the boy left. He wanted to find out if Cherry and Ophelia were close, but barraging the girl with questions was apt to be counterproductive.

"Yep," Cherry replied.

"Charley doesn't have a vehicle, does he?" Jax asked.

"Nope. But a couple of his buddies do, and he borrows one sometimes." Cherry pursed her lips. "He ought to be helping with a regular job after school, but Ma babies him. I s'pose I do too, even though he's only three years younger and a head taller than me."

"That's natural enough," Bella assured her.

Jax privately thought Charley needed more supervision, but Kamalie Ammers had her hands full. "Did Charley get a ride today?"

Cherry cleared her throat and glanced away. "He might've gotten one. I was working when he took off."

"What time did you last see him?" Jax knew the question sounded accusatory, but the answer could prove important.

The girl shifted in her chair. "I didn't see him cuz I started work about seven. I heard him banging around."

Mrs. Ammer's return interrupted the conversation. "I got all the connections for the second call. Not many operators involved. The first one will take longer. Seems like it went through several places. Same with the others." She handed a slip of paper to Bella. "I may have more by the end of the day. I'll sure try."

"Thank you," Bella said. "Both of you. Do you have other questions, Jax?"

She must know he did, so Jax nodded. "We were wondering what time Charley left for school this morning."

The color left the operator's face. "Just after seven-thirty."

"School doesn't start until nine," Jax observed. Children from area farms helped with morning chores, so the hours accommodated them. Why would the boy rise and leave ahead of time? Most kids liked to sleep later. Jax had at Charley's age.

"He was meeting a friend, who needed help with his car. I told him not to get dirty, because he's done that before. But he'd rather tinker with some old vehicle than go to class," Mrs. Ammers said.

Since that was hardly unusual, Jax offered a smile. "That's true of many boys his age." He paused briefly before asking his next question with care. "Who is this friend?"

"I'm not sure," Mrs. Ammers replied. "More than one has a vehicle."

"Have you heard about any local boys being hired and fired by Mrs. Lackner?" Jax asked.

She answered quickly. "I haven't. Cherry, have you?"

The woman's daughter again shifted in her seat. "No, I haven't"

Was it possible neither knew Charley had done work for the dressmaker? Jax didn't think Mrs. Ammers would lie to him, but he wasn't as sure about her daughter. Jax rose from the settee. "If either of you think of something else, please call the office."

After mother and daughter offered assurances they would, Bella and Jax left. When they were on the road again, Bella spoke. "You looked taken aback when Cherry mentioned her brother being upset over Mrs. Lackner chastising Cherry."

Jax inhaled deeply. "Him saying he'd tell Mrs. Lackner to leave them alone could be a boy pretending to be tough. Leaving early is another matter. If he didn't help a friend work on his car, that's a cause for concern. We know the dressmaker was killed this morning, but pinpointing the exact time is impossible. It could've happened as early as eight. I want to know about Cherry and Ophelia, but squeezing those questions in didn't feel right at this point."

"I agree. Ophelia paying people to wreak havoc seems possible but not probable, at least to me. But I don't know the girl well. None of that means Charley wasn't out there. Along with a friend, since Charley has no vehicle."

"Unfortunately, you're right. We need to find a lot more, and I'd like to know if he was in school this morning. We can call the principal from the office. I've only met the new one twice, but he seems like a good man. From what I hear, he reaches out to the boys without fathers, so he's undoubtedly spoken with Charley on multiple occasions."

"That's wonderful," Bella said.

"Nolen may have some insight, too. More interesting is the man using *dear heart* with Mrs. Lackner," Jax said. "It's not a lot, but it's a start."

"I was thinking the same things. The endearment is especially intriguing considering Mrs. Placette's comment about Mrs. Lackner possibly still being married."

"Definitely," Jax agreed. "I don't want to go back to the Placette house until we have more details, but I'm sure we'll need to talk with her again."

"I agree, but you have a sound strategy. If we have more background material to share, she may reveal what else she knows. Maybe Mrs. Placette didn't want to say more out of fear. Or for some other reason." A chuckle left Bella. "Or she was nervous, and I'm misreading her."

"I'd bet on your insight any day of the week," Jax put in. "There's something she's not sharing."

"And it could be insignificant, at least regarding the case," Bella observed.

Jax sighed. "Possibly. We'll have to wait and see. What about Cherry's attitude? She hesitated to reply when I asked about local boys working at the Lackner place."

"I noticed. Mrs. Marren will know more." Bella sighed. "So, we head to your office now?"

"Yep. If Nolen and Newton aren't back, I may go to the Lackner house again. With luck, Jillian found the housekeeper. I want to hear what she has to say."

"So do I," Bella agreed.

Within minutes, they were inside the constable's station. Jillian, who was behind the counter, glanced up. "Nolen and Newton got back a few minutes ago. They're in your office, Jax."

He expressed his thanks before asking, "Did you reach Mrs. Marren?"

Jillian shook her head. "When I spoke with Mrs. Ammers earlier to get a connection, she knew about Mrs. Marren's sister living in Boxwood, said the pair speak on the telephone about once a week. I asked Mrs. Ammers to keep trying to reach Mrs. Tillis—that's Mrs. Marren's sister. When someone answers, the call will be put through to us."

"Wonderful." Jax ushered Bella into the other office. Both deputies looked up. "Anyone come to the house after we left?" Jax asked.

"Nope," Newton replied. "Nolen got photographs while I made notes. We searched high and low. Didn't find anything important, so we left the crime scene as is, and locked the place up."

"Good," Jax replied. "We can get everything later today or tomorrow, but I'd like to look at it again." He turned his attention to Nolen. "Have you called over to the newspaper to see about using the black room?"

"Not yet, but it shouldn't be a problem," Nolen replied. "The paper came out yesterday, so they won't need to develop photographs for next week's edition right off. I'll call now. Unless the two of you want to discuss what you learned."

"Let's talk first," Jax said.

In moments, the three men and Bella were seated at the table in the corner. Both she and Newton pulled out their notes. "Why don't you go ahead?" the deputy asked her.

Bella nodded before covering what she and Jax had seen at the house and learned from interviews. "We need to look into the delivery man and the caller. The Ammers boy needs to be questioned, too," she said as wrap up.

"You think Charley could be the killer?" Nolen asked, dismay clear in his tone and expression. "I know he skips school, but I can't imagine him harming anyone."

The deputy's reaction surprised Bella. "How well do you know him?"

A half-shrug lifted one of Nolen's shoulders. "I've talked to him some, mostly about staying in school and helping his mother. I know how it is to grow up without a father, so we have things in common."

"It's good of you to befriend him," Bella observed.

"It is," Jax agreed. "Maybe you should talk with him, Nolen. Casually. I doubt if he's involved, but we have to check out each possibility, and he's the only one we've identified as even a remote suspect. Also, we heard about a couple of local boys working at the Lackner house and getting fired after stealing. I'm not saying Charley is involved, but he could know who was."

Nolen nodded. "Charley is usually at the park with some buddies after school. I'll go by later and see."

"I'll call Vera Placette's maid of honor," Jax said. "I want to know if Ophelia Upchurch really issued a threat."

"Ophelia is full of herself," Newton observed. "She definitely doesn't chat with people below her social level, unless they can help her."

A chortle escaped Nolen. "Moreley doesn't really have social levels, but that girl has had her nose in the air ever since moving here. Which is why her mother sent her to Boxmore School for Young Ladies after one year at Moreley Grammar. Boarding so close to home seems stupid to me, but she was with other snobs."

"The girls aren't all snobby," Bella put in. "Ida went there, and she isn't snooty. She's been teaching there, and I substituted. Most of the girls are pleasant."

Nolen rolled his eyes. "You weren't there much more than a week, and you were mostly busy investigating a disappearance."

"Two disappearances." Jax made the correction. "And Bella is right. Going to a private school doesn't make someone a snob."

A slight flush rose in Nolen's freckled face. "Sorry, Bella."

"It's fine. But I agree about sending Ophelia a few miles away," Bella replied. "She met her husband-to-be through a classmate, so that was her primary goal."

"At least she'll be leaving after her wedding," Newton added. "I'm still surprised she's getting married here. I figured she'd want fancy doings in a big city."

"According to Vera Placette, Ophelia is set on supporting Moreley," Bella said.

"Her uncle is set on that," Jax put in. "Since he's paying for the whole deal, including their honeymoon to Europe, Mayor Cawlings has control. Or so I've heard."

"You've heard, have you?" Bella asked with amusement in her voice. "Constable Hastings, I'm surprised you listen to gossip."

"You can learn a lot that way," he said with a wink and a chuckle.

"True," Bella agreed. "So, we know why she wanted Mrs. Lackner to make her gown. Now, we need to find out if Ophelia was angry enough to hire someone to destroy the other dresses."

"We need better clues, for sure," Nolen said.

"Maybe something will turn up in the photographs." Jax turned to Nolen. "Go on over to the newspaper office. You can take the film along."

"Will do," Nolen replied.

Jax looked from Nolen to Newton. "Did either of you find a date book?"

The other two men shook their heads. "No, and we combed the house," Newton replied.

"A lot of the upstairs rooms are virtually empty. Some have no furniture at all. We looked in the closets and drawers everywhere. We even went up to the attic. Trunks, crates, and such. The trunks are locked, but the crates contained nothing of interest," Nolen added. "Is the book important?"

A shrug moved Jax's shoulders. "Bella says it's always been in the same place, but it was gone today."

She nodded. "Mrs. Lackner always had it in the outer display room, and she never failed to make a note of future fittings."

"Why would the killer take it?" Newton asked.

"Maybe Mrs. Lackner had an appointment before Ida and I were scheduled," Bella replied. "If so, it must've been recorded. Knowing who was coming could be a critical piece of evidence."

"It would be if the killer was on her schedule. Did she keep all her meetings in it, or only ones related to her business?" Newton posed the question.

The query evoked a new possibility for Bella. "I'm not sure. Since she never talked about her personal life, I don't know if she had many social engagements. I've seldom seen her in town. The housekeeper does all the shopping and other errands."

Jax glanced at Newton. "Do you know the housekeeper's sister? Jillian found out her name is Mrs. Tillis."

The deputy nodded. "That's right. Mrs. Heloise Tillis is her name. I'm not acquainted with her, since I'd already moved when she got to town. But a newcomer is always cause for talk." His forehead furrowed, as if in concentration. "Nice lady. Maybe in her mid-fifties. From what I heard, she's a widow. No children. Same with her sister, I think."

Bella listened carefully before replying. "Mrs. Marren told Ida and me about losing her husband. She had a son, but he died in a fire a few years back."

"Where did they come from?" Jax asked.

"Columbus," Bella replied. "Mrs. Marren came to Moreley because Mrs. Lackner needed a housekeeper. Her sister is her only family, and the two of them wanted to be near each other. I don't know why Mrs. Tillis moved to Boxwood. There are still homes for sale here, and the boardinghouse is only full during busy times."

"Interesting." Jax drummed his fingers on the battered table top. "We know little about where Mrs. Lackner has lived. Supposedly, she went to Toledo when she originally left Moreley, and she lived in Columbus before arriving here. Is that how Mrs. Marren found out about the housekeeping job?"

"She mentioned hearing about the job at her church," Bella murmured.

"In Columbus?" Nolen asked.

"Yes," Bella replied. "Unfortunately, she didn't mention the church's name."

"We really need to talk with the housekeeper. Evidently, Jillian hasn't gotten a call yet." With a sigh, Jax slumped back in his chair and folded his arms over his lean waist. "I hope the woman has additional information. I'd like to know more about who called, since Mrs. Lackner wanted to avoid him. Of course, we have other leads to pursue."

"Maybe the caller is the killer. If so, we might solve this case quickly." Bella hoped that would happen. Weaving loose threads into a tapestry was challenging. Just as hard as sorting out the unnecessary material.

Jax offered a faint smile. "Maybe so. Discovering his name would be a good starting point."

"And we need to know about the itinerant workers and the local boys," Bella put in before explaining Mrs. Placette's revelation about part-time help. She turned to Newton. "Is there anyone in Boxwood who might hire out for short-term jobs? Supposedly, one man grew up with Mrs. Marren, but that's all we know. And that she's the one who located them."

"Several men could fit the description of needing a job. What with work scarce, odd jobs are all some fellows can find," the older deputy replied. "Same with some in Moreley. I haven't heard about anyone local going out there to work, though."

"Neither have I," Nolen added.

With one hand, Jax massaged his neck. "I haven't, either, which seems pretty strange. The boys evidently got fired in short order, but it sounded like the men were there off-and-on for a time."

The telephone rang in the outer office, which halted the conversation. Within moments, Jillian appeared in the doorway "That was Mrs. Tillis. They were out earlier, and Mrs. Ammers got through to her. Her sister left for Moreley about ten minutes ago."

A harsh breath left Jax as he pushed back his chair and stood. "I need to get to the house before she does."

Bella got to her feet. "I'll go along." A niggling finger of doubt traced her spine. The housekeeper normally did not come back until Tuesday morning. Why was she arriving a day early? Had word about her employer's murder already reached Boxwood?

Chapter Five

Within a few minutes, Jax was pulling to a stop in front of the Lackner home. He went around the vehicle to help Bella out. "Since it's chilly, let's step inside. We can watch the driveway from the foyer."

Bella readily agreed.

After unlocking the door, Jax ushered Bella into the foyer. "I hope Mrs. Marren comes straight home. If she stops in town, she might hear the news. I'd rather tell her myself and gauge her reaction."

"I'm interested in why she's back ahead of her normal schedule," Bella commented. "Do you think word has spread as far as Boxwood?"

"Doubtful, so I'd like to know what brought her back, too." His jaw tightened until a small muscle twitched.

"You're suspicious about her returning today. Why?"

He shifted to face Bella. "Like you, I get an occasional insight."

Bella rolled her eyes. "You are an excellent detective, and you have a great feel for clues."

"I try," he said with a lilt of amusement in his voice.

The exchange evoked a chuckle from Bella before she returned to the case. "You don't suspect the housekeeper, do you? Mrs. Lackner was definitely killed this morning, right?"

Jax nodded. "She was, and I'm not pinpointing anyone as the culprit. I'd like to know how Mrs. Marren reacts and why she's changed her pattern. Maybe she got a bad feeling. Who knows? Possibly, she'll think of someone suspicious. The caller, the temporary workers, the local boys who got fired, or another person who clashed with Mrs. Lackner."

"That makes sense."

Her comment made him smile. "I like to think I'm sensible."

Bella shook her head. "You're very sensible and skilled. Moreley is lucky to have you as the constable."

While her observation was positive, her expression was not. Months had passed since Bella had lobbied for him to return to his career as a golf pro. Was it still on her mind? He would not be surprised. Before the war, being the co-professional at Ballantyne had been Jax's dream. So had marrying Bella. For a long while, he had put all dreams aside. Not anymore. "I suppose so."

She shot him a questioning look. Before Bella could speak, footsteps sounded on the front porch. She turned toward the door. "That must be Mrs. Marren."

"Probably, but let's be cautious." Jax pulled his service revolver out. "Come over here, out of the direct line of the door, and I'll see who it is." While he didn't expect trouble, Jax wanted to be safe rather than sorry.

Only a minute's hesitation preceded Bella moving to the side. Jax stepped to the door and opened it to see a sturdily built, middle-aged woman with her graying hair pulled into a bun. A frown furrowed her long, lined face.

"Constable Hastings?" the woman asked as dismay turned to surprise. "What are you doing here?"

Although he had seldom crossed paths with the housekeeper, Jax wasn't shocked that she immediately recognized him Moreley was a small town, and the constable was well-known to the entire population, even relative newcomers. "Come in, Mrs. Marren." He ushered her into the foyer. "I'm afraid we have bad news."

The woman's attention moved to Bella. "Miss Stewart, your fitting was earlier today." Marren glanced around. "Where is your friend Miss Byington?"

"Maybe we should go into the front parlor and sit down," Bella suggested.

Mrs. Marren shook her head. "I'm the housekeeper, miss. That wouldn't be fitting." Suddenly, the woman looked past Bella and Jax to the side hall and staircase. "Who tracked in the mud?"

"I think we should sit down and talk, ma'am," Jax said.

The woman's gaze, wide with some undefinable emotion focused on Jax. "Where is the missus?" An edge of alarm crept into her voice.

Bella went to Mrs. Marren's side, took her arm, and led her into the parlor, which was right off the foyer. Jax followed.

After the two women took the loveseat, he settled on the rocker across from them and addressed the housekeeper. "I'm sorry, but we have bad news about Mrs. Lackner." He continued by providing the basic facts.

While Jax spoke, the color drained from the older woman's face as she folded her shaking hands in her lap. "I told her I should stay here with her. My sister would've come and spent time with me. I didn't have to go over to her place."

Jax glanced at Bella, who looked as solemn as he felt. "What made you think you shouldn't leave Mrs. Lackner alone?" he asked.

The woman ran one hand over her gray bun. Not a single strand escaped, but she fingered the locks as if they had. She glanced from Jax to Bella. "The missus got some calls from a man. After the first couple, she didn't answer herself anymore. Afterward, she told me to dismiss him. When I said not to telephone again, especially the last time. He were angry."

"When was the last call?" Bella asked. Getting confirmation of other evidence would be useful.

"A week ago." Mrs. Marren shook her head. "He told me he'd talk to the missus, one way or another. If she wouldn't come to the telephone, he'd come here."

Bella and Jax exchanged a long look before he spoke. "Do you know the man's name and location?"

The woman licked her lips. "No. He never told me and the missus didn't, either. I asked about him, of course." The housekeeper looked at Bella. "You know how reserved she were. She held her personal business close."

"She did," Bella agreed. "But she knew the man?"

"Seems so," the older woman replied. "The first time he telephoned, she answered because it was my day off. When he called again, I called her to the telephone because she hadn't told me about not wanting to speak with him until then. But he kept calling back and got her when I were off. The missus acted odd about the whole thing. One time, she snatched up the telephone like she were expecting a call. From him maybe, cuz she talked for a few minutes. Again, she said no more calls, and she told Cherry as much. The girl was s'posed to tell her ma. Missus was plenty mad when Kamalie Ammers let the man get through." She glanced at the empty fireplace. "I suggested we ask Mrs. Ammers if she knew who was calling. She didn't, and the calls went through other operators before she got them. I don't know how all that works, but you were an operator in France, weren't you?" She posed the question to Bella.

"I was," Bella agreed. "We talked to Mrs. Ammers, and she'll trace all the calls back. It will take time, but we should be able to get the origins of them. But it would help if we knew who this man is. Mrs. Lackner never used his name?"

"Never," the woman said. "She was very careful not to."

"But she knew who he was," Bella suggested, trying to confirm the facts.

"Yep, I'm sure she did," the housekeeper replied.

"Did you get any sense of where and how she knew him?" Jax wondered why Bella hadn't said Mrs. Ammers gave them information on one call. Or that they talked with Cherry. Knowing his betrothed, she had a good reason.

Mrs. Marren released a long exhalation. "The missus didn't give no details, but when she refused to talk with him one time, he told me her running away was foolish. Said he was plenty mad about coming home to find her gone, and that weren't no way to treat a hard-working man."

The response only increased Jax's curiosity. "We've heard she was married. Could this man have been her husband?"

"I don't know," the housekeeper replied. "When I first hired on, she told me about being a widow. Said her man worked on the railroad and died in some accident."

"Did she say how long ago he died?" Bella asked.

A half-shrug lifted one of the woman's broad shoulders. "Nope. I figured it had to be a while back, because she didn't act upset. Mostly matter of fact, but some folks hide their feelings."

"True. Mrs. Lackner never told Ida and me anything about her personal life. She made it clear her time was short and getting our dresses done was the priority," Bella said.

As Bella jotted down more notes, Jax wondered about the dressmaker's demeanor and actions. Had her husband died recently? If so, that would explain her return to Moreley. If not, why come back now?

"She says the same to everyone," the housekeeper replied. "We never chitchatted, neither. But she paid well and give me time off." She pulled out a handkerchief and dabbed at her eyes. "If I had been here, she would still be alive."

"Or you might've been a victim, too," Bella said.

Mrs. Marren sniffled again. "Maybe."

The housekeeper's offhand reaction struck Jax as strange. Didn't her narrow escape trouble her? "Speaking of time off," Jax began. "You rarely return until Tuesday morning. What brought you back early today?"

Mrs. Marren's eyes widened. For a moment, she was speechless. When she finally responded, her tone was curt. "Do you keep track of the comings and goings of all townsfolk, Constable? I've never lived in a little burg like Moreley, but I can see now why the missus kept to herself. Wanting to avoid gossip and nosiness."

Bella spoke before Jax formed a reply. "As far as where you were, Ida and I told the constable when he arrived on scene this morning. Every fact is important in a murder case, and revealing pertinent information isn't gossip."

Briefly, Mrs. Marren pursed her thick lips. "I suppose you're doing your job," she admitted in a grudging voice.

Her annoyance was another oddity, but Jax didn't allow his curiosity to surface. "I am, ma'am. So, what brought you back early?"

"I knew missus had appointments today. That's different from a normal Monday." The housekeeper's expression didn't soften. "Anyhow, I figured she might need me for something or another. Sometimes, she does when customers come and go."

The explanation seemed reasonable, but Jax didn't like the woman's attitude. She had seemed genuinely upset over her boss's death. Why be annoyed about him running a thorough investigation? Jax tucked the question into the back of his mind. Her comments led him to another query. "If she rarely saw clients on Mondays, what did Mrs. Lackner do?" They'd heard the dressmaker's usual habit of taking a drive, something Bella and Ida knew about, but would Mrs. Marren reveal more?

After shifting around a bit, the woman replied. "She took a long drive sometimes. Loved that vehicle of hers. Some old friend of hers went along or the missus went to visit the woman in town."

"I don't recall ever seeing her driving into Moreley," Jax commented. "What make is it?"

"I don't remember. It's an open two-seater," the housekeeper replied.

"It's an original Winton, according to what Mrs. Lackner told Ida and me," Bella put in. "Ida asked when she saw it in the carriage house."

Jax shifted to face her. "Those were expensive, but dependable. More than a few are still on the road in this state, since they were made in Cleveland. Has she had it a long time?"

"She didn't say," Bella replied before glancing at the other woman. "What about the friend?"

The housekeeper shrugged. "I dunno about her. A school chum."

After a moment, Jax turned back to the housekeeper. "Do you know if Mrs. Lackner had an early appointment? One before Bella's and Ida's fittings?"

The woman stared at him for a long moment before saying, "Not that she told me. Just said three brides was coming, and I knew who she meant."

When Marren didn't expand on the observation, Jax asked another question. "Does she ever keep her appointment book some place other than her display room?"

Again, the housekeeper took a minute to answer. "At times, she's carried it to her bedroom or down here."

Beside Jax, Bella stiffened. "I've seen it in the same place every time Ida and I have been here."

"Dunno. I weren't supposed to be in those rooms, since the missus didn't want no items disturbed." After the quick response, the housekeeper again dabbed at her eyes. "This is so terrible. Poor, poor thing."

Jax watched as Mrs. Marren's lips trembled. Her reaction seemed genuine, so he offered empathy. "I'm sorry, ma'am. We won't keep you much longer, but I would like to go through the kitchen and your suite with you. Just to see if anything is out of place."

The woman looked stricken. "I need to clean up. All that mud..." Her voice trailed off.

"We don't want the place cleaned up yet," he said. "Before we look around, I have another question. Mrs. Placette said some boys did odd jobs around here, but she didn't know who. You must, though."

Mrs. Marren's lips worked before she spoke. "The Ammers boy did yard work last fall into winter. Some other chores. Didn't show up regular and took some stuff, so missus fired him. Same with the one who came after that."

"Who came after Charley Ammers?" Jax asked.

"Another young hooligan. Abner something or other," the housekeeper replied with a grimace.

"Abner Crater?" Jax posed the query.

"That's him. Didn't last long." Mrs. Marren shook her gray head. "Younguns now are bone-lazy and dishonest."

"Did Abner steal anything?" Jax asked.

The housekeeper harrumphed. "Some things was missing. Same after the Ammers boy left."

"No one reported thefts to my office," Jax said.

"The missus said not to," Mrs. Marren replied. "Didn't agree, but it were her belongings that disappeared."

"What belongings?" Jax asked.

"Sterling silver, mostly," the housekeeper said.

Bella jotted more notes before speaking again. "We also heard about a childhood friend of yours who worked mostly for room and board. He and another man remodeled the upstairs rooms for Mrs. Lackner."

The housekeeper went rigid before flinging a hand in the air, as if to brush off the observation. "He weren't no childhood friend. I don't know who said such a thing but there ain't no truth to it. I run across them down around Marion. My sister and me stopped there for a meal. The two was to do renovations, so I told them to come up when they was done there. When they come, we needed wood hauled and the rooms fixed up. Since missus had other odd jobs, she let them stay in the carriage house. There's old cots in the little room off to one side. A woodstove, too. The fellows here off-and-on for a while."

"Ida and I never saw them," Bella said.

"After fixing up her work area, they sometimes took jobs elsewhere," the older woman replied.

"What are their names?" Bella asked.

A momentary silence ensued while the housekeeper's glance flickered from Bella to Jax and, then at a point behind them. "One called himself Joe Smith. The other went by Bill Johnson. It took the two of them a couple weeks or better to fix up the rooms. After that, they come and went. Did chores when they was here. Mostly cutting and hauling firewood. Bill did a few other repairs." Once again, Mrs. Marren folded her arms across her substantial middle.

"It's funny neither came to town." Jax watched the house-keeper's face for some telltale sign, but none appeared. Exactly what sign, he wasn't sure, but something didn't ring true.

Mrs. Marren made a dismissive gesture with one hand. "Neither one had much money. Never shared where they was from or where they was headed, and I didn't ask."

"When was the last time you saw them?" Jax asked.

A half-shrug lifted one of the housekeeper's hefty shoulders. "Last week mebbe. Not sure. Coulda been a couple of weeks. I'm too busy to watch for comings and goings of hired hands."

Jax issued another question. "What kind of automobile did they have?"

"Joe didn't have no transportation. Bill hauled him around, when needed. Some old black rattletrap."

The color was the same as the one seen by Jillian, but many automobiles were black. And some were junkers. Both Jillian and Mrs. Placette mentioned a vehicle fitting that description, which piqued his interest. Jax glanced at Bella, who posed an additional query.

"Did Mrs. Lackner ever hire other extra help? This is a big place."

The housekeeper shook her head. "The missus watched her pennies. I were surprised she hired any menfolk, but we had some heavy work done besides the remodeling."

"These men were skilled carpenters?" Jax suggested.

"They knowed how to use hammer and saw. Mostly, the rooms needed shelving, a platform, dressing screens, and such. Of course, the furniture had to be moved, and supplies hauled up. There'd been water damage around a couple of windows, so that needed fixing." Mrs. Marren shrugged. "Didn't require no special talents."

"You said you met the men in Marion at a restaurant," Bella said.

Mrs. Marren pressed her palms together and put her hands to her chin. "Heloise, my sister, and I were down near Marion. We'd visited with an old neighbor of mine down in Columbus and stopped to eat on the way home. It's a good sixty miles north of the city, so we needed a break by then. Stopped in a little town café, and two men was doing some work for the owner. Since the missus had been wanting to redo the rooms upstairs for her dressmaking, I asked the pair how much they charged and such. They was real interested, since they was out of work with no place to stay once that job were done. I give them the directions, and they come a few days later."

"When and where was that?" Jax asked.

"Right after Christmas," Mrs. Marren said. "Don't recall the town's name."

Jax's suspicion grew, but he didn't call her out on not knowing where she had met the men. They could do that later, if no other leads arose. Why was the housekeeper acting anxious and being obtuse? Knowing her employer had been murdered was enough to make the woman uneasy, but was it the entire reason? Jax was not sure. "Let's look around your suite and the rest of this floor to see if anything is missing," he said as he got to his feet.

Mrs. Marren heaved herself out of her chair. "Of course."

Bella followed close behind the housekeeper, while Jax brought up the rear. As they made their way through the downstairs rooms, nothing seemed out of order until they reached the kitchen, where mud covered much of the floor.

"Oh, what a mess," Mrs. Marren said as she looked around the room. "I wish you'd let me mop it up." Her attention went to Jax as she made the last statement.

"Not yet, ma'am." He pointed toward the door to her room. "My deputies checked your suite, but I'd like to know if you notice anything out of the ordinary."

With a sigh, she nodded and led the way into the compact room. A double bed, covered in a patchwork quilt, stood against one wall. On the opposite side was a bureau. A rocker and a small table were tucked into an alcove near a window. The door to the attached lavatory stood ajar.

Slowly, Mrs. Marren turned to survey each part of the room. "Nothing missing or disturbed."

"All right," Jax said. "If you don't mind, I'd also like you to look upstairs."

The color drained from the woman's face. "I don't want to see her body."

Bella laid a hand on Mrs. Marren's shoulder. "Doc Smedlay and Mr. Forrester were here, so she's gone."

A shudder rippled through the housekeeper. "All right."

Jax again let the women precede him. When they reached the seamstress's rooms, he opened the door. "Please don't touch anything. My deputies took photographs and logged evidence, but we may come back to gather more."

"Of course," the older woman replied.

Bella noted Mrs. Marren's continuing pallor. "Try not to be upset by what you see. Both rooms are in disarray and garments are badly damaged."

"I understand," the woman replied, "but I don't know what goes where no how. The missus don't allow me in her domain."

"Not even to clean?" Bella asked.

"No, miss. She tidied up her workroom and the display area. I only ever got glimpses in there. The missus were a fussy one," the housekeeper said, but she gasped when they entered the display area. "All these beautiful gowns is ruined. Completely ruined."

When Jax saw a shiver ripple through Bella, he laid a reassuring hand on her shoulder. "You don't have to be in here. You could wait downstairs."

She offered a tremulous smile. "I'll be fine. It's a bit of a shock seeing it all again."

His expression solemn, Jax nodded. "I'm sure it is. Why don't you stay out here while Mrs. Marren and I look in the workroom?"

"I don't mind going along," Bella assured him.

A moment passed before Jax replied. "All right." Maybe she wanted to gauge Mrs. Marren's reaction. Although the woman seemed upset by the news of her employer's demise, Jax was equally curious. He ushered the women into the adjacent area.

"Why is that veil on the floor?" the housekeeper asked, bending toward it.

Bella glanced at Jax, who shook his head. "Please leave it alone, ma'am. We haven't collected everything yet. For now, I want nothing disturbed."

The woman turned toward him with a scowl. "This place is a mess. It's my job to keep things in order."

"Jax already explained about not moving things yet," Bella said. "Besides, you said this area was off-limits to you."

Something akin to alarm crossed the housekeeper's face. For several moments, silence reverberated through the room. Then, Mrs. Marren's sharp tone cut through it. "Who else will clean up?"

"That's the least of my worries at present," Jax said. "If you'll just look around and see if something seems odd to you, in here and in the closet."

Mrs. Marren searched the designated areas. "Lots of fabric in this here closet. The missus loved expensive materials. Got stacks of stuff piled up."

"If you never came in here, who brought up the bolts?" Jax asked.

"She got one of the hired hands to do those chores. Too heavy for me," the housekeeper said.

"Not the mailman or delivery men?" Jax nodded.

"The mailman always leaves packages on the front porch," the housekeeper replied. "If a delivery come by train, the stationmaster would usually send a porter out with it, but none bring stuff up here. It woulda been easier to take the stuff to the main attic, since a regular staircase goes to it. But she wanted what she wanted."

"I see," Jax murmured. "We can go back downstairs and you can head to your sister's house."

"To my sister's place? I live here." The housekeeper folded her arms across her ample bosom as she stared at him.

Jax's jaw tightened. "I'm afraid that isn't possible now. We can help you pack your things. If they don't all fit into your vehicle, my deputies can assist you later in the week."

"What?" Mrs. Marren looked and sounded aghast. "It's bad enough you're forcing me out of this house, Constable Hastings. My sister and I will be back to get the rest of my belongings." Her voice took on a sharp edge.

A harsh breath left him. "You'll need to give your key to me before you leave and, as I said, my deputies will assist you later in the week. I'd rather no one else come into the house yet. Right now, our focus is finding Mrs. Lackner's killer, and we don't want people in-and-out of the crime scene."

A harrumph emanated from the housekeeper. "Well, I never."

"The constable is doing his job, ma'am. You must be terribly upset by the entire ordeal. If you note nothing being amiss here, why don't I go to your suite with you? We can pack up a few things, and you can be on the road before darkness sets in." Bella spoke in a reassuring, but firm, tone.

The annoyed expression didn't leave the older woman's face, but she nodded. "I don't know where things should be up here. As I said." As she spoke the last three words, Mrs. Marren glowered at Jax.

Bella, standing to the side where the housekeeper could not see her expression, rolled her eyes. Jax's response was a slight nod. He turned back to Mrs. Marren. "Did the hired men only bring materials up here? Anything else?"

The woman maintained her scowl but shook her head. "Renovating supplies and, a bit ago, the missus ordered new dress forms, material, and other items from up Sandusky way. Paid to have the kit-and-caboodle brought here."

"The mannequins she had when Ida and I first came looked fine," Bella said.

"She were fussy," the housekeeper replied.

"Where are the old forms?" Bella asked.

"The men hauled them off, I s'pose. They was used in her mother's store, so pretty old," the housekeeper replied.

"They seemed serviceable when Ida and I first came. Mrs. Lackner watched her budget, didn't she?" Bella posed the query.

"She did, but she were fussy." Mrs. Marren turned a stony stare on Bella as she repeated the assertion.

As he listened to the exchange, Jax wondered why the dressmaker would replace functional equipment. "I see," Jax murmured, even though what he saw was murky. "If you could jot down the name of the store, that would be helpful."

Another harrumph left Mrs. Marren. "I've got paper and pencil in the kitchen, but you wanted to look around here. I haven't seen both rooms, in detail."

Bella turned to Jax. "I'll meet you in the foyer."

"Fine. I want to take one more look at the entire scene," he replied. "Thank you for your help, Mrs. Marren."

To that, the older woman had no response.

Thirty minutes later, Jax and Bella were on the road to town. "What did you think about the housekeeper?" he asked.

A low laugh left Bella. "At first, she seemed helpful. Then, she acted strangely. Wanting to clean up when you'd said she couldn't. And never venturing into the showroom or work-room? I'm not sure I believed her. Mrs. Lackner didn't seem like the type to straighten up after herself, when she had hired help. Plus, Mrs. Marren mentioned it not being safe in that big, isolated house, but she planned to stay alone with a killer on the loose."

"I agree. She was inconsistent with some of her comments, and wanting to be in an empty, solitary house where a murder just took place makes no sense. If Newton talks with her sister, he may get some insight."

"I'd like to know what the sister says about running into the two men near Marion. That story also seemed off-key. Actually, driving all the way to Columbus for a day trip is odd."

He nodded. "As is Mrs. Marren not recalling the name of the town? I know she's new to this part of the state, but that was strange."

"It sure was," Bella said. "Her description of the two men didn't match what Mrs. Placette told us. Why would she think one of them was a childhood friend of Mrs. Marren, if he wasn't?"

"Yep. That's odd," Jax put in. "Then, there's their vehicle looking like the one Jillian saw on Saturday, and Mrs. Placette noticed at one point. Things don't mesh. I'm not sure how to assess Mrs. Marren, but I want to find out more about her."

"Do you suspect her?" Bella asked. He hadn't earlier, but Jax might have changed his mind after the woman had been brusque and evasive.

"Not really, but I want to cover every possibility. Like when she arrived in Boxwood yesterday, when she left today, and what the two sisters did in-between."

"Newton can also ask about Mrs. Tillis in Boxwood. He may learn more about both sisters."

A chuckle escaped Jax. "Now, who's being suspicious?"

"You're right about not overlooking anyone," Bella said, "and Mrs. Marren acted strangely. She seemed upset about the murder, but that ebbed. She fussed a lot over the mud. About as much as over the murder. And she got critical of Mrs. Lackner. When Ida and I went for fittings, Mrs. Marren was deferential to her employer and about her. She praised Mrs. Lackner more than once."

"In what ways?"

Bella hesitated a moment before responding. "She was effusive about having a lovely suite and a pleasant boss. She also mentioned getting time off to visit her sister, but she told us that much just now."

"At the end, she sounded like Mrs. Lackner was demanding and snobbish. Mrs. Marren never indicated that before?"

"Not to Ida and me."

"Interesting. I'm not sure what it means, if anything. Same with her changing her pattern and returning early. Perhaps, she really wanted to be around when customers were coming and going."

"That seems feasible. But her criticism seems odd, as do her inconsistencies. Usually, folks have nothing bad to say about the dead, especially a murder victim. Particularly when they've previously had all good words to share. It isn't a sign of guilt, but you're right about looking more into Mrs. Marren." A soft sigh left Bella. "I wish we didn't have so many possibilities. But we always do. And we often solve the case in short order. I'm sure we will this time, too." The trouble was, Bella didn't feel as optimistic as she tried to sound. How many cases had they wrapped up in less than five days? "We've also got to find out more about Charley and Abner."

"And the two vagrants. Their names are common, too common for me to believe they're real," Jax observed. "Then, there's Mrs. Marren denying one was a childhood friend."

"Someone isn't telling the truth, and we've got multiple scenarios on the table."

"We may find a focus yet today," he said. "Not that we have any strong suspects, just vague possibilities. As for Mrs. Marren, she seemed pretty peeved with me over not being able to stay in the house, but she isn't the owner. Surely, she didn't expect to continue living there."

"Part of that could be shock. It takes time to accept a sudden death," Bella murmured.

Jax moved his hand from the gearshift to clasp hers. "You know too much about that kind of grief."

"You do, too," she murmured. Her thoughts returned to their impending nuptials. "You must wish your parents could be here for our wedding day."

"I do. I wish yours could be, and I wish Matt could be my best man." Emotion resonated in his deep voice. "Lots of wishes."

She wasn't surprised Jax kept thinking about her brother because she did, too. The three of them had been a close-knit trio growing up. Several moments passed before Bella replied. "They'll all be with us in spirit," she assured him. "And we have wonderful friends to share our joy."

"You always find the good in every situation."

"I try." After losing her parents and brother, Bella had come home to discover her hometown and family resort in dire straits due to wartime losses and the Spanish flu. Then, she had found a murdered neighbor, which had turned out to be the last and worst crime in a months-long spree. Since Moreley depended on visitors, halting the binge had been essential. Eager to help, Bella had horned her way into the investigation, much to Jax's dismay. But, with his job hanging in the balance and war wounds hampering him, he had grudgingly let her take part. When she glanced at him now, those days seemed far off. The misunderstandings between them were over. Thank heavens. "Right now, I want to help you solve this case, so a cloud isn't hanging over the ceremony. If we don't find the killer, you won't want to leave town for a honeymoon, will you?" Her question echoed inside the confines of the Chummy.

He released her hand. His fingers tightened on the steering wheel until his knuckles showed white. "No, I couldn't go away with a murder investigation pending." Jax glanced at her and back at the road. "I'm so sorry, Bella. You don't deserve uncertainty dimming our day."

"You don't, either," she pointed out. "But there's time left. The rest of today and four more before the wedding. We may get a big break. We have in other cases."

"Very possible," he agreed.

Although Jax didn't sound positive, Bella avoided further comment about the timeframe. "What about Mrs. Marren's attitude toward Charley Ammers and Abner Crater? She seemed to have a low opinion of both boys," Bella said. "You've told me about them flirting with trouble, and Cherry mentioned Charley threatening to confront Mrs. Lackner."

"Cherry not revealing her brother did odd jobs for the woman bothers me. Why not say so?" Jax asked.

"It sounded like he didn't last long, and he wouldn't want his mother finding out about him being accused of stealing."

"That makes sense, but no one in town knew. At least not that I've heard. Where did they put the stolen items? Selling the stuff in Moreley would've caused comment."

"What about the two men? Mrs. Lackner probably hired them to save money, but why did they never come to town?" Bella inquired.

"I'm surprised my deputies and I didn't hear about those two. I'll ask around town and have Nolen and Newton do the same. Maybe one or both hired hand was around at some point."

"You three have so much to handle," Bella murmured.

A moment passed before Jax replied. "When we get back to the office, I'm calling Richard Jenkins. He, Jenny, and her mother will be here for the wedding anyhow. I'm sure they'd come early. Then, he and Jenny could help. What do you think?"

Richard was a retired senior constable who had worked with them on other cases, and his wife had also taken part occasionally. Both had become friends with Bella and Jax. "That's a wonderful idea. They're coming for the wedding and planning to be at your house, aren't they? Jenny's mother could come along, and they could all stay, even if we solve the case quickly."

"True. There's plenty of room, and they've stayed before. At this point, I'd like as much assistance as I can muster. More eyes and ears could lead to a speedier solution."

"That'd be wonderful." She and Jax had waited a long time to get married, and Bella didn't want the event spoiled by him rushing back to work.

He shot a sidelong glance at her. "If they come now, you'd have more time to prepare for the wedding because you wouldn't have to help me so much."

"I enjoy helping you. Besides, most everything is ready. Ida and I can see about our dresses this evening. Jenny's mother was a seamstress, so she might help us alter them. She'll probably come along now, so they don't have to go back to Karston for her on Saturday morning."

"How do you know she sews?" Jax asked.

Bella furrowed her brow. "Jenny mentioned it at some point. I don't recall exactly when. What about you? Are you ready?"

Jax grinned. "I've been ready to marry you for years. My suit is in order, if that's what you mean. Griff and I talked to your employees last week, and they're going to set up chairs in the big parlor on Friday. He and Mac will oversee all that. We have music, courtesy of Mrs. Smedlay, who is an accomplished pianist. Mac will walk you down the aisle and is excited about doing it, from what he's told me."

Warmth spread through Bella. "He is, bless him, and our staff is more than happy to pitch in. The final decorations will go up a day ahead of the ceremonies."

"What are the decorations?"

She beamed at him. "You'll see them Friday night at dinner. I hope everyone can make the pre-wedding festivities." Bella's concern crept into her voice. More than that, she hoped their honeymoon would not be delayed. Bella always felt pressure to solve a murder quickly but never more so than now.

Jax called Richard as soon as they stepped inside the constable's office. While he waited for the connection, Bella chatted with Jillian, who was concerned about the wedding gowns. "You must be disheartened about your dress being ruined."

"We are, but Ida and I have our mothers' gowns. Jenny's mother may help us fix them. Ida is stylish, so I'm sure she has ideas on how to alter the dresses. My mother was my size, so it should be fine." Bella, who was taller than average, sometimes regretted her height, but the top of her head came to Jax's chin, which he said was perfect. The thought made her smile.

"You look happy," he commented after hanging up the telephone.

"I am," she said without further explanation.

He grinned. "Keep your secret, but you'll be even happier to know the Jenkinses and Mrs. Burtis will be here later this evening. Jenny's mother is more than willing to work on the dresses, so the two of them will be at Ballantyne in the morning." Jax looked at his clerk. "You're welcome to be late to work, so you can talk to her, too. I know you picked up your dress already, but you probably want to be in on the bridal gowns. Just be here by noon."

"Thank you, Jax," the younger woman said, excitement glittering in her eyes.

He turned to Bella. "We'll all gather here around that time. If you can come, that'd be great."

"Of course, I'll be in," she assured him.

The bell over the front door jingled, which interrupted their by-play. Newton entered, swept off his cap, and hung it on the wall hook along with his jacket.

"Were you able to speak with Mrs. Tillis?" Jax asked.

"I was." Newton's forehead furrowed. "She hedged a lot. Uncertain and uneasy are the best words to describe her attitude. After we talked, I went to the diner and chatted with a few folks. I don't have the key to the case, but I got some information."

Disquiet prickled along Bella's nerves, and she saw a similar emotion cross Jax's face.

"Let's talk in my office," Jax said. He gestured for Bella to go ahead of him.

As soon as the three were at the table in the corner, Jax focused on his deputy. "What do you mean about her not being open with you?"

Newton pulled a pad out of his pocket and flipped it open. "I went over the basics, like when her sister got there. We knew she usually left Mrs. Lackner's place on Sunday around noon, but I asked when Mrs. Marren arrived in Boxwood, like I wasn't aware of her typical schedule. Mrs. Tillis said she didn't know exactly when, since she was gone until late in the day. Then, I asked what the two of them did today, and she sort of hem-hawed around. Said they chatted at her house for a while and didn't give a reason for her sister leaving early."

"Interesting," Jax murmured.

"I thought so," Newton replied. "No stores are open on Sunday, of course, but I stopped at all of them to see if anyone had seen either sister today. No one had, but a couple mentioned Mrs. Tillis not being at church yesterday, which is unusual for her. I went to the parsonage, and the pastor confirmed she didn't attend services."

Bella frowned. "We don't know exactly when Mrs. Marren left for Boxwood. Maybe it was later than usual, but she didn't mention staying at the Lackner place until late yesterday. She sounded like she followed her usual schedule."

"She did," Jax agreed.

"Mrs. Tillis acted like her sister didn't come on a regular schedule, which doesn't fit what the two of you learned. Anyhow, I asked people in the diner if they saw Mrs. Marren on Sunday, but they hadn't."

"Do they usually?" Jax asked.

Newton tapped his notepad. "Some mentioned often seeing Mrs. Marren driving through downtown Boxwood to get to her sister's house, which is in a well-populated neighborhood. It's odd no one noticed her vehicle, since she's a frequent visitor, and it'd be easily recognized. She drives an old Packard. Although, if she went after dark, probably not as likely to be seen."

"I should've asked when she left to visit her sister," Jax said. "I will when we talk to her again."

Newton glanced from Bella to Jax. "You caught Mrs. Marren at the Lackner house?"

"We did." Jax continued with a summary of their discussion. "She's acting oddly, too, which means we need to learn more about them both. That's why I plan to speak with her again. We also have to find out about several others."

"That's more than a half-dozen suspects," Newton observed. "Ophelia, Abner, Charley, Mrs. Marren, maybe Mrs. Tillis, the caller, and the two men."

"Exactly," Jax said.

A tap on the door preceded Nolen stepping into the room. "I've got photographs from the crime scene."

Jax waved him inside. "Anything stand out to you?" he asked as his other deputy sat down and put the pictures in the middle of the table.

"Something that's odd is the mud on some dresses." Nolen glanced at Bella. "One is partially soiled, but another is pretty bad. The muddy trails led to the back door. When we looked out there, the drive had a lot of puddles from the weekend's heavy rain. With the front drive being gravel, it's funny whoever came in the house parked and walked in mud."

"Customers come to the front," Bella put in, "so the intruder was most likely being cautious. If he'd made clear footprints, he might've cleaned up."

"That makes sense, because it was impossible to get sharp images of the muddy splotches inside or out," Nolen said before pointing to a couple of the pictures.

The observation had Bella studying the black-and-white prints. She and Jax had noticed the gown with large splotches of mud. Now, she realized her dress also had a bunch of streaks. "The dirt may be more obvious because it shows up as much darker in the photographs." While she kept her tone even, Bella felt twin surges of anxiety and uncertainty. While doing interviews with Jax, she had focused on the murder—not on the note or the method. Now, she again wondered why the killer had chosen her veil as a weapon. Was it pure happenstance? And what about the threat? Was it genuine? The questions reverberated in her mind, but Jax's voice broke into her thoughts.

"Didn't the other gowns also have mud?" he asked his deputy.

"A bit. I think there's more on these two." Nolen glanced at the pictures again. "I wonder who planned to wear them."

Bella took a deep breath before pointing to one image. "That was going to be my bridal gown."

Silence followed her revelation. Finally, Jax spoke. "Does the other one belong to Ida?"

"No," Bella replied before pointing at another photo. "This was to be hers."

The men bent their heads. Nolen was the first to look back at Bella. "It's not as soiled, but there are a lot of slashes in it. Maybe not more than in yours. More than the other one, though."

"I agree with you, Nolen," she said.

"The killer could've started with the first one in the row," Jax pointed out. "Bella's gown was on the model closest to the workroom. If he started there, he probably had less mud on his shoes as he went through the group." He gestured to the wide shot of all three dresses.

"True," Newton put in. "And we can't be sure the perpetrator knew which veils and dresses went with individual brides."

The observations eased Bella's mind a little, but she couldn't completely shake her fear. "What do you all think about the note? Nothing Jax and I have learned has been useful in that regard."

Several moments passed before Nolen answered. "We know Mrs. Lackner was married, but she could be a widow or a divorcee. Maybe she planned to remarry. She's only been back a few months, and she could have a suitor somewhere else. The threat could be directed at her."

Bella mulled over the suggestion, which presented a new avenue of interest. "If so, the note might refer to her remarriage. It seems like the housekeeper would know about that. Unless the man only visited when Mrs. Marren was away. That's possible, I suppose. Mrs. Marren told us the male caller said it wasn't fair of Mrs. Lackner to leave a hard-working man without a word. It sounded like he was her husband."

Jax drummed his fingers on the table. "As for Mrs. Lackner having a jealous suitor, it's not out of the question. Mrs. Marren said nothing about an impending wedding, and she ought to know."

"If she knows, she might want to keep the secret," Bella suggested.

"That's a possibility," Newton said. "The house is a ways out of town with no close neighbors to watch comings and goings. A suitor could park in back and not be noticed."

"That must've happened this morning," Bella said. "Someone came and wasn't seen."

"Probably, but the caller concerns me," Jax put in. "He was overheard referring to her as *dear heart*."

"What is she wasn't really a widow?" Nolen made the observation.

Bella rolled the pencil between her palms. "Why wait until now to call her? She came in late August. As far as we know, the man didn't telephone until a few weeks ago."

With a sigh, Jax slumped back in his chair. "That's a good question, and we've got a lot of those."

"We do," Bella agreed, "but bringing them all out usually helps hone our focus."

A weary smile lifted his lips. "You're right."

Bella couldn't repress a grin. "Thank you."

Nolen pulled more photos out of a large envelope and spread them across the table.

Bella scanned the array before focusing on one of the dressmaker's body and Bella's veil. "Strangulation is such an awful way to die. Do you think she was still alive when the end was shoved into her mouth?"

Jax studied the photo. "Not necessarily. It could be a statement about wanting her to be quiet. Hard to say." He pushed the picture toward Newton and Nolen. "Either of you see anything else of importance?"

Both men shook their heads prior to Nolen commenting. "You can't tell from the black-and-white film, but the bruising was a lot more obvious when Doc Smedlay and Mr. Forrester took her away."

"Strangulation requires effort and strength." A sigh escaped Jax as he leaned back in his chair. "I should go over and talk with Doc, since he'll have completed an examination by now."

"I can go along," Bella said.

"Don't you want to get back to Ballantyne? You still need to sort out what you're wearing to our wedding." Concern darkened Jax's eyes. "I know alterations can't start until tomorrow, but don't you want to get the dress out? Look at it and so forth."

"Ida and I will do that this evening, and it won't take a lot of time. It's not like we need to study every stitch," she replied. Bella liked to look nice, especially to Jax, but she was no clothes horse. "I assume you won't be coming out for dinner tonight, as we planned."

Regret lined his face. "I'm afraid not. I want this case solved as soon as possible. There's so much to find out and more to follow up on."

"True." Bella failed to keep all of her anxiety out of her voice.

"We'll catch the killer, Bella," Nolen said. "Don't worry about that."

"We sure will," Newton added. "If we have to work around the clock, we'll do it within the next few days."

Moisture pricked at Bella's eyes, but she blinked it back. "Thank you."

Jax laid his hand over hers. "Let's go see Doc. Then, you can go home."

Part of her wanted to disagree and vow to work around the clock, too, but common sense intervened. Not only did she need a wedding gown, Bella would help Ida with last-minute arrangements. "All right."

Chapter Six

A few minutes later, Bella and Jax entered the Smedlay home. Doc's wife, a pleasant woman in her late fifties, ushered them into the physician's domain. "He's back from the mortuary, but he's changing clothes before late office hours. Colds and bronchitis are going around." She pursed her lips. "Such terrible news about Mrs. Lackner. I remember her from when we first moved to Moreley."

"You met when your husband took over her father's practice?" Bella asked.

Mrs. Smedlay nodded. "We did. She was a sad little girl. Losing both siblings and her papa so close together took a toll. Then, there was their financial situation. Her mother started the dressmaking business in order to keep the house, but I'm sure it was a struggle. Elsie had to help, which she resented. I can't say I blame her. Until then, the family had ample means. Hard for a child to adjust to reduced circumstances."

"I'm sure it was," Bella agreed, but her mind went to the revelations from Mrs. Placette. Some confirmation would be useful.

"We've heard Mrs. Walling often charged items at local stores." She didn't elaborate, but Mrs. Smedlay's troubled expression supported what they'd already learned. Her response put an exclamation point on the details.

"It was common gossip when we arrived in town. Almost immediately, shopkeepers told us they didn't want to barter for medical care. I was taken aback because folks often give the town doctor goods instead of money. Finally, Mrs. Downing, the mercantile proprietor, was kind enough to explain the situation. Mrs. Walling ran up big bills, far beyond what could be evenly bartered. When the doctor died, more than one merchant had extended over one-hundred dollars of credit to her," Mrs. Smedlay said.

"That's an enormous debt, especially if they owed several stores," Jax said. "What in the world did she buy?"

"All sorts of things. Many were special ordered," Mrs. Smedlay replied. "Sterling silver cutlery and serving pieces, expensive jewelry, the best linens, custom-made furniture, Tiffany lamps. The list goes on. She was from a wealthy family and expected to have the best of everything. Each shopkeeper thought he was the only one giving her so much credit. When Doc Walling died, the truth came out. Then, everyone wanted to be paid."

"How in the world did she pay them off with a little dress shop?" Bella asked.

"For a long while, she had little money because she owed so much." Mrs. Smedlay shook her head.

"Did you get to know the two of them—mother and daughter— well?" Jax inquired.

"Mostly Mrs. Walling," Mrs. Smedlay replied. "I made my own clothes when we were first married, but I occasionally splurged on a special outfit. Later, I took all my business to the shop. They needed it, and we could afford the expense."

"You must've met Mrs. Lackner's stepfather," Jax put in.

"I did, but Elsie never referred to him as her stepfather. She always called him *my mother's husband*."

Jax shot a glance at Bella, who looked as put off as he felt. "I take it they weren't close," he said with a trace of asperity.

"Not at all," the older woman replied. "Major Birtinger was a bachelor before the marriage. A nice man but reserved and older than Mrs. Walling. He probably seemed almost grandfatherly to Elsie. Dr. Walling spoiled his children from what we heard when we got here. Nothing wrong with that, but the major wasn't cut from the same cloth. He was a retired Army officer, used to giving orders and having them followed without demur."

"We heard Mrs. Lackner was close to her father," Bella observed.

"She went on calls with him, so I'd say so. The major was stricter, but his funds added to their coffers. He saw that much needed repairs were made to the home, which had fallen into disarray after Dr. Walling passed. It was most likely his largess that got them out of debt."

Doc Smedlay's appearance interrupted the conversation. He smiled at his wife. "Thank you for ushering them in, my dear."

"Of course. I'll bring refreshments. I baked cookies earlier, and I can make coffee or tea." The older woman glanced from Bella to Jax.

"Tea and cookies sound good, ma'am," he said.

Bella repressed a smile. Jax had a sweet tooth, so he was always ready for a treat. Besides, the noon hour had passed a while back, with neither of them eating. Had it only been a few hours ago that she and Ida had anticipated the final fittings of their gowns?

"Be right back." Mrs. Smedlay hurried out and closed the door behind her.

Doc settled at his desk. "You're here about the autopsy results."

"We'd like to know what your preliminary findings are," Jax replied.

The physician pushed his spectacles up his nose. "As we figured at the scene, she was strangled. The slight cuts on her hands most likely came from struggling with her killer when he was vandalizing the gowns. The sewing scissors caused those wounds, and that probably happened in the front area. There was bruising on her upper arms. I'm guessing he dragged her into the workroom and killed her there."

"So, the small blood spatters on the dresses come from the tussle with her murderer?" Bella asked.

"I believe so." Doc leaned back and folded his arm across his chest. "The two of you are better at figuring out hows and wherefores, but she might've caught him destroying her work and tried to stop him. Or her. I can't determine the killer's gender."

"That scenario seems likely to me," Jax put in.

"To me, as well." Bella pulled her notepad and pencil out.

"I can give you my notes, but I'll need them back." Doc reached into his middle desk drawer and pulled out a sheaf of papers before handing them to Jax.

"I'll have one of my deputies take down the highlights. We'll get your original to you tomorrow," Jax said.

"Fine by me," Doc agreed. "I'll keep them for a trial, since I'm confident you two will find the killer. As far as any other particulars, Mrs. Lackner died within a few hours of when you and Miss Byington found her, Arabella."

"Which is what we figured," Jax put in, "so she could've been killed as early as eight o'clock."

"Perhaps even an hour before then." Doc drummed his fingers on his desk. "I'm surprised she left her doors unlocked when she was there all alone. The house isn't terribly far from town, but it's a ways back from the road. Hard to see, even with bare trees. At night, I've noticed lights in the windows, but that's all."

"We've heard the doors were always locked, which Ida and I found to be true. We've never gone for fittings on Mondays when Mrs. Lackner is there alone. Usually, she takes that day for design or to get out for a while. She's very talented. Was very talented," Bella tapped her pencil against the notepad. "On previous visits, the housekeeper answered, and we always heard the lock disengaging before the door opened." She shifted toward Jax. "I mentioned that earlier, but it seems like more of an issue now because we could walk in, and anyone could, too.."

"I agree," he replied. Jax watched her scribble more notes. "We're gathering lots of evidence."

"And some suspects?" Doc made it an inquiry.

Jax offered a rueful grin. "We have a few possibilities, which is more than I like."

"But it's typical," Bella put in. "There are always several people who appear to have motive, and some may have means and opportunity. We'll work on eliminating them until we find the killer, like always."

Her certitude eased some of Jax's anxiety. If she could be positive, so would he. After all, Bella was as invested in ensuring their wedding went ahead without a hitch as he was. Dashing off after saying *I do* seemed like a poor way to begin a marriage. Not that she wouldn't insist on coming with him to complete the investigation. "Good points."

Doc beamed at them. "I have faith in the two of you. You've solved a lot of cases together, and I know you'll crack this one, as well."

"You might help us more," Bella commented. "Have you heard about a couple of itinerant handymen working for Mrs. Lackner? They lived in the carriage house for a while."

"No, not at all. We don't get many drifters around here," Doc replied, "and I'm surprised she'd take a chance on hiring a couple of strangers."

Jax explained the situation before asking about the local boys. "We also heard about two kids doing odd jobs. Charley Ammers and Abner Crater. Both got fired."

Dismay blanketed the physician's face. "Young Crater hasn't had a lick of supervision since his mother passed. I understand his father's grief, but the boy needs attention." Doc ran one hand over his face. "Charley could use a man in his life, too. Kamalie does her best, but she's got the burden of raising two children alone. Cherry helps, but she's only nineteen."

"You're right about both boys," Jax said.

Doc looked from Bella to Jax. "I hope we don't have more murders around here, but will you still investigate cases after you marry, if any arise?"

Jax braced his elbows on the chair arms and folded his hands in front of him. "Who knows?" Out of the corner of his eye, Jax saw Bella shift toward him. He kept his attention on Doc.

"I'm certainly willing to work on investigations, if they come along," she put in.

Since Jax didn't want to discuss the idea further, he got the conversation back on track. "My current concern is finding Mrs. Lackner's killer."

"Of course," Bella agreed.

The slight edge in her tone influenced Jax to modify his statement. "If I have to pursue another killer, I definitely want you as my partner."

A smile lifted Bella's lips. "Good." She again put pencil to paper. "Anything else I should add to my notes?"

"Nothing from me." Doc drummed his fingers on his desk. "You'll want to talk with Forrester, I'm sure, and he'd like to speak with you, Jax. He's tried to reach the housekeeper with no luck. He needs to plan funeral arrangements, and we don't know about next-of-kin."

With one hand, Jax rubbed his taut neck muscles. "We talked with Mrs. Marren. She's on her way back to her sister's place in Boxwood, but I'm not sure she'll be any help in reaching next of kin. From what she told us, Mrs. Lackner didn't have any family left. We're going to talk with a couple of her other school friends. Maybe one will have details."

"I hope someone does," Doc said. "Any leads on what the note means?"

"I'm afraid not," Jax said. "Since an expensive piece of jewelry was missing, we can't be sure the missive isn't intended to mislead us."

"You're the lawman, but it makes sense." Doc put his elbows on his desk. "A lot of folks around here know the housekeeper is off on Mondays. Maybe someone thought Mrs. Lackner would be gone, too."

"We've discussed the possibility. Another issue is the missing appointment book. Maybe an entry would reveal an earlier appointment," Jax said.

Mrs. Smedlay returned with a tray holding a teapot, four cups and saucers, and a plate of cookies. Her husband immediately rose to help her.

"This looks good, my dear," he said with a smile. "We're still discussing the case. Since you knew Mrs. Lackner better than I did, I'm sure Arabella and Jax would like to hear your thoughts."

His wife poured tea and distributed the cups before passing the sweets around. "I told them a little."

"We'd love to hear more," Bella said.

"Yep, we would," Jax agreed.

Mrs. Smedlay settled in the extra chair and helped herself to tea and a cookie. "I heard you discussing Elsie going places on Mondays. I believe she liked to take a drive, although occasionally she and Mrs. Baggeley got together. Most often, at the Baggeley home, although sometimes out at the Walling place." A slight smile tugged up one corner of her mouth. "It hasn't belonged to the Wallings for years, but I always think of it that way."

"A lot of the old-timers do," her husband agreed.

"Mac calls it the Walling house," Bella put in, "and he refers to Mrs. Lackner as Elsie Walling."

"He would've known the family," Mrs. Smedlay observed. "Dr. Walling and the other children died about the time your grandfather and Mac moved to the area."

"Mac mostly recalled the dress shop in town," Bella said. "My mother and grandmother traded there. He's indicated not really being acquainted with Mrs. Walling or Mrs. Lackner. Elsie."

"Understandable," the older woman observed. "What with all that's gone on as far as influenza, businesses suffering, and the war...people haven't gossiped about all the old doings much."

"We heard Mrs. Lackner left town to get married, or she married shortly after leaving. Do you know anything about that?" Bella asked.

"Her mother spread the story," Mrs. Smedlay replied. "I was never sure about it being true."

The comment surprised Jax. He looked at Bella, who seemed equally off-kilter.

"Do you suspect she was never wed?" Bella asked.

A half-shrug lifted one of the older woman's shoulders. "It's hard to say. Elsie told the same story when she returned. No details included, though. I didn't pry." She briefly gazed into her teacup. "It's just that she and Bradley Farber were more than smitten. When they were in school, the two of them started stepping out. It quickly became courtship. They seemed deeply in love, and that sort of profound emotion doesn't disappear."

"No, it sure doesn't," Jax agreed. When Bella turned to him with a smile, his heart swelled with joy and gratitude.

"So, Mrs. Lackner had a childhood sweetheart," Bella suggested.

"Exactly right." the older woman replied.

"I can see why her mother might concoct a story," Bella said. "Marrying is a good excuse to leave home. As far as Mrs. Lackner, I suppose she might've gone along with it to save embarrassment. Few young women went off on their own in those days. It might've seemed scandalous to some."

"I agree, dear." Mrs. Smedlay took another bite of cookie. "It's a harmless fabrication."

"Then, Mrs. Lackner didn't meet her supposed husband-to-be before leaving here?" Jax made the inquiry.

"Her mother promoted that idea, mostly to save face and quell gossip." Mrs. Smedlay glanced at her husband. "We don't engage in tittle-tattle, but it's common knowledge that Bradley's father was president of the local bank. There was trouble when Doc Walling died, but we hadn't moved here yet, of course. Everyone knew about Mrs. Walling owing merchants, or I wouldn't have mentioned it to you even now. A doctor and his wife hear a lot from patients about their money troubles, especially when they need care but can't pay."

"If there's something that might help us solve the murder, I hope you'll share it. Neither Bella nor I will reveal anything personal," Jax assured the older couple.

Doc released a long, low breath. "A few years after Dr. Walling died, we heard his widow was behind in mortgage payments, and the bank was about to foreclose."

"I was in the bank when Mrs. Walling stomped out of Mr. Farber's office. She berated him all the way to the sidewalk." Mrs. Smedlay sat her cup and saucer aside. "Elsie and Bradley were spending a good deal of time together. That ended in short order. Not long afterward, he went off to college. Both of his parents died while he was in school. Brad returned for the services, sold their home, and never came back. Shortly after their funerals, Elsie turned twenty-one and left, too."

"How did word come that she was married?" Bella asked.

"Even though she and her mother weren't close, Elsie wrote occasionally. Her mother said the news came in one of those letters."

"Where was she living then?" Bella asked.

"The letter was postmarked Toledo. Her mother commented on that because there was no return address. Just the postmark. Not that I actually saw the letter, but Lila, her mother, said at least she knew where Elsie was." The older woman shook her head. "So sad for them not to reconcile."

"It is," Bella agreed. "Do you know if Mrs. Lackner stayed in Toledo for long?"

Mrs. Smedlay put her hands out, palms up. "She evidently moved around. No one else seems to be sure where or when. When Elsie came back to Moreley last year, she mentioned styles Back East, although she never admitted to living there. She could've seen fashions in magazines."

"She mentioned wanting to ensure our gowns were chic." Bella chewed on her lower lip. "And they were."

Jax laid a hand on her arm, which brought her gaze to meet his.

Bella answered his unasked question. "I'm happily wearing my mother's gown. Really. The main thing is the ceremony going ahead, as planned."

Jax nodded. They had agreed on that, but the logistics of proceeding would be impaired if the murder was not solved. He hadn't mentioned details to Bella, but they had plagued him. Nolen was Jax's best man. Newton was ferrying guests to Ballantyne from the train station that morning, and Jillian was serving as a bridesmaid. The Jenkinses would help with the investigation, but Richard couldn't stay at the office during the ceremonies. Not when he and Jenny were honored guests. Jax had made a call to another sheriff already, but one lawman wouldn't be enough to cover the day if the case wasn't cracked. Mrs. Smedlay broke into his troubled thoughts.

"Doc and I went to your parents' wedding, Arabella," the older woman said. "Your mother's dress was lovely, and I'm sure you'll be beautiful in it. I doubt if many alterations are necessary."

"I don't think so, either," Bella replied. "It's hanging in her closet. I haven't seen Mrs. Byington's, but the styles should be similar."

"If your mother and Ida's mother married around the same time, I'm sure they are." Mrs. Smedlay smiled. "And there's plenty of time to ensure it fits you well. What is the Placette girl going to do? She's getting married Friday evening, so she must be at her wit's end."

Jax and Bella exchanged glances before he spoke. "She is." After a moment's hesitation, he revealed Vera's accusations. "I need to speak with her maid of honor to confirm the exchange, but I don't know that Ophelia would carry through with her threat."

Mrs. Smedlay met his gaze. "I can imagine Ophelia saying what she did. She's quite full of herself, and I'm sure she was angry about Vera swooping in and getting Elsie to do all the gowns for her wedding party. She's almost as snooty as Ophelia." A flush rose in her lined cheeks. "I shouldn't say such things. I know my words won't go any further."

"They won't," Jax assured her. "Everything we say in this room is confidential."

"Although a doctor and his family shouldn't gossip about patients, I agree with my wife. Both girls are pretentious and proud. I'm sure Ophelia wouldn't ask anyone to kill, but ruining dresses...I can see her paying someone to destroy the gowns. Are you planning to talk with Ophelia?"

"Not yet," Jax said. "I want solid evidence she may be involved. Otherwise, the mayor will be mighty upset."

Bella laid her hand on Jax's arm. "If he fires you, you can always work at Ballantyne."

He clasped her fingers. "Always good to have something to fall back on." Jax kept his tone light, but being the golf professional at the resort had been his dream for most of his life, not an afterthought or a last recourse. No, not at all.

After a few more minutes of conversation, Bella and Jax left the Smedlay house.

Before they got back to the constable's office, she turned to him. "You don't believe we'll solve this case quickly."

Jax's gaze flickered over Bella before returning to the road. "I'm not sure we will, but we'll do our best."

For several moments, neither spoke. Then, Bella voiced the issue in the back of her mind. "You're not thinking we should postpone the wedding, are you?"

He was quick to respond. "I don't want to do that anymore than you do. We already agreed it will go ahead."

Again, a period of silence ensued while Bella considered the issues. "I know, but your deputies are involved, and so is Jillian. Jenny and Richard are dear friends, who want to be at the wedding. I'm sure the mayor will be displeased if no one is at the station for a couple of hours. He probably is already." Mayor Cawlings was always most concerned with how things appeared and, if the entire staff of the constable's office was at a celebration while a killer ran loose, Cawlings would air his displeasure far and wide.

"You're reading my mind, because I was thinking the same things already. As far as the mayor, he mentioned that last week, so I called another offer and asked if they could send one of his deputies for the day. They're happy to do that. I may ask for a second deputy."

Some of her tension seeped away. "I'm not surprised you planned ahead, but even with reinforcements during the ceremonies and reception, you'll have to go back to work if we don't solve the case before the weekend. I suppose I'll have to learn to live with a husband who's a lawman." Resignation and resolve combined inside Bella. Working out the details of married life would take time, but the effort would be more than worth it. When Jax didn't immediately comment, Bella turned to look at him. A muscle worked in his jaw as he stared out the windshield "Are you worried I won't adjust? We've talked very little about me moving into your house. I won't change everything around, if that's what you're thinking. I may not have time to do much except basic housework until fall, since the resort season will start shortly after we return from our honeymoon. If you want everything to stay the same forever, that's fine."

Another interlude passed before he replied. "You work long days at Ballantyne from spring through the holidays with only a brief respite in October and November. Maybe we should live there."

"Really?" Surprise rippled through Bella. The resort was close to town, so Jax could get to work quickly.

"Really. I'm sure it'd work out, and I can rent the house out or sell it."

His quick replies surprised her. "You've already thought about all this."

Jax cleared his throat. "I've thought about everything since we announced our wedding date."

"I see." Why hadn't he mentioned his contemplation before now?

After Jax parked the vehicle in front of his office, he turned to Bella. "You love Ballantyne, and I don't want to take you away from there."

"I love you more than the resort," she murmured without a second's hesitation.

A broad grin lit his handsome face. "Good to know." With one hand, he cupped her cheek. "Maybe I should've discussed it with you, but you'd say living at my place was fine. As for cracking the case, I'll admit I'm concerned about getting it done before our wedding. But you heard Nolen and Newton. They're determined to do all they can. Richard and Jenny will, as well. And it's a given that you and I are steadfast in wanting a solution as soon as possible."

She pressed her fingers against his. "That's all true." Bella let her hand fall away. "Before I go home, let's see if Nolen and Newton have news."

His thumb brushed her lower lip before Jax moved his hand away. "I suppose we should."

Inside the constable's station, Bella and Jax found Jillian and Nolen studying a paper on the counter. "Anything new?" Jax asked.

As the young couple glanced up, Nolen nodded. "It's an old news clipping. The newspaper editor called. Hearing about the murder got him thinking back to when Mrs. Lackner was a girl. After I had the photographs developed, he looked in the files and found an article about her being in a Christmas play."

Bella and Jax crossed the room to study the paper. After scanning the story, she glanced up. "Mrs. Lackner and Bradley Farber had the starring roles. They played sweethearts."

"Interesting, considering what Mrs. Smedlay told us," Jax replied.

"What did she say?" Jillian asked.

"They'd been stepping out when they were in high school," Bella said. "Some folks thought it was getting serious."

The younger girl's eyes widened. "What happened?"

Bella turned to Jax. Although Jillian and Nolen were involved in the investigation, she wasn't sure how much Jax wanted to reveal to the clerk.

"A problem at the bank," he said. "The senior Farber was the president, and there was an issue with the mortgage on the Walling home. Neither Doc nor Mrs. Smedlay had details, but Mrs. Walling berated Mr. Farber publicly. Shortly afterward, Mrs. Lackner and young Farber split up."

"How sad," Jillian murmured.

"I don't remember the Farber family." Nolen made the observation.

"You wouldn't," Jax told him. "Bradley Farber went away to college. Both of his parents died while he was at school. He sold the house and didn't come back. That would've been before you were born."

"I wonder where he is now," Jillian said.

"He went to Toledo University, but we don't know how long he stayed in the city after graduating. If he finished. Evidently he lost touch with everyone from Moreley." Jax shifted from one foot to the other. "Letters from Mrs. Lackner to her mother were postmarked Toledo, which interests me. At least that's what Mrs. Walling told folks. So far, we haven't heard about anyone seeing those letters or getting any themselves."

"I imagine that part is true," Bella put in. "And it interests me, as well."

Jillian and Nolen concurred.

"I want to speak with Mrs. Placette again." Jax glanced at the wall clock. "They're expecting dinner guests. We have other leads to pursue, so I'll call and set up another meeting for tomorrow."

"I want to be there," Bella told him. "I'll try my dress on as soon as Jenny and her mother arrive, which means I should be here by eleven o'clock."

"I'd like you to go along with me," Jax agreed. "In the meantime, we'll talk to Charley Ammers, the principal, Abner Crater, Sam Push, and some others. That's if we can track them all down yet tonight."

"We can definitely speak with Sam," Nolen said. "I don't know about you, but I'm ready for supper."

When Jax's stomach growled, everyone chuckled. He flushed bright red.

"You missed lunch, so supper is necessary," Bella said. "Besides, someone at the café might know about the two men who worked for Mrs. Lackner."

"That's a good place to start," Jax agreed, "since it's hard to understand why they supposedly kept to themselves. Not normal behavior."

"I agree," Bella replied. "I suppose I should head to Ballantyne, but I'll see all of you tomorrow."

"I want to follow you home. Just to be on the safe side." Jax stood up as he spoke.

Because she knew he'd worry if she didn't acquiesce, Bella agreed.

The drive to Ballantyne took the usual ten minutes. Jax pulled his Chummy to a stop behind the Buick roadster and joined Bella by the porch steps. "Ida will be glad to have her precious vehicle back," she observed with a smile.

"I'm sure she will." Jax shifted from one foot to the other. There was so much more he wanted to say. Pressed for time, he forced himself to keep to the case. "If we turn up anything big before ten o'clock, I'll call."

"Good. I'd love to hear you know who the killer is," she replied.

"I'd love to know, but that's not likely yet tonight. We have some suspects, but none stands out." Jax didn't quell his frustration, which stemmed from wanting to crack the case before Saturday.

Bella's next words went to the core of the matter. "You wouldn't feel as pressured if our wedding wasn't less than five days away. Neither would I." She laid one hand on his chest. "We've never found a killer in fewer than twelve hours, and we can't expect to now."

Jax put his fingers over hers. "You're right. I'll gather as much evidence as I can this evening, and we can go over everything with the team tomorrow."

"I'll be at your office around eleven o'clock. Jenny will call when they arrive at your place later tonight, and we'll set a time to meet for early tomorrow."

Dismay assailed Jax. "Take whatever time you need."

"I won't need much," she assured him. "I'll have to try on the gown, so Mrs. Burtis can work on it. Since Mother and I were almost the same in height and build, it shouldn't need many alterations. I can come back and try it on again later in the day. I'm sure Ida will let me use the Buick again. Both Griff's vehicle and the Ford will be here."

Since he valued Bella's sleuthing ability, Jax agreed with a caveat. "As long as you take whatever time you need for wedding plans and resort issues, I'd like you to join me as soon as you can tomorrow."

She beamed at him. "I'll see you around eleven o'clock."

Jax brushed a kiss across her forehead and reluctantly took his leave.

Chapter Seven

O n Tuesday morning, shortly before eleven o'clock, Bella, Jillian, and Jenny Jenkins climbed into Ida's Buick and headed to town. Earlier, Nolen had dropped his sweetheart off at the resort, along with his mother, the Ballantyne cook and housekeeper. Shortly afterward, Richard had done the same for his wife and mother-in-law. The five women, along with Ida and her mother, tackled the wedding gown issue in short order. Mrs. Burtis was enthusiastic about working on the dresses, and the others contributed their ideas. Nips and tucks were the only necessities. Within two hours, Bella and Ida both felt confident and pleased with the plans to alter their mothers' dresses. Since her best friend encouraged her to work on the investigation, Bella left with a clear conscience.

When the trio of women entered the constable's office, Jax and Nolen were standing at the front counter. Richard Jenkins, who was seated at the clerk's desk, immediately rose. "How lovely to see both of you again." He focused on Bella and Jillian, before looking at his wife. "It's always wonderful to see you, dear."

Jenny beamed at him. "And the same for me seeing you."

The warm by-play between the long-married couple made Bella wish for the day when she and Jax would have similar exchanges. Soon, she thought. Soon, they would embark on a lifetime together.

After Jillian sat at her desk, Jax gestured toward his office. As everyone assembled at the round table where their group meetings typically took place, Bella got out her notepad and pencil. Nolen did the same. "We've discussed the basics of the case, since Richard got here." Jax went on to reveal the latest information. The main takeaway was the Geneves and the Coopers confirming what the Smedlays had revealed. Unfortunately, the two couples added nothing substantive, and no one knew anything about the two men who had temporarily worked for Mrs. Lackner.

"I haven't been able to find Charley Ammers. He wasn't at home last night or at school this morning," the young deputy said. "I talked to his mother twice. Late yesterday and early today. He wasn't back, and he left class yesterday after lunch. Both Newton and I have asked around town, but no one has seen him."

"Did Mrs. Ammers say if he's stayed out all night in the past?" Bella asked.

"He has a few times," Nolen replied. "I've talked to him about it before, because him disappearing worries his mother."

"What does he do? Where does he go?" Bella asked.

"Usually, he's with Abner Crater," Nolen replied.

Apprehension stalked Bella. "Both boys worked for Mrs. Lackner, and both got fired. Cherry told us her brother planned to confront Mrs. Lackner about her planning to report

Mrs. Ammers and Cherry for putting through calls from the stranger. If the man was a stranger."

Jax ran his fingers through his clipped blonde hair. "Since we haven't tracked Abner down, I'm concerned about where the two of them are."

Bella studied her betrothed. Dark smudges shadowed his red-rimmed eyes, and his handsome face was lined with fatigue. She didn't need to ask if he'd gotten any sleep. If she knew him at all, and Bella knew Jax well, he had stayed up to work on the case and had probably driven around town looking for the boys. Later, she would suggest some rest was in order. For now, she responded to his comment. "I agree. We need to find both of them, but what about the calls? Has Mrs. Ammers learned anymore?"

A shake of the head preceded Jax's reply. "I talked to her last night and this morning. She hasn't traced all the calls yet, but she's hoping to hear from other operators today. We can stop there later." He directed the comment to Bella, who nodded.

Richard leaned back in his chair. "From what Jax, Nolen, and Newton told me, details of the calls could be key. We may even get a name and location, so we can talk with the man."

"I hope so," Bella replied. "That could be significant if he has an alibi for yesterday morning."

"Then, we'd eliminate someone," Jax put in, "but I wish we had more hard facts."

The retired constable glanced around the table before speaking again. "Earlier, you mentioned going back to talk with Mrs. Placette. Having Arabella along on that interview is a good idea. Same with interviewing Mrs. Marren, if you can locate her."

Bella looked from the senior constable to Jax. "Didn't Mrs. Marren go back to her sister's house?"

Jax drummed his fingers on the table. "Newton called twice this morning. No answer, so he contacted the diner over there.

The owner hasn't seen either woman, but he's been busy. Lots of customers in-and-out, and a couple of his workers are sick. I sent Newton over to check the Tillis house. If the sisters aren't there, he'll ask around town."

"Surely, someone has seen one of them. If no one has, that's a bad sign." Mrs. Marren seemed to be an unlikely killer. But how well did Bella know the woman? Not well enough to be sure of her innocence. Or that she hadn't fallen victim herself.

"We'll find out," Jax said.

"Which means we have four strong possibilities," Nolen said. "The housekeeper, the unknown caller, Charley, and Abner. I hate to include those two boys, but until we find them..." His voice trailed off.

The frustration in the deputy's voice echoed inside Bella. "What about the two men who worked for Mrs. Lackner?"

"Richard, Newton, Nolen, and I all asked around town this morning. No one recalls seeing them. Not even the regular mailman, who comes in the afternoon," Jax replied. "On the other hand, he saw Charley working after school and on weekends for a time. Abner didn't last as long, and the mailman never saw him."

For a few moments, Bella considered the revelations. "Since the mailman would come and go quickly, he might not notice who was working. But shouldn't he have seen the black car?" Even as she expressed the sentiment, Bella wondered why the boys or the men would always have been out of sight. Pondering the idea any longer slipped away as the discussion continued.

"That's likely," Nolen put in.

"But it leaves us with more questions." Bella didn't hide her dismay.

"Take heart, Arabella," Richard told her. "Not having the actual killer among our current suspects doesn't mean we won't solve the case before your wedding day."

"We're getting married, no matter what." As he spoke, Jax clasped Bella's hand.

The reiteration of his promise touched her deeply, but apprehension remained. Although their nuptials were the top priority, Bella had been looking forward to the honeymoon. If they couldn't get away now, they would have to wait until fall. Then, they wouldn't be going with Ida and Griff, as they had planned The two young women had spent hours poring over magazine articles about their destination. Niagara Falls looked to be spectacular, and Bella was excited about the trip. She brushed off her disappointment and smiled at him. "Yes, we are."

He nodded and released her hand. "Back to the case. When I spoke with Sam Push, he mentioned names of their schoolmates. He thinks a couple of women tried to befriend Mrs. Lackner again. She was in the café when one of her schoolmates invited her to share a table, but Mrs. Lackner gave her the cold shoulder." Jax yanked a sheet of paper off his desk, which sat beside the table. "Ruth Baggeley and Sadie Duckson are her two old friends. Since Mrs. Placette mentioned them, I'd already tried to contact both. Mrs. Baggeley took the train to Sandusky yesterday but should be home this afternoon. Miss Duckson went to Boxwood after school yesterday, but I stopped today while her class was in morning recess. She definitely got an icy response from the dressmaker. Mrs. Lackner told her not to call again and, when they crossed paths in town one time, she hurried past Miss Duckson."

"Any idea of why?" Bella asked.

"Miss Duckson thought it was jealousy. Evidently, they were competitive in school. Mrs. Lackner didn't have as much time for her studies after her father passed, and she didn't earn top honors in their class after that. Miss Duckson did. And she went on to normal school." Jax turned to Richard. "I hadn't gotten around to sharing all this, but she's been a teacher at Moreley Grade School for years."

"Then, envy is a possibility," Richard commented. "Or is this teacher the kind to brag?"

"I wasn't in her class. Were either of you?" Bella asked Jax and Nolen.

"I had her for second grade," Nolen replied. "Sweet lady."

Jax shook his head. "She was never my teacher, but I recall my mother liking her."

"So, Mrs. Lackner was probably jealous, but Miss Duckson doesn't harbor bad feelings herself, does she?" Bella asked.

"Not that I could tell," Jax responded. "She seemed sad they didn't renew their friendship. Said so many from their class moved away or died in recent years. A few from influenza."

Bella rolled the pencil between her fingers. "But they were friends in school, even though they competed."

"They were," Jax agreed. "Miss Duckson thought Mrs. Baggeley and Mrs. Lackner were closer. Best friends growing up, and we've heard they still get together."

"I talked to Mr. Forrester," Nolen put in. "He's a little older, but he recalled Mrs. Lackner and Bradley being smitten with each other. He didn't know what happened to Farber after college or where Mrs. Lackner headed from here."

"The information is useful as corroboration," Jax said. "Sam didn't hear the exchange between Vera Placette and Ophelia Upchurch at the café, did he?"

Nolen shook his head. "He didn't even remember the two girls being there at the same time. Ophelia comes in often, since Sam is providing food for her wedding reception. He mentioned her being persnickety." The deputy glanced at Bella. "Said it's too bad she wasn't getting married at Ballantyne."

Bella chuckled. "I'm glad we had an excuse. I can't imagine how we'd meet her lofty expectations."

"Or why you'd want to try," Newton added.

After a moment, Richard brought the conversation back to the case. "Maybe there's someone else who's still around that she had issues with. Or one could have information about why she went to Toledo, where Bradley Farber was in school."

"The last interests me most," Bella said. "Toledo isn't far, but neither is Columbus. Or even Cleveland. If she wanted to get away, any of those cities would've offered work possibilities."

Jenny nodded. "Earlier today, Bella mentioned Mrs. Lackner and young Farber being a couple before outside forces intervened. I'd like to know why she went to where he was. It doesn't seem like a happenstance."

"I agree, dear," her husband said.

"But why wouldn't she tell anyone they were married?" Nolen asked.

"A good question," Jax replied. "One that we haven't answered yet."

Fresh frustration assailed Bella. "There are several dangling threads."

"We'll get them tied up," Richard commented. "What do you want Jenny and me to do?"

"I'd like someone to stay here in case any important calls come in," Jax said.

"Then, we'll stay," Richard said.

"Thanks." Jax turned to Bella. "We need to see the Ammers women before heading to the Baggeley house."

"And I need to make the regular rounds," Nolen said with no enthusiasm.

"That's important, too," Jax told him.

"Right," the young deputy replied.

Bella had to bite her lip to keep from chuckling, but she didn't blame Nolen for being disappointed. Walking the business area and neighborhoods wasn't half as intriguing as investigating a murder. But this time, she didn't feel as enthusiastic as usual. Instead, Bella felt apprehensive. Not only did they have no solid direction to follow, they didn't know if the note was a genuine threat or an attempted deflection. Uncertainty hung as heavily as a shroud.

After a final discussion of their next steps, the meeting broke up a few minutes later. When Bella and Jax got on the road, he turned to her. "I plan to ask tougher questions, especially of Cherry. I'm not sure the girl has been forthright with us, and I'm wondering if she knows where her brother is."

"I am, too, and I could have asked more pointed questions myself."

"You had to still feel shock over finding the body and, although you're a great amateur detective, I'm a lawman. The onus is on me." Jax could not keep a note of frustration from his tone.

With one forefinger, she tapped the steering wheel. "You may be right about someone from long ago holding a grudge. Someone from Moreley. I know that adds another potential suspect. A vague one."

"We have to examine all possibilities. If Mrs. Baggeley has any clues, we can loop back to talk with Mrs. Placette. And follow-up with the person, or persons."

"If we talk with Mrs. Ammers first, we see Mrs. Baggeley afterward, since she should be home in about an hour-and-a-half."

After Bella pulled to a stop in front of the Ammers' home, Jax escorted her to the door. A few moments passed before

Cherry answered. The girl frowned. "What do you need? Mama is working, and I'm about to meet a friend at the café."

The greeting, hardly warm, surprised Jax, but he maintained an outwardly calm demeanor. "Maybe you should call the café and let your friend know you'll be late. We need to talk with your mother again, and possibly you, too."

A mutinous expression darkened Cherry's face. "All right," she replied in an affronted tone before turning away and stalking down the narrow hallway to the tiny room where her mother was handling calls.

Mrs. Ammers sat at the small switchboard, which resembled an upright piano. Only four of the plugs were filled, indicating active lines. No lights were lit to signal incoming calls. Within moments, the operator shifted to face the trio after she finished a connection. "You must be back for more information." Concern etched her weary expression. "I don't have details about all the calls yet. I'll have to wait until the operators contact me."

"I understand," Jax replied, "and if you have any new information about the male caller, we'd like to know."

"Of course," the operator said as she removed her headset, rose from her chair, and took a paper off the desk. "Cherry, I'll need you to take over for a short time."

"I gotta call Ophelia and hope she isn't already at the café," the girl replied.

"If she isn't at home, telephone the restaurant and explain." Mrs. Ammers gestured to Bella and Jax. "We can talk in the parlor."

Jax glanced at Bella. Her expression revealed she'd also noted the name of Cherry's friend. How close were the two girls?

After they were all seated, Jax spoke. "Thank you for speaking with us again. We're sorry to infringe on Cherry's time off, but we may need to talk to her, too."

"She isn't a little girl anymore, and she needs to understand work comes before play. It won't hurt her to be late for lunch. Ophelia doesn't have a job, so she can wait for Cherry. They're likely discussing the wedding, which is next week. Cherry is part of the wedding party." Mrs. Ammers chewed on her lower lip.

"Ophelia and Cherry must be good friends," Bella observed. The news surprised her, but Bella didn't keep track of town goings-on. She had plenty to do with her own wedding, sleuthing, and Ballantyne.

Kamalie Ammers ran one hand over her face. "Ophelia enjoys being admired and copied. Not that we can afford what she buys. If Mrs. Upchurch hadn't offered to pay for Cherry's dress, my daughter couldn't be a bridesmaid. I hate taking charity, and I feel like we owe a debt to the family despite what they've said."

"I'm sure Cherry would've been terribly disappointed not to be in her friend's wedding," Bella said.

"Cherry believes Ophelia is a friend, but Ophelia likely regards my daughter as a loyal follower. Nothing more. After the ceremony, I doubt if she'll stay in touch," Mrs. Ammers replied.

The observations were revealing. Jax watched as Bella duly jotted notes down. Later, they could review this conversation, and her view was apt to match his: the relationship between Ophelia and Cherry was cause for concern.

"But they meet to talk about wedding plans often?" Jax inquired.

One of Kamalie Ammers' thin shoulders lifted in a half-shrug. "Usually, Ophelia has a list of duties for Cherry to handle. All the other attendants, including the maid of honor and matron of honor, live out-of-town. Mostly schoolmates of Ophelia."

"How many are in the wedding party?" Bella asked.

"Eight girls, in all. I'm sure Cherry was only included because she's willing to help with any type of tasks." The operator clasped her hands together. "I hope she's not hurt when Ophelia drops her after the wedding."

Jax hoped Cherry hadn't included getting her brother to do Ophelia's dirty work in her task list. The girl's nervousness took on a different aspect, considering the latest revelations.

"Perhaps, they will stay in touch," Bella said.

"Perhaps," Mrs. Ammers repeated, without a trace of certainty. "Cherry might not really be meeting Ophelia. She could have plans with Abner Crater. She knows I don't approve of the boy, so she pretends to meet others."

Another disclosure that put Jax on alert. Young Abner was a troublemaker, so Jax understood the woman's objection. He had known nothing about the young couple spending time together. Most likely, they kept their dates secret, so word did not get back to Mrs. Ammers—although she had obviously found out. The situation was complicated by both Abner and Charley being fired for stealing, and by Cherry's friendship with Ophelia Upchurch. Jax was considering an appropriate response when Bella spoke.

"Young girls sometimes have crushes on boys who don't meet with their parents' approval," she said.

"I s'pose so, but Charley also spends time with Abner. I know the boy grew up like a weed, with virtually no tending after his mother passed. Quit school at fourteen and has worked at odd jobs ever since. If he works at all." The older woman shook her head. "I'm sorry. You're here to talk about the murder." She handed the paper to Jax. "Since I last spoke with you, I traced back another call."

He scanned the contents before passing it on to Bella. "This one evidently originated in Columbus."

"I'm sure that's true because I spoke with the operator who initially handled the connection," Mrs. Ammers replied. "I put her name at the bottom of the sheet. She knows you may contact her."

"Thanks," Jax said. "She didn't ask for a name and no one along the way did, either."

"No, but it isn't unusual." Kamalie made the confirmation. "You'll see the call was made from a hotel in Columbus. Would a guest have to get permission for long-distance?"

"He would, so we'll look into that aspect," Jax replied. "But what about the other calls? Didn't you know who connected to you?" The other operator, even if not known to Kamalie Ammers, would surely have named her location.

Color climbed into the woman's face as she wrung her hands together. "Cherry was working those times. She knows to take down information about long-distance connections, but she doesn't always. Particularly if she gets distracted by a friend ringing her. I should've said so right off, but I'm trying hard to get details for you. I need to contact all the operators who connect with us."

Dismay flickered through Jax. Tracing the additional call backs to their sources should not be impossible, but the girl's distraction would make it more difficult than he had figured. "If you have a time frame, we'll work on locating the callers ourselves."

Mrs. Ammers put a hand to her mouth. "I'm so sorry. I'll make sure she does better." Her lips trembled. "This is a good job, and I don't want to lose it."

"We won't do or say anything to get you fired," Bella assured her.

"But if people know Cherry didn't note all the calls..." The woman's quavering voice trailed off.

Jax broke into the response. "No one else needs to know."

A shuddering breath left the operator. "Thank you. As for the time, it was last Wednesday in the early afternoon. I had an appointment with Doc Smedlay. On my way home, I shopped, so I was gone for a couple of hours. About two o'clock to four."

Since Bella had already retrieved her notepad and pencil, she was busy writing. Jax smiled to himself. She was a remarkable sleuth and a wonderful partner. "That'll help us a lot," he said.

"It should," Bella agreed. "Does Cherry know where the last connecting operator was?"

Mrs. Ammers nodded. "Over in Karston."

Bella made another notation. "I'm not acquainted with her, but the Jenkinses must be."

"We'll ask them," Jax put in. "Can we take these notes? If you need them back, let me know."

"I keep a call log, so you can have those." She gestured at the papers in Jax's hand. "I wrote what I thought might be useful."

"Thank you," he replied. "Now, if we can speak with Cherry, you're free to go back to work."

After a nod, the woman hurried from the room.

Jax turned to Bella. "We should be able to trace the call back to the source, shouldn't we?"

"I believe so, but I wasn't ever a domestic operator."

"You trained to be one, so you know the basics," he observed. Jax remembered Bella revealing the Signal Corps had looked for French speakers and taught them as operators, since it was an easier process than the other way around. Since Bella had been fluent in French, due to several years of studying the language in high school and college, she'd gotten accepted immediately.

"We learned about using the switchboards and such, but that was several years ago. Processes may have changed some. If the Karston operator keeps an accurate log, that'll be key," Bella replied.

"Let's hope she does."

"You didn't mention Charley working for Mrs. Lackner."

Jax shook his head. "I doubt if Mrs. Ammers knows, but I bet Cherry does. I'd rather catch her off-guard. We've got more than expected to go over with the girl."

Bella rolled her eyes. "I had no idea about her being in Ophelia's wedding. Of course, I haven't been in town much, since the holidays."

"And you've been busy planning our wedding." Jax clasped her hand. "But I've been around every day, and I know nothing about the Upchurch ceremony, except that it's the weekend after ours, which gave us an out as far as attending."

"Our honeymoon plans also provided an excellent excuse for me to turn down scheduling the event at Ballantyne. Mrs. Upchurch and Ophelia weren't pleased, but the mayor understood."

"It means a lot of business for the town," Jax pointed out. "The hotel is booked up, and the boardinghouse is accepting overflow guests." Whatever else Jax might have said was cut off by Cherry walking in. Her sulky expression didn't surprise him. Although he wanted to chastise the girl for not being responsible, and possibly putting her mother's job in jeopardy, Jax minded his own business on that score. There was plenty more to cover. "We have a few questions for you."

Cherry's response was to plunk down in a chair with a loud sigh. Jax and Bella exchanged a glance before she addressed the girl. "We won't keep you long."

"I hope not. I'm already late," Cherry replied.

"You called your friend, didn't you?" Bella asked.

"She'd already left home." Cherry didn't meet Bella's gaze. Instead, she shifted restlessly.

"I'm sure Mr. Push at the café will give her the message," Bella said.

"I didn't telephone there."

"Why not? Don't you want your friend to know you're going to be late?" Jax made the inquiries.

The girl folded her hands in her lap. "I'll get there soon enough."

When Jax turned to Bella, he saw her gaze narrow on Cherry. "Were you really meeting a girlfriend?" he inquired.

Cherry's head came up, and she stared at Jax for a long moment. "I suppose my mother told you about my beau."

"Are you and Abner courting?" Bella asked.

Color crept into the younger woman's cheeks. "No, not exactly."

Several seconds elapsed before Bella responded. "Are you just stepping out with the boy?"

"He isn't a boy," Cherry said. "He's a man."

Jax felt sure Abner had insisted on that designation. "He's nineteen, which is still young, and he hasn't reached his majority yet."

"He's been on his own, making his own way for a while," Cherry observed.

"The last I knew, he didn't have a full-time job." Jax tried to sound nonjudgmental, but he didn't like the girl being involved with young Crater. Uneasiness crept through him, as he considered if Cherry knew the whereabouts of her brother and her beau. If they had reason to hide, was she aware of why? Had she instigated them going to the Lackner home? Had Ophelia asked her to do the dirty work? The questions disturbed him.

"No, but he works when he can." Cherry lifted her chin a fraction.

The girl's snippy tone grated on Jax, who knew better. The boy only worked when he wanted pocket money. Several shopkeepers in town had revealed as much to Jax and his deputies some time ago. "He's not working now?" A general query wouldn't garner information about Abner being hired by Mrs.

Lackner, but Jax wanted to proceed with caution. Jumping to Abner's defense would likely be Cherry's knee-jerk reaction. Better to slowly lead into queries about his job at the Lackner house and her brother's tenure there, as well. Then, Jax could go on to her relationship with Ophelia Upchurch.

"No, he's been looking for something worthwhile," Cherry replied. "But why ask about him? He's got nothing to do with the calls."

Jax shrugged. "He might, if you were talking with him when any came in. Your mother says you're supposed to log all of them. But you didn't. Maybe because you wanted to get back to Abner."

Color surged into the girl's heart-shaped face. "Sometimes, I forget to jot down long-distance calls."

She sounded recalcitrant, which matched her previous comments. Jax ground his teeth and glanced at Bella, who moved one forefinger from side-to-side. He let her address Cherry.

"Your mother needs her job," Bella pointed out, "and she depends on you to help. Business in Moreley has rebounded, so calls are on the increase. That's likely to continue, since more and more people are getting telephones. No one can work twenty-four hours a day, seven days a week. A second operator might be hired, if you no longer want to assist your mother. There aren't many other jobs open right now, but summer help is always needed at various places. You could make a change then."

The girl's jaw dropped. "Those jobs are mostly cleaning or clerking. Sometimes, evenings, too. Ma is pretty good about allowing me to choose my times off, and I enjoy being able to go right to the telephone room here at home."

"I'm sure you do," Bella replied, "especially in bad weather. You don't need to leave the house to go to work." When Cherry bowed her head, Bella looked at Jax.

He winked. She was more adept at handling the girl than he was. Jax waited for Cherry to respond.

"I oughta be more responsible," the younger woman said. "I won't skip noting long-distances calls again."

"That's good," Jax put in, "but we could use more information about the calls you didn't record. Do you remember anything at all that might help? Did the other operator say something of note?"

Cherry gnawed on her lower lip. "One mentioned the call taking time to come through, and the caller being annoyed with the operator at his end. People don't like to wait."

"Which happens when a long-distance request requires multiple connections. The caller often needs to wait for a return call," Bella observed. "That might've occurred. We can ask the operator who spoke with you."

"And that will help?" Cherry asked.

"It should," Bella replied, "although it'd be better if you had recorded more details."

A soft sigh left the girl. "I will from now on."

Since Cherry was now contrite, at least in one regard, Jax asked about her young swain. "Are you meeting Abner for lunch?" He hoped she was. Otherwise, finding the kid could be a problem.

Surprise flashed in her gaze. For several moments, the girl seemed to wage an internal debate. Finally, she released a pent-up breath. "I'm meeting him at the park. Don't tell Ma. Please."

Bella and Jax exchanged a long look before she said, "We won't, if you also let us know where your brother is."

Cherry put both hands to her face. "Staying at Abner's place. Mr. Crater went up to the lakeshore for a few days."

Probably to meet a boat with bootlegged booze, Jax thought with dismay. The man had gotten involved in the illegal trade to pay his bills, and his participation took him out of town often. "Why didn't he come home last night? Your mother is plenty worried about him."

"He'd been smoking with his friends," Cherry replied.

"And drinking, too," Jax suggested.

A half-shrug lifted one of her slender shoulders. "Maybe."

Bella focused on the girl. "He tells you things that you both hide from your mother." When Cherry nodded, Bella continued. "How long did your brother work for Mrs. Lackner?"

The girl looked stricken. "I should've told you about that yesterday."

"Yes, you should have," Bella agreed in a calm tone. "I assume your mother didn't know."

"She didn't because he went out there when he should've been in class," Cherry replied. "He told Mrs. Lackner he'd quit school. Since she's hardly ever in town, she didn't know the difference."

"So, when your brother threatened to go out there and tell her off, he knew her. And she knew him." Jax made the statements.

"Yes, but he didn't go. He was just blustering," Cherry said. "He only worked there a few weeks. The housekeeper and Mrs. Lackner were demanding, and he didn't get paid much. Then, the principal found out what he'd been doing and threatened to tell Ma. Charley quit then."

"He wasn't fired?" Bella asked.

"No. Like I said, Charley didn't want Ma to know about skipping school," Cherry replied.

"What about Abner? Why did he leave?" Jax asked.

Cherry looked crestfallen at the query. "Some silver came up missing, and they accused him. But he didn't take nothing."

"It wasn't reported to my office," Jax said.

"Mrs. Lackner didn't pay him for the last week of work. Said that would help even out what he owed her. Abner agreed cuz he's been accused before," Cherry said. "Mostly cuz of his pa."

While Jax didn't concur with her assessment about Abner being wrongly implicated in thievery, he didn't argue. If the girl knew more, Jax wanted to hear it. "So, he's done nothing wrong."

"Not that I know about." She worried her lower lip. "Well, maybe some little things when he was younger. He wants to be better now."

Although Jax wasn't convinced, he continued with more questions. "And your brother? When is he coming home?"

"Probably this afternoon. Charley called early today when Ma was bathing. He's lying low until school is out," Cherry explained.

"When he gets here, tell him I want to talk with him," Jax said. "It'll go better for him if he comes to the station, and we don't have to search anymore."

"Yes, sir." Cherry shifted restlessly. "Can I go now?"

"We'd like to know about your friendship with Ophelia," Bella put in. "You're going to be one of her attendants. You two must've gotten close since she's been living in Moreley."

Pleasure sparkled in the girl's eyes. "She went to school here for the first year, and we were in the same class. Since she's usually in town for part of the summer, I've seen her sometimes. This last year, Ophelia has spent a lot of time in Moreley, especially since the holidays. She's needed help with her wedding plans."

"And you've pitched in," Bella said.

"Yes, it's so exciting. Ophelia has such wonderful ideas, and my gown is gorgeous. I'm lucky one of her cousins can't be in the wedding, since she's with child," Cherry responded. "We're about the same height, so I'll fit in with the other girls."

"Are all of Ophelia's attendants the same size?" Bella asked.

Jax detected the note of incredulity in her voice.

Cherry, still beaming, seemed oblivious. "Close. The tallest will go down the aisle last and be on the outside edge at the altar. Same with the groomsmen. It'll look lovely."

"I'm sure it will," Bella observed with little enthusiasm. "You mentioned how pretty your dress is. Where did Ophelia go to have them made? I know she wanted Mrs. Lackner to make them, but she couldn't take on another client."

All cheerfulness left the girl's expression as a scowl blanketed her features. "We had to go to Sandusky. The dressmakers are highly skilled, which was good, but Ophelia wanted every aspect of her wedding to support Moreley businesses. Vera Placette ruined those plans."

"How so?" Bella asked.

A smile formed on Jax's face as he observed his betrothed at work. Bella was a skilled sleuth, and watching her in action riveted him.

"Around Christmas, some of Ophelia's friends came to town for the engagement party. The day before, we ate at the hotel. Vera and her bridesmaids were there for the special luncheon, too. We ended up sitting at the same big table. Ophelia was talking about her mother calling Mrs. Lackner the next afternoon to settle on our gowns. Supposedly, Vera was getting hers made in Toledo. Or so she had said before Ophelia mentioned wanting to support Moreley businesses. Until then, Vera planned to see her grandmother's dressmaker, since the woman makes gowns for all the wealthy ladies in the city."

"Do you know what happened?" Jax asked, even though he already did.

A harrumph left Cherry. "That awful brat, Vera, went home and got her mother to call Mrs. Lackner that very evening. When Mrs. Upchurch tried to set up an appointment the next day, it was too late. Vera thought it was funny that she got Mrs.

Lackner before Ophelia could. Can you imagine? She lorded it over Ophelia more than once." The girl's voice grew shriller with each word. "I'm glad someone ruined her dress. She deserved it."

"The same person destroyed other gowns, including mine." Bella laid her pencil down.

A flush rose in Cherry's cheeks. "I'm sorry about that," she murmured.

Jax didn't allow any time to elapse before he pressed for the most important information. "Do you know anything about who did it?"

Cherry's eyes went wide, and she swallowed convulsively. "Of course not."

For a long moment, he stared at the girl, who failed to maintain eye contact. "Are you sure you didn't mention a way to see that Vera Placette's gown was unwearable?"

Silence echoed in the tiny parlor, while Cherry clasped and unclasped her hands. In the interlude, Jax turned to Bella with a silent query. She nodded before speaking.

"What did you say to Ophelia about getting even with Vera?" Bella asked.

After putting her hands over her eyes, Cherry responded. "I only said it would be too bad if someone broke in and ruined Vera's dress ahead of her wedding. I never said to do it, or who could do it." When she looked at Jax and Bella, Cherry wiped at the tears streaming down her face. "Ophelia only agreed it would. Not that she'd get it done, and I don't think she'd do such a thing. I'm sure she wouldn't have wanted Mrs. Lackner harmed."

"Did you suggest someone who might break in and ruin the dress?" Jax asked.

Cherry licked her lips. "I didn't."

Something in her manner put him further on edge. "But you told others about the idea. Maybe your brother or Abner?"

A shuddering breath left the girl. "I mentioned Vera going behind Ophelia's back to both of them. Neither of them liked Mrs. Lackner much, and they talked about getting some money by breaking in on a Monday when no one was home. I said *no* right off."

Jax was not sure about the veracity of her claim, but he wondered about the two boys more. "How did they respond?"

"They promised not to do anything," she replied. "I said they better not."

The worry darkening her watery eyes telegraphed her fear that the pair hadn't listened. "Did Ophelia mention the idea again?" Cherry shook her head.

"You're sure she didn't talk to Charley or Abner?" Jax asked. "Or that neither of them talked to her?"

Moisture spilled down her cheeks, and Cherry wiped at it with the back of one hand. She cleared her throat, but no words came out.

"Cherry, if you know something significant, it'd be better all-around if you tell us." Bella spoke in a soft, reassuring tone.

Finally, the girl looked up. "I saw Abner talking with Ophelia a couple weeks ago. She knew I was meeting him at the park and got there before me. They claimed it was happenstance, but they looked guilty." She pulled out a hanky and swiped away an errant tear. "I thought she handed him something, but he swore that wasn't the case. He said he wouldn't vandalize Mrs. Lackner's house for fear of getting arrested. He doesn't want to hurt or embarrass me. I believe him."

Although Jax felt sure the girl wanted to believe her young beau, he was equally certain the boy could have lied. "What about your brother?" He made sure the question was not an accusation.

"Charley wouldn't do it on his own," Cherry said. "He's foolish but not stupid."

Again, Jax was not convinced, which he kept to himself. He and Bella could do more digging, as would the rest of their team.

After wrapping up their exchange with Cherry, Bella and Jax went back to the car. She turned to him before driving off. "I'm not sure what to think about the situation with Ophelia Upchurch."

"Neither am I. While I don't think she or either boy would plan to kill anyone, I can see her contemplating revenge, and maybe planning for it. Same with Charley and Abner taking money to destroy Vera's dress. Since they wouldn't know which one it was, they could've ruined all the gowns."

"And there was a fight with Mrs. Lackner if she surprised them," Bella added.

"I'm afraid that's what happened, although I still hope there's another explanation. Mrs. Marren, her sister, and the hired men aren't off my suspect list."

"Mine, either," Bella said. "Charley and Abner are closer than I figured, which is a concern. And the silver missing weeks ago is troubling, even though it probably doesn't relate to the murder."

Jax nodded. "I agree. Abner has skirted the edge of the law, and may have fallen over it, although we haven't caught him stealing stuff."

Dismay hit Bella. "You think he's burglarized other homes or businesses?"

He lifted one shoulder in a half-shrug. "Abner worked at the mercantile last year for a time, and the Downings noticed some items missing. They asked him, and he got huffy about it. When Mr. Downing talked to me, he didn't want Abner charged, but he thought I should know. Then, the kid was a stock boy at the drugstore. Again, things disappeared. That time, Nolen talked to him, to no avail."

"That's not good," Bella said, "especially when items disappeared from the Lackner house."

"It's worrisome. There were a couple of home break-ins last fall and again this past month. I can't say it's Abner, but my deputies and I discussed him as a suspect and questioned him. Without solid evidence, we couldn't make an arrest."

"You didn't mention all this to me." Bella wondered why Jax hadn't.

A chuckle left him. "There isn't a trail of clues to follow. Besides, Nolen and Newton handled the cases that occurred when I was gone." His expression softened. "You've been busy enough with the resort and rescuing me twice in the past six months."

Jax's gratitude touched her. "I only rescued you in September. In December, I spearheaded the effort proving your innocence."

More low laughter rumbled out of him. "Indeed, you did, and I appreciate all your efforts on my behalf."

Matching amusement filled Bella, but apprehension soon displaced it. "I hope we solve this murder soon and without more complications. We're not paring down the list." For a long moment, she gazed steadily into his leaf green eyes. "Only Ophelia's warning to Vera explains why that note was left."

"Unless there's more to know, and Mrs. Lackner planned to remarry."

Frustration rose inside Bella like steam in a teakettle. "We need to know who was calling to find out if that's a possibility."

"For now, let's focus on what we know. Mrs. Smedlay mentioned Mrs. Walling buying a lot of expensive goods. Maybe some things are still in the house. I never saw silver, but they wouldn't accuse Abner if none existed." He clasped her hand. "We can ask Abner about it. As far as the note, the Placettes are already on alert about a perpetrator wanting to stop one wedding."

"And since we could be the target, we'll be on guard, too."

"We should make plans, just in case the killer isn't caught before our wedding day," Jax said. "I'll talk with Richard, Nolen, and Newton later this afternoon. Then, we can discuss the situation with Mac, Griff, and Mr. Byington. They all know about the note, but more definite actions need to be considered, just in case it's a valid threat."

"Our staff will help, too." Bella hated thinking about security for what was supposed to be a joyous day, but being ready for trouble was important.

"We can meet with them in a couple of days." Jax released her hand and sat back in the passenger seat. "If Abner and Charley are involved, they aren't apt to lash out at anyone else, since they're probably scared. That could be why they've been hiding out since yesterday morning."

Neither boy was cruel or mean, so Jax had a good point. "But it could be someone else. I don't want to believe someone is targeting us. Have you heard from Mick?"

"Not yet, but he'll be thorough. We may not get word until this evening or tomorrow." He released an audible sigh. "Now, let's talk to Abner before we run down Charley."

"You mentioned the note being a coverup."

"It's still a possibility. We know the ruby pin was missing. The thieves might've planned to take other items and got nervous before they could grab anything else."

"But why damage the gowns?"

"That's a question that keeps going through my head. Mrs. Marren gave no reason for the hired men to hold grudges against Mrs. Lackner, but we've both agreed she wasn't forthcoming. Now, she's disappeared. That's all troubling."

Renewed uneasiness blanketed Bella. "We might eliminate Abner, if he has an alibi. Charley, too." She hoped that would prove true.

"That would be useful," Jax replied.

"Where do you think we'll find him?"

"He was supposed to meet Cherry at the park, so let's head over there. I'm guessing he's still waiting, and we'll get there ahead of her."

Chapter Eight

T hey reached their destination in moments. "There's someone on that bench." After pulling to a stop, Bella gestured toward a figure sitting about a hundred yards away.

"That's him." When Bella exited the car, Jax clasped her hand. "Why don't you wait here?"

"Because I can take notes for you." Bella forced a calm note into her voice. Surely, Jax didn't think the boy, sitting in a public place with other people walking about, was a threat. Besides, she wanted to assess Abner's attitude.

A sharp exhalation left Jax. "I suppose it'll be fine."

While Bella understood his protective instincts, she disliked being hemmed in when there was no danger. She bit her tongue to keep from saying so, since it had been a bone of contention in the past...and would likely continue to be in the future. Jax would forever fret about her well-being, and vice versa. With those thoughts in mind, she strove for a calm tone and benign observation. "Look around. Other folks are taking advantage of the pleasant weather, so he isn't likely to attack either of us."

Dull color rose in his face, and Jax released his hold on her. "You're right."

"How I love when you say that." She offered a triumphant grin and jumped out.

"I know you do." Jax chuckled.

Buoyed by his reaction, Bella tucked her hand into the crook of his arm.

As the pair approached Abner, the boy sat up straight and stared at Jax. "I ain't doing nothin' wrong, Constable Hastings."

The angry edge in his tone and the sneer on his youthful face telegraphed belligerence. Bella let Jax reply.

"We just want to talk with you briefly," Jax said. "Here is fine, but we can head to my office if you prefer."

Abner's nostrils flared with a sharp intake of breath. "Here, I s'pose." His gaze went to Bella. "Why's she gotta be involved? Oughta be at home doing women's work."

Bella's hackles rose, and she bit her tongue to keep from telling the kid off. Chastising him wasn't apt to glean pertinent information. After a moment, she glanced at Jax, whose jaw had tightened.

"You owe Miss Stewart an apology and respect," he said from between gritted teeth. "In fact, you owe respect to all women."

Long moments of silence passed before Abner finally spoke. "Sorry."

Although it was grudging regret, Bella gave a slight nod before sitting down on the bench at a right angle to where the boy lounged. Jax joined her, placing himself closer to Abner.

"This won't take long," Jax said, "but I'd like to know where you were yesterday morning."

"With a friend," Abner replied without missing a beat.

"What's the friend's name?" Jax asked.

"I don't have to tell you nothing." The boy glared at Jax. "I can meet someone without the law gettin' involved."

Jax allowed quiet to fill the air for several moments before he reacted. "You must've heard about the incident at Mrs. Lackner's home."

Although Bella had her notetaking supplies out, she focused on Abner. Moreley was a small town where news traveled far and fast, so most everyone knew about even minor infractions, eventually. A major crime generated town tittle-tattle in short order.

Abner shrugged. "That snooty old lady. Thought she was better than everybody else, so I ain't surprised she bought it. Wasn't me who got her, though."

The total dearth of compassion stunned Bella, as did the description of the dressmaker, who had been in her late forties. "Those are strong opinions. Did you get them before or after she accused you of stealing?"

The boy looked taken aback as he stared at Bella.

When Abner didn't reply, Jax spoke. "How well did you know Mrs. Lackner?"

This time, the boy reacted quickly. "Hardly at all."

"You didn't talk with her when you worked there?" Bella asked.

Abner shifted restlessly on the bench. "A little. She were demanding, even though I worked real hard. That housekeeper had me doing some of her chores. Lazy thing."

"Like what?" Jax posed the question.

"Hauling dishes and silver to the kitchen for her to clean and taking it back to the dining room. I did it twice. Second time, there weren't as many pieces in the breakfront. Mentioned that to her, and she accused me of stealing." Abner scowled. "I didn't take nothing."

"Were pieces of sterling silver missing?" Bella asked.

Abner shrugged. "I guess. I don't know sterling from no other kind of silver, but there were some bowls and trays tucked in the cupboard's bottom. The old bat housekeeper said I shouldn't have been snooping in there, since she'd cleaned that stuff the week before. She had me hauling bolts of fabric upstairs, too. Heavy stuff."

"We saw the materials in the closet off the workroom," Jax said. "It looked like they were piled up pretty far back."

"Yep, them and other junk. I said the stuff oughta get straightened out, and I'd do it. Figured I could make more money if I worked longer. I started, but Lackner accused me of snooping in there." Abner shook his head.

"Was there anything to pry into?" Jax asked. "Papers and such."

"I dunno for sure," Abner said, "but there's a trapdoor in the ceiling. Toward the back of the closet. It were partially open, and I could see a pull-down stairway. I suggested the old dress forms could go up there and be out of the way. Lackner had a fit, told me to stay out of the closet, and not tell nobody about the door or stairs."

While Bella jotted down more notes, she considered the revelations. A glance at Jax revealed he was as intrigued as she was.

"Could you tell what was up there?" Jax kept his voice even as he made the inquiry.

"Nope, but I never went to the second floor again. Course, it weren't too long before I got canned," Abner said. "Old lady Marren told Lackner I took stuff from up there. But I never did."

"That's when you got fired?" Bella picked up the interrogation.

"Yep. Told me to git with no pay for the entire week. I said it were wrong, but Lackner threatened to turn me in." Abner shot a glare at Jax. "I didn't want you putting me in jail."

"I wouldn't do that without proof," Jax assured him. "The two women accusing you isn't enough."

For several moments, the boy studied Jax. "I know the druggist thinks I stole from him, too, and you didn't arrest me."

Bella watched the play of emotions on Jax's face and realized he thought Abner was guilty on that count. But she also noted his look of concern. His time as an army lieutenant had taught Jax how to assess and handle young men, and she wasn't surprised he used the same discretion as a constable.

"No proof," was Jax's response.

Abner ran both hands over his face. "I haven't always done right since my ma died, but I want to do better."

Cherry had asserted much the same, and Bella hoped it was true. Maybe the young couple had a chance. But she wanted to know more. "Did you meet Cherry Ammers yesterday morning?"

His gaze narrowed on Bella. "What if I did? Her ma don't like me, but Cherry's a grown woman, not a girl. We can step out," Abner replied.

"She's still under age," Jax pointed out, "which means her mother has say-so over her. You'd best keep that in mind."

The boy turned his surly look on Jax. "Yeah, I'll do that," Abner said in a tone belying his words.

Next to Bella, Jax inhaled long and deep. His irritation was obvious, and little wonder. Abner was back to being obnoxious.

"Look," Jax began, "I can take you to the station and talk there. Or you can tell us where you were yesterday morning."

Seconds of silence ensued before the boy finally answered. "I helped old man Thomley for a few hours. Needed some money for food, since my old man never has any. Don't keep many groceries in the house, either. Mostly booze." He stared hard at Jax. "You was a Prohi, and you're still a copper. Why don't you arrest him?"

Bella cringed at the use of Prohi. The derogatory term for federal agents from the Prohibition Bureau always incensed her, especially when it was directed at Jax.

"We focus on bootleggers, rum rummers, and speakeasy owners, since it's not illegal for folks to consume liquor at home. Only to make, sell, or distribute it," Jax pointed out.

A snort left Abner. "Somebody did all three for my pa to buy the stuff."

"But proving he bought it since Prohibition went into effect would be difficult," Bella pointed out. "And it has nothing to do with Mrs. Lackner's murder."

"I have nothin' to do with it, either," the boy shot back.

Beside Bella, Jax sighed. "What time did you leave the Thomley place?"

Abner shrugged, as if in indifference. "About eleven."

Bella jotted down the detail. They needed to check with Mr. Thomley about the exact time, and hope the elderly man remembered. His mind was no longer sharp, but his will to stay in his own home was strong.

"Where did you go from there?" Jax asked.

"Rode around for a while," Abner replied. "The weather were good for a spin."

Jax didn't refute the statement. "What about Charley Ammers? Where is he right now?"

For a moment, the boy looked like he might balk, but he eventually answered. "At my house. My pa's away for a day, maybe more."

Abruptly, Jax got to his feet. "Thanks for your time, Abner."

"Sure," the kid replied.

"Don't disappear," Jax warned. "We may need to talk with you again."

Abner's reply was a scowl and a shrug.

Bella stowed her notetaking supplies in her pocketbook before taking Jax's arm. Once they were back in the automobile, she turned to him. "He's obnoxious, although that doesn't make him a killer."

"True enough," Jax replied. "Mr. Thomley may be his alibi. In the past, Abner has done odd jobs out there, so it's possible."

"I hope he was there. It's good of Mr. Thomley to hire Abner."

"I wish the kid would take a full-time job. Then, he could get a place of his own and get away from his father, who is a terrible influence."

"Has Mr. Crater always been a drinker? I don't recall seeing him often. I sometimes ran into Mrs. Crater, who was a sweet lady."

"He drank very little, as far as I ever knew. His wife died while we were in France. A tooth infection went through her system." Jax's expression grew bleak. "It had to hit him hard. Abner, too. Mr. Crater lost his job a couple of years ago, which is when his alcohol problem increased, although his boozing was an issue at work after he became a widower. Hungover too often."

"And when Abner started getting into trouble."

"The kid skipped school before then, but that seemed to be a turning point. If the house hadn't been in the family for generations, they'd have lost it. As it is, Mr. Crater can't pay his bills. Folks try to be understanding, but they can only wait so long. It's why he's working with bootleggers along the lake. He needs money. As a former agent, I shouldn't say this, but I hope he doesn't get arrested. Abner needs a father, one who sets a decent example."

"It's a terrible situation," Bella murmured. "I hope it isn't complicated by Abner robbing Mrs. Lackner."

"Or worse, killing her."

"That'd be much worse," Bella agreed. "For starters, we ought to find out if the sterling silver and other expensive items are, or were, still in the house."

"We should," Jax agreed. "Nolen and Newton checked the attic. They found crates and trunks." He ran a hand over his face. "There's a lot to do yet today, including another talk with Mrs. Marren, when we find her."

"Do you have a lock pick at your office?"

"I brought it along," he replied while tapping his jacket pocket.

"You're well-prepared."

"I'm trying."

"Do you want to head to the Lackner house now?" Bella asked.

Jax pulled out his pocket watch. "Mrs. Baggeley's train won't be in for another half-hour, so yes. That stairway may lead to the attic, where Nolen and Newton saw the trunks and such. But we'll find out."

"It seems odd to have a trapdoor and pull-down steps if there's easy access to the third floor from the main staircase," Bella commented. "And why would Mrs. Lackner be so adamant about Abner staying out of there?"

"Good points. Maybe it's a separate attic space. Some of the other big old houses around here have two attics."

"That's a valid point. It could be a place where she stored valuables. What if whoever killed her knew about it?"

"It'd be a motive for robbery." Jax drummed his fingers on his knees. "Abner is aware of its existence, so Charley must be, too. We can guess Mrs. Marren knows about what's up there."

"She could've shared the information with her sister and the workmen. I'm not convinced she didn't know one before he came here."

"Conflicting stories make it impossible to know for sure."

"With some luck, we may locate more than just valuables in the attic. If we don't find anything above the closet, we could get into the trunks with your lock pick. Maybe she tucked old letters up there somewhere. A marriage license would be better. People usually keep those papers, and your deputies didn't run across any."

"I've been planning to search those trunks, but we've all been on the go constantly. Although it seems iffy about a license and letter, we can hope to find something."

When Bella pulled to a stop in front of the Lackner house, Jax helped her out before the pair ascended the porch stairs. Jax unlocked the front door and turned to Bella. "Let me go in first." After a moment, he gestured for her to follow.

She watched as he scanned the interior. Jax was always cautious. "Everything looks just like we left it yesterday," she remarked.

"Yep, it does," he agreed. "Let's head to the workroom."

Once there, Jax entered the closet. After he moved the first half-dozen fabric bolts, Jax turned to Bella. "The first bunch were neatly stacked, but there are more and they're in disarray. Turn on your flashlight, so you can see."

Bella pointed the beam at a point past Jax. "The closet is much deeper than I figured, and the back is a mess. Someone had to disturb it. Mrs. Lackner would never keep her materials so hap- hazardously. Maybe it really was a robbery gone wrong."

"If so, the thieves knew where to look." Jax moved the other bolts out of the way. "Here's the trapdoor."

As Jax pushed it open, the high-pitched creaking pierced Bella's ears. "It needs oil."

"That could be what alerted Mrs. Lackner. Her bedroom is on the other side of this wall, as I recall from searching the house." Jax pulled down the stairs. "Let me go up."

Impatience had Bella shifting from one foot to the other. "Can you see or do you need the flashlight?"

"Light is coming in through a small window. There are crates, and they've all been opened and shoved around."

Curiosity overcoming her, Bella followed Jax up the narrow, steep ladder. She glanced around to see his assessment was correct. "The mess is almost as bad as it was in the showroom." Every container was upside-down or on its side. Toward the back, papers spilled out of a box. "Look. Those could be letters."

"I'll get them after I put gloves on. I'm going to have Nolen come up later and see if he can get fingerprints." Jax crawled carefully across the floor, shoved the missives into their container, and came back to where Bella waited. "Here. There's a carpet bag way in the corner. I'm going to grab that, too."

"I don't suppose you see any sterling silver or other valuables?" Bella asked.

"None, but from the detritus, I'd say something valuable was stored in the empty crates."

"Which means there was a robbery."

"All signs point in that direction," Jax confirmed before handing the bag to her. "If you take this down, I'll scoop up the papers and anything else that looks useful."

Bella slung the bag over her shoulders and descended the steps. When Jax joined her in the workroom, he had a train case in one hand and a box cradled against his chest. "Surmising there was a robbery is a step forward, but I still want to look through these bags and that box before we leave." He pointed at the bags. "The tags have the initials, EWF."

"Elsie Walling Farber?" Bella's pulse sped up at the possibility.

"That could be. Both are dusty, so no one got into these yesterday."

Bella pursed her lips, pulled a hanky out of her pocket, and wiped them off. "That's an understatement. Where should we start?"

"Let's look in the bags. Going through the papers will take a while."

With that, Bella opened the carpetbag. Inside were several books, an old medical bag, and a kaleidoscope. She picked up the last item first and looked through it. The beautiful colorscapes had fascinated Bella when she was a girl. Evidently, Mrs. Lackner had been a fan of them, too. When Jax's voice interrupted her survey, Bella started in surprise.

"Is there something unusual in that thing?" he asked.

Bella laid it aside. "Just the usual chips of colored glass and mirrors to reflect them. But I've always thought they were magical."

A soft smile curved his lips. "I remember you getting one from a fair some years ago. Do you still have it?"

She nodded. "I don't look at it often anymore. I'm surprised at Mrs. Lackner keeping one. She doesn't seem the type."

"Perhaps there was more under the surface than anyone knew."

"Perhaps," Bella agreed as she turned back to her task. But what was below the dressmaker's no-nonsense outer shell? Something that would lead them to her killer? And what about the monogram? Bella hurried to unearth the rest of the contents. "Nothing of note. What about the luggage?"

Jax unsnapped the closures and flipped the top back. "I think these are framed photographs."

With both hands, Bella reached into the farthest recess and carefully pulled out a stack of wrapped items. The yellowed newsprint, used as protection, indicated they'd been stored for a while. Bella carefully unwrapped the top one to find a family portrait. "Jax, here's a picture of what has to be Mrs. Lackner's parents, siblings, and her."

He leaned forward for a closer look. "The woman bears a striking resemblance to Mrs. Lackner."

"There's a definite similarity," Bella agreed. "It's sad they grew apart." With one forefinger, she pointed to each figure.

"It is," he replied. "What about the other photographs?"

Bella laid the first one aside and took the paper off the one under it. Two young couples, all smiles, looked up at them. "The girls have to be Mrs. Lackner and Mrs. Baggeley. Easily recognizable, even after decades." She turned the frame so Jax could get a better look. "They must've been in high school."

"I'd say so." Jax pointed at the men. "I vaguely remember Mr. Baggeley from when I was a kid. He's been gone for over ten years, but this boy is him. I never saw Brad Farber, but I'm sure you're right, since no one has mentioned Mrs. Lackner stepping out with anyone else."

"From the background, this photograph was taken near the lake. Going away from Moreley would've kept people from knowing they courted."

A grin kicked up one corner of his mouth. "Very observant, but you always are."

His compliments never failed to touch Bella. "Thank you." With determination, she returned her focus to the case. "There are several more." After unwrapping the next picture, Bella frowned. "This must be Brad Farber in his college cap and gown."

"Which means he and Mrs. Lackner stayed in touch, even after they supposedly went their separate ways. Or she got the picture when they reunited."

Bella rubbed her temple. "Mrs. Lackner didn't leave Moreley until her twenty-first birthday. Bradley Farber was two years older. He went off to college several years before she turned twenty-one, but he remained in Toledo after graduation."

Jax picked up the litany of events. "His parents didn't die until his senior year of college, so he probably came home summers and holidays until then. He and Mrs. Lackner undoubtedly had opportunities to see each other. Mr. and Mrs. Baggeley might've helped the pair, if they all stayed friends."

"I'm even more eager to talk with her." Bella laid the frame aside, picked up another one, and unwrapped it. "It's Mrs. Lackner with the same man, probably Bradley Farber." She turned the picture, so Jax had a better view.

"She and Farber look a little older than in the shot with the Baggeleys. He appears much the same as in his commencement portrait. To me, this confirms they stayed in touch," Jax said. "and I'd wager she moved to Toledo because he was there."

His assertions made sense, but uneasiness plagued Bella "There aren't any wedding photographs, which seems odd, but the monogram is telling. Mrs. Baggeley must know they wed, but what about others here?"

"If the two women were best friends, they'd keep each other's secrets, don't you think?"

"Absolutely," Bella stated. "I wonder what else Mrs. Baggeley knows."

"Let's look through the letters quickly, so we can catch her shortly after she gets home."

Bella nodded and pulled out the first bunch. With utmost care, she untied the faded ribbon holding the stack together. The papers were fragile, and she did not want to damage them. Getting prints off paper was something Nolen hadn't mastered yet, so she didn't worry about touching them.

"How are they addressed?" Jax asked.

Bella riffled through the stack. "The top few are written to Mr. Bradley Farber in Toledo. No return address." She took one, opened the envelope, and scanned the contents. "It's from Mrs. Lackner—Elsie is what she signed. News from Moreley and complaints about having to spend all her time helping in the dress shop." She passed it to Jax and opened another missive. "This one is about the same." After skimming several more, she sighed. "They all have the same sort of messages, except for the last two. She can't wait to see him again in both. They were written in May 1896, so he must've been coming home for the summer."

"What about the ones in the next bunch?" Jax pointed to another set of envelopes, also secured with a worn ribbon.

"These have a return address in Toledo, but they were sent to Mr. and Mrs. Baggeley." Bella hurried to open the first ones. After a quick glance at a few, she looked back at Jax. "They're from Bradley to Elsie. Very short, but he promises they'll marry as soon as she turns twenty-one."

"More and more interesting," Jax observed.

"Mrs. Baggeley was the go-between." Bella felt sure of that.

"Evidently. What about the ones at the bottom?"

After laying the other stacks aside, Bella extracted the last group and glanced through them. "They're all addressed to Mrs. Elsie Farber at an address in Toledo." She moved them so Jax could see.

"From Lieutenant Bradley Farber at an army camp in Virginia," he said. "They were married, something Mrs. Baggeley ought to know. Or guess, especially since Brad mailed letters for Elsie to her and her husband."

"There are only a dozen. Let's see what he wrote."

"Read them out loud."

With great caution, Bella untied the ribbon and opened the first note.

Dearest Elsie, I hope you've gotten over your anger with me, which I understand. Perhaps I should have discussed joining the army with you, but I feared you'd convince me to stay home. Heaven knows, I wish I was with you now. Military life is arduous, but doing my duty is important to me. All my male ancestors served our country, going back as far as the Revolutionary War. My father was with the 8th Ohio and helped turn back Pickett's charge at Gettysburg. My grandfather fought in the Mexican War, and a great-uncle was a soldier in the War of 1812. Their father and uncles were all in the Continental Army. One was on Washington's staff. I don't claim the current conflict is as important as those, but the call to arms is strong. Please try to understand why I had to leave you. I know your stepfather was your only example of a soldier, but his strictness had more to do with his personality than with his service. Please write to me, my sweet wife. We ship out soon, and mail may not reach me after we do. With love and devotion, your husband, Bradley.

"He must've joined to serve in the Spanish-American War down in Cuba," Jax said.

"Evidently, and she didn't want him going," Bella murmured, putting the letter back in the envelope and retrieving the next in line. Her heart hammered hard against her ribs. The anguish in Brad's words was obvious.

"I can't say I blame her," Jax put in. "But I understand his feelings."

Bella glanced at him. "Because you did the same."

"Not exactly. After all, I was in the Ohio National Guard before America went to war. When we were called up, I had to go."

"But, in the beginning, you joined out of a sense of duty."

"I did, as did Matt," he agreed, "and you became a Signal Corps operator for similar reasons."

165

"Pretty much," she agreed, before looking back at the note. "I vaguely remember hearing about the Farber men being in the army and serving in various wars."

"I do, too," Jax said. "Their military memorabilia was in the library, along with mementoes from other Moreley men who served in various wars. As a kid, I was enthralled."

"Most little boys would be. I recall Matt always going into the history room when we went to get books. I was more interested in checking out as many stories as possible." Bella went on to the next letter.

Jax chuckled. "Not surprising. You've always loved to read." He pointed to the missive in her hands. "What does it say?"

"The same things. It was written a few days after the first one, and she still hadn't responded." Bella shuffled through the remaining correspondence. "Every letter is more pleading until the last two get accusatory. He writes she is a terrible wife with no concern for his welfare."

Jax took one letter from Bella. "It says ...*maybe you hope I'll die. If I do, it's on your conscience. Live with that, Elsie. We ship out tomorrow, and I won't try to contact you again.*"

Bella's heart lurched at the anguish underlying those words. How awful for both Elsie and Bradley to part in such a way. She and Jax had come close to a similar situation while he served on the line. If he had died when they'd been at odds...Bella forced the thought away. He hadn't, and they weren't. "Judging from the dates, it was the last letter she received. Or the last one she saved."

"More likely his final message to her, but why keep them?"

"I don't know. It seems cruel to send her husband to war without a word. Especially after they argued over him joining the army." Bella cast a glance at Jax, who was chewing on his lower lip. "What are you thinking?" Did he disagree? Or did he see the letters like she did—tragic remnants from a love gone wrong?

His green gaze met hers. "I shouldn't have discouraged you from going to France, especially after you'd decided. You deserved my support."

Bella studied his solemn expression. Jax's letter, sent right before she left for the Signal Corps, had opened a gulf between them. During that time, he had strongly advised her to stay home, which had infuriated Bella. After that, neither of them wrote again—not until they partially reconciled in Paris when Jax and Matt had leave. Her heart constricted. That weekend was the last time all three had been together. "I didn't appreciate the warning, as you know, but all that's behind us." She beamed at him as proof.

He nodded. "It is, and we're lucky." Jax studied the letter in his hand. "I wonder what happened to Brad Farber. Nothing here gives a hint."

"We may find out when we talk with Mrs. Baggeley."

"I didn't see any silver or jewelry in the other boxes, so we can go. On our way out, let's check the breakfront, just in case some valuables are still there."

A few minutes later, after finding the bottom of the dining room cabinet empty, they were at the Baggeley home. Jax escorted Bella to the front door before ringing the bell. The lady of the house, tall and elegant in a traveling suit of gray serge, answered. "Arabella and Jackson, how lovely to see the two of you together, even though these are not the best circumstances. Come in, please."

Jax let Bella precede him as they followed the older lady to the front parlor. Clearly, Mrs. Baggeley had guessed their reason for coming. That could make their mission easier.

"May I get some refreshments?" their hostess asked.

"No, thank you, ma'am," Jax replied. "We have a few questions, if you don't mind."

A soft sigh escaped her. "When my train got in, I heard about Elsie. Such a terrible thing to happen." She put one hand to her mouth. "When she first got home, I told her she ought to have a handyman or such live on-site. I especially didn't like the housekeeper being away two nights."

"It sounds like you and Mrs. Lackner renewed your friendship after she returned." Jax hoped that was the case because they sorely needed more insight into the dead woman's life.

Mrs. Baggeley folded her hands in her lap. "I welcomed her back with open arms. We were such good friends growing up. Lots of little adventures. I was sad when she left, but I understood. After her father died, Elsie had to give up her dream of becoming a doctor. That would've been a challenge even with his support, but she could've gotten into medical school since his best friend was the dean at one. A few women had already been admitted there. But money was a problem after his death. You already know about her mother opening a dress shop, I'm sure."

"From what we know, she and Miss Duckson competed for scholastic honors before Mrs. Lackner had to work," Jax said.

"They did," Mrs. Baggeley replied. "Before Doc died, the competition was amiable. But afterward, as Elsie struggled to find time for schoolwork, she got more competitive. That led to a breach between her and Sadie."

"But the two of you stayed good friends," Bella said.

A rueful smile played across Mrs. Baggeley's lips. "I was no scholar, so no threat. I managed Bs and Cs, and that was satisfactory to me and to my parents. Aloysius, my husband, and I began courting while we were still in high school, and being with him took precedence over class work. We married shortly after my nineteenth birthday."

"Mrs. Lackner was your maid of honor," Bella offered the observation.

Surprise flashed in Mrs. Baggeley's blue eyes. "She was. How did you know?"

Jax explained about their conversation with Abner Crater and their exploration of the lower attic. He finished by describing one photograph.

Realization replaced surprise. "Then, you must know Elsie and Brad married later."

"We found letters between the two of them. The first ones from him to her were sent to your address," Jax said.

Mrs. Baggeley rested her hands on the chair arms. For several moments, quiet filled the parlor. Finally, she spoke. "My husband and I facilitated their correspondence. When you're young and in love, being separated from your sweetheart is agony." A soft smile touched her mouth. "You two already know that."

With one hand, Jax squeezed Bella's fingers. "We do."

"At least you didn't have to deal with a mother intent on keeping you apart. Poor Elsie did," Mrs. Baggeley said.

"Why doesn't anyone else here know about them marrying? We've heard about Elsie writing her mother, but never revealing her husband's name." Bella laced her fingers with Jax's. "I can't imagine keeping it a secret."

"Mrs. Walling never got over being angry with Mr. Farber about the bank almost foreclosing. She told folks that Elsie married, but many thought she made up the wedding. My husband and I honored our friends' wishes and kept quiet."

"But you knew they wed," Bella suggested.

Again, Mrs. Baggeley smiled. "We were their attendants."

"Really? We didn't find any photographs of their wedding," Bella said.

"Two were taken. One of the four of us and one of just them," the older woman replied. "They had a single copy of each, and Brad took them with him to the army. At least she had other pictures of him, and of the two of them."

"But they were in the lower attic, so she didn't look at them much," Bella observed.

"She put some things there when she first moved back," Mrs. Baggeley replied. "The housekeeper helped her. That was mostly sterling silver and jewelry collected by her mother. Elsie didn't want many valuables out. I suppose you found those, too."

Jax shook his head. "I saw empty crates and cartons turned on their sides."

The color fled from Mrs. Baggeley's face. "Whoever killed her must've been there to rob the place. Someone who knew about the valuables being stored up there."

"It looks that way," Jax agreed.

A look of utter dismay blanketed Mrs. Baggeley's features. "Most Mondays, Elsie takes a drive. Often, I go along. Or she comes here for lunch. In fact, we've been together almost every week. Maybe her killer thought she'd follow the same pattern." She put both hands on her forehead. "I went to visit a cousin in Columbus for a few days. Otherwise, Elsie wouldn't have been at home."

"It isn't your fault, ma'am," Jax said.

Mrs. Baggeley looked stricken. "There's more, Jackson." A shuddering breath escaped her.

"Did she tell you about the telephone calls from some man?" Bella asked, wondering if that was disturbing the older woman.

"She did. She was terribly upset because the man gave his name as Brad."

A gasp escaped Bella. "Her husband was contacting her?" No wonder the dressmaker had been uneasy. "We read the letters about her being angry with him for joining the army. It sounded like they parted on ugly terms."

"They did. Elsie feared Brad would come back like her stepfather—domineering and demanding. Brad wasn't at all like that." Mrs. Baggeley put one hand to her mouth. "And he never came back."

Bella glanced at Jax, who looked as perplexed as she felt. "Was he killed in action?" Jax asked.

"We never knew for sure. She got word that he was missing. After the war, which didn't last long, Elsie tried to get details but never did. Instead, there were conflicting stories. He was sick and nursed by a local woman. He deserted or died. No one seemed to know exactly what happened. Eventually, after years, she moved from Toledo to Columbus. That's where she met Ike Lackner." The woman shook her head. "I only saw him once when I visited. He was a sweet-talking ne'er-do-well. Died after getting drunk and walking in front of an automobile on his way home from a tavern. He'd gone through most of her money, but there was the house here, so she moved back."

For several moments, Bella absorbed the details. "You stayed in touch with her all along?"

"Not so much after Brad was lost. It was like she wanted to put the past behind her for a while. Then, we corresponded, and I visited once. When she first came back, she was still standoffish, but we talked some. Then, we began getting together every Monday. Just a week ago, Elsie confided about the telephone calls. She didn't want anyone to know who was calling. Or who she thought it might be. She was never convinced the man was Bradley, but part of her wasn't sure. She regretted letting him go to war with hard feelings between them, so repairing the breach appealed to her. On the other hand, Elsie feared being exposed as a bigamist."

"Her second husband is dead, so she wouldn't have been guilty of that now," Jax pointed out.

"Elsie wasn't concerned until the man pretending to be Brad started calling." She put one hand to her chest. "You don't think it could've been him, do you?"

"It's highly unlikely," Jax replied.

"It is," Bella agreed, "but I can understand her concern." Unlikely was not the same as impossible.

"It seemed odd to me she never got a firm answer from the army. They must know what happened to Brad." Mrs. Baggeley frowned. "Very unfair."

"Even though the war didn't last long, combat conditions are chaotic. It's possible he was killed and found by locals, who buried him without notifying army brass." Jax made the observations.

"I suppose," the older woman murmured. "The uncertainty wasn't good for her. Neither was the way they parted. I never read their letters. She didn't offer to show them to me, and I didn't ask to see them. I only know they were pleas from Brad for her to write him."

Although her question had little to do with the case, Bella couldn't withhold it. "Why didn't she correspond with him?"

"Pride and stubbornness. She admitted to both recently." Mrs. Baggeley wiped more tears away. "Besides, Elsie thought he'd come back hale and hardy. Said she couldn't believe another loved one would be taken away from her. And it was unfair, but life can be that way. You both know as much."

Bella glanced at Jax, who nodded. His parents were dead by the time he was eighteen, and she had only had hers a little longer. Losing Matt had been, and still was, hard on both of them. "We do," she murmured. "But we're lucky because we have each other."

"We are lucky." When he turned toward her, Jax smiled, although pain clouded his gaze. His sensitivity was a big part of what made him a good lawman. He wanted to provide justice in an unjust world. Bella shared the sentiment, which was an important part of why she loved sleuthing. Solving crimes helped victims, the ones left behind, and those who were gone.

"You are," Mrs. Baggeley said.

Bella returned to the case. "So, Mrs. Lackner never revealed her first marriage to anyone in Moreley except you and your husband."

The older woman shook her head. "She didn't mingle with folks in town after her father died. Too much gossip about their finances. When she came back, she held hard feelings. Then, when the calls started, she feared word had gotten out about her and Bradley. If he was still alive, she would've been humiliated and maybe shunned. The scandal might have kept customers away from her dressmaking business."

"But she could've moved elsewhere," Bella said.

"Despite everything, she was happy to be home," Mrs. Baggeley said.

"Is there anything else that might help us?" Jax asked.

The woman paused for a long moment. "The caller wanted to meet with her, and she planned to do that. I didn't like the idea at all."

"Did she meet him or arrange for him to come to the house?" Bella's pulse raced as she wondered if the caller was the killer.

"She planned to see him yesterday morning in Marion," the older woman replied.

Bella felt her jaw drop. "Maybe he followed her home."

"No, I convinced her not to go. But he could've come to her." A shiver rippled through Mrs. Baggeley. "I've been in a tizzy since I heard the terrible news. If only I'd been home and gotten Elsie to stay here while Mrs. Marren was with her sister."

"You couldn't possibly know something terrible would happen," Bella pointed out. "Besides, we can't be sure the caller is the killer. We have several suspects."

"We do," Jax agreed.

Mrs. Baggeley's stricken expression didn't lighten.

"Do you know anything about her temporary help?" Jax asked.

The older woman's expression didn't lighten. "You mentioned Abner, so I suppose you know Charley Ammers also did odd jobs for a time. The housekeeper accused Abner of stealing, so Elsie fired him. He runs wild, so it wouldn't surprise me." She paused for a moment. "Do you suppose he broke in yesterday? Elsie caught him in the closet once. It seemed odd to her, like maybe he'd looked up there and seen valuables."

"We can't discuss suspects and such, but we're looking into a few possibilities," Jax replied. "Do you know anything about the other two men who worked out there?"

"Elsie mentioned some friend of the housekeeper doing heavy work around the place. She said a buddy picked him up a few times, and they went elsewhere for odd jobs. The two of them remodeled upstairs, so she'd have a nice workspace. But I never met them."

"One man was a friend of Mrs. Marren?" Bella made it a query, although the housekeeper had nixed the idea.

"That's what Elsie told me," the woman replied.

"They had transportation of their own, didn't they?" Jax posed the question.

"Once, when I drove out to pick up Elsie, I saw two men take off in a beaten-up Colonial Tourer," she replied.

"You know your automobiles," Jax put in. "Not many of those on the road around here."

She smiled. "My husband had a passion for horseless carriages and bought one of the first ones. He purchased a new vehicle every few years. Among them was a Colonial."

While the tip might not make a difference, Bella took it down. "We've heard Mrs. Walling had a lot of bills when her husband died, so I'm wondering why she didn't sell off more valuables?"

Dismay darkened the woman's face. "Elsie's mother was a spendthrift. That's no secret to anyone who was here after Doc died. Elsie was humiliated when their financial problems came out. Some of our classmates weren't sympathetic, which made matters worse."

A surge of sympathy rose inside Bella. Gossip could be hurtful, especially to a child. "Did Mrs. Walling sell any possessions to pay the bills?"

Mrs. Baggeley ran a hand over her face. "Perhaps a few, but she was attached to her things. Especially the jewelry and sterling silver."

"Mrs. Lackner often wore a ruby pin," Bella put in. "When Ida and I admired it, she said it had belonged to her mother."

A smile turned up Mrs. Baggeley's lips. "I remember that piece. Truly lovely. I believe it was purchased in the city. So were some others." A frown furrowed her forehead. "Elsie kept them in her workroom's attic. She shared that with me when I complimented the pin. I stopped to visit not long after she moved back. She had it on, and we briefly spoke about her mother's love for beautiful things. Elsie treasured the pin."

Bella heard the note of uncertainty and answered the unasked question. "It was gone when Ida and I found her."

Mrs. Baggeley's head fell forward. "I feared that."

Silence hung heavily in the room for a long moment. Finally, Jax broke it. "We're both sorry about the loss of your friend, ma'am. I don't want to keep you, but is there anything more you can think of? Something that might point us to the killer?"

When the woman looked up, tears were in her eyes. "I don't want to believe those young boys killed Elsie because she walked in on them stealing, but I could see both of them wanting to make money the easy way. Still, I wonder about the man who was calling her. It's not likely that Brad's alive. If he is, he might've gone to the house when she didn't meet him."

"She didn't tell the caller about not going?" Bella could see how that would upset a man. But could the caller be Bradley Farber? The question continued to nag at Bella.

"She had no way to contact him," Mrs. Baggeley said.

Jax leaned forward and braced his elbows on his knees. "What time was the meeting supposed to be?"

"Eight o'clock."

Bella and Jax exchanged a look before she spoke. "Which means he had plenty of time to get here from Marion."

"They were supposed to meet at a little diner called The Coffee Spot," Mrs. Baggeley said. "Maybe someone there can help."

After jotting the name down, Bella said, "Thank you."

"Yes, we're indebted to you for your time and contributions," Jax added.

"If I think of anything else, I'll call the station. I want you to find her killer and bring him to justice, and I'm beholden to both of you for trying."

Jax rose to his feet. "Thank you, ma'am, for your time. We'll be back in touch if we have other questions."

After stowing her notepad and pencil, Bella expressed their condolences again. Then, they were on their way.

Jax waited until they got into the Chummy to speak. "I wish we had solid evidence about Brad Farber's fate. The war didn't last long, so few soldiers were missing."

"Maybe he was killed and buried by the Spanish or the Cubans."

"Maybe. From what I know, a lot more men died from yellow fever than in combat. In either case, you're right. He may be buried in Cuba."

"Which means it's unlikely we can find out what happened to him."

With one hand, Jax massaged his taut neck muscles. "True."

Bella shifted to face him. "Perhaps my imagination is running away with me, but is it possible he didn't die?"

"Sure. Not probable but possible. You know how many men simply disappeared in France. Some died, and their remains were never found. Others were captured and died in a prison camp. But there were more than a few who never returned home after the war. The reasons vary, I'm sure." He rubbed his chin. "I know some soldiers who wished they'd stayed in France due to the extent of their injuries—physical and mental."

Sadness clouded her gaze. "We met some at the sanatorium."

He nodded. The two of them had gone undercover to investigate deaths and disappearances at a hospital for shell-shocked soldiers. "What are you imagining might've happened?" Jax didn't repress his interest. Bella often had good ideas that might seem far-fetched to most lawmen. As always, he wanted to hear them.

"It may seem unlikely, but he could've been wounded or gotten sick and been nursed by local folks. You mentioned that much. Afterward, Brad might've had no impetus to come right home. Not when Elsie never wrote to him."

"But why would he return now?" Jax really wanted to know Bella's perspective. The Spanish-American war had started and ended in 1898, twenty-four years ago. What would keep a man on foreign soil for so long? Jax had been beyond eager to leave France and get home.

"I don't know. Maybe he came back long ago. Maybe he tracked her down. If he found her in Columbus, he knew she was married again. If he loved her, he might've wanted her to be happy, so he didn't interfere."

"And he might've known when her second husband died."

"Exactly," Bella said with obvious enthusiasm. "Brad could've wanted to renew their relationship. Or he could've been angry she never wrote and had another spouse. Either seems possible."

"So, where was he all this time?"

Bella's gaze narrowed on him. "You think I'm having a flight of fancy?" Her tone was accusatory.

He put up one hand. "Not necessarily. It's hard to say when we don't know for sure. Brad, no matter how pleasant he was as a young man, could've gotten bitter. His last couple of notes to Elsie were harsh. And who can blame him? That's not the send-off a soldier wants."

"Or deserves," she murmured.

Jax took her hand. "You gave Matt and me a lovely farewell. Both when we were called up in 1917 and the next year after the three of us met in Paris and before we went back to the line." Warmth spread through him at the memories. That long weekend, he had tried to make amends for his insistence she stay home. And they'd come to better terms. Getting back together had taken much longer.

"I'm glad."

For several moments, neither spoke. Then, Bella broke the silence. "What if Brad Farber deserted? Mrs. Baggeley said it was one rumor. That'd be a reason for him to lie low all these years."

"It would." Jax dropped her hand and shifted gears. "And that's something we can uncover, but it'll take time. If that's the case, Elsie's reaction to his calling is more understandable. Maybe she got confirmation he deserted and kept it a secret, even from her best friend."

A sharp exhalation left Bella. "A lot of possibilities."

"Along those lines, we know Elsie didn't want him calling back. If he was accusatory or threatening, that'd be unnerving."

"It seems like, on one hand, she wanted to believe it was him. On the other, she didn't. That could result from him being harsh or from her being afraid to hope."

"If he was the caller, he might've accused her of bigamy. That worried Elsie."

A slight smile touched Bella's lips. "Since we found the letters, we're both calling her Elsie instead of Mrs. Lackner."

Jax shrugged. "Those notes brought a high level of familiarity, and I feel like we know both of them much better."

"I do, too."

"One of the biggest unknowns is: what happened to Bradley Farber?" Jax returned to the issue that could be key.

"I realize it's far-fetched to believe he's been hiding for twenty years. Even if he was a deserter."

"We've experienced some odd goings-on in previous cases, so I don't want to dismiss the possibility. Richard can call his buddy in Washington and get him on the case."

"Good idea. Since Elsie kept her first marriage a secret, she wouldn't have confided in Mrs. Marren."

"Probably not, but what if the housekeeper snooped around?" Jax paused before continuing with another thought. "Mrs. Marren wasn't supposed to go into the sewing spaces. Or so she told us. We both agree that may not be true."

Bella steepled her fingers. "Mrs. Marren definitely knew about valuables. Maybe Abner did, too."

"Sterling silver was taken, but Elsie was aware of that," Jax said.

"Both of them blamed Abner, and he could've stolen other items. But how would he know where they were? Was he alone in the workroom long enough to go into the lower attic? The idea plagues me."

"Me, too. We've got to find out if he was at Thomley's farm yesterday morning," he put in. "It's not too far out of our way, so I'll stop and run in."

"All right."

Bella tapped her fingertips together while she waited for Jax to come back from speaking with Mr. Thomley. When he got behind the steering wheel, she couldn't wait to find out what he had learned. "Was Abner here?"

"Very early in the day. He left over two hours before you found Elsie's body, said he was picking up a friend at the park."

Dismay hung over Bella like a storm cloud. "The friend could be Charley Ammers."

"That's my concern. We need to talk with Charley and see if Newton found Mrs. Marren and her sister."

"Nolen, Richard, and Jenny might have news," Bella replied as she leaned back in the passenger seat.

"We'll head to my office and find out. We can share ours, too."

Chapter Nine

B ack at the constable's office, Bella and Jax found the two deputies and the clerk at work. "Jillian," he began, "it's past time for you to go home."

The young woman shook her head. "I wanted to see what you two uncovered and hear what you think about what Newton found out."

"Our story is long. Is yours?" Bella asked Newton.

The deputy shook his head. "Not the crucial fact. It turns out Mrs. Marren isn't a widow. Her husband is alive and well."

Bella and Jax exchanged a long look. He found his voice first. "How did you discover that?"

Newton leaned against the counter. "The two sisters weren't at Mrs. Tillis's house, so I checked around town, talked to a few folks, and ended up at the old tavern. It's a coffeehouse since Prohibition started, but a lot of the men still head there after work or on breaks. Anyhow, turns out one guy recently moved to Boxwood from Columbus. He didn't know either of the sisters, but he heard about them. He was mighty surprised to find out Mrs. Marren had told one and all that her man had died. Not so according to this one guy who lived in the housekeeper's old Columbus neighborhood."

"Did this man know where the husband is?" Jax asked.

"No, but he told me Mr. Marren was well-known as a shady character. Got fired for stealing from his boss." Newton folded his arms over his chest. "Before this guy in Boxwood left Columbus, he heard Marren and another jailbird who ran with him had left town for parts unknown."

"How long ago was this?" Bella posed the query.

"The guy at the tavern moved to Boxwood about a month ago, and he got the news right before that," Newton replied. "He seems honest enough. When I left the coffeehouse, I stopped at a few other places. Everyone I asked said the guy is a good man, not prone to dishonesty or exaggeration."

"And someone with interesting information," Nolen put in.

"Very interesting," Jax confirmed. "We learned some things that may mesh with your clue."

The front door opened, and the Jenkinses stepped inside. "Looks like we're right in time for a meeting," Richard observed.

"An impromptu one," Jax said. "Let's go to my office and we can trade details."

"Can I come, too?" Jillian asked.

"Sure. You can be our main notetaker," Jax replied.

Bella saw the young woman's pleasure at being included. When Jax looked at her, she winked, and he smiled. In future investigations, Bella might have to cede her secretarial duties to Jillian, so she might as well get used to the idea. Her life would be changing. All for the better, Bella was sure, but poignancy swelled her heart. One person could only do so much, and Bella already had multiple roles. Adding wife, and eventually she hoped, mother, could crowd out detective.

Jax shared everything they had discovered, and Bella chimed in. He wrapped up by saying, "I'd love to know exactly what happened to Brad Farber, but first I want to interview Mrs. Marren again, and find her spouse and his buddy. I'm pretty sure they're the vagrants who did itinerant work at the Lackner place."

"Which might eliminate Charley and Abner as murder suspects," Nolen observed.

"I'm not ready to do that," Jax replied, "because we haven't found them. Hiding out isn't a sign of innocence."

"You're right," Nolen said.

"As far as the housekeeper and her sister, Mrs. Tillis's neighbor promised to call when they get back to the house," Newton said. "The woman is a long-time Boxwood resident and a lovely lady, so I asked her not to say anything to them about me being there."

Jax leaned back in his chair. "We have a lot of information, but without knowing where the Marrens are, we're stuck in one regard." He looked at Newton. "Did the neighbor see the sisters leave?"

"She did," the deputy replied. "They planned to be home this evening."

"She didn't see two men?" Bella asked.

Newton shook his head. "Afraid not."

"What about you, Nolen?" Jax asked.

"Mrs. Ammers called, so I jotted everything down." He laid a paper on the table. "Three of the calls came from Columbus. They all originated at a hotel there. When she spoke with the first operator, the woman told her the place is a flea bag inn. The other call originated in Marion. It was after the other calls," Nolen said, "and from a boardinghouse. I telephoned the place, but the landlady was evasive. She has a heavy accent, not sure what. I think she understood me, but she pretended not to."

"Still, it's more useful information." Jax looked at his deputies. "I'd like you two to head down to Marion when we finish talking. We don't know the name of that restaurant, but start with the one Mrs. Baggeley mentioned. You might get lucky and find out if a man was there yesterday morning to meet Mrs. Lackner."

The pair nodded.

"You've gotten conflicting information about one worker being an old friend of the housekeeper," Richard observed.

"We have," Bella confirmed, "which bothers me, especially considering what we know about Mrs. Marren now, and what we learned about Mrs. Lackner and Bradley Farber." Bella glanced at Jax, who nodded. "They were married." After a round of gasps, she provided the additional information from the letters and from Mrs. Baggeley.

"That puts a new spin on the entire case," Richard replied.

"It certainly does," his wife agreed. "The letters are revealing and sad, and you've only shared snippets."

"They are tragic," Bella agreed.

"But, from what Mrs. Baggeley told you two, Mrs. Lackner didn't believe the calls came from Brad Farber," Nolen put in.

"Neither of them did, although Mrs. Lackner felt uncertain. Now, I'm more concerned about Mrs. Marren's friend being the one who planned the morning meeting," Jax said.

"With the intention of actually showing up?" Jenny asked.

"I'd say it's more likely he and his partner wanted her out of the way," Jax replied.

"If so, it was an inside job," Richard commented.

Jax nodded. "Mrs. Marren knew her employer had appointments late yesterday morning."

"Which meant Mrs. Lackner wasn't following her usual pattern of being out for the day. If the housekeeper is involved, she would've told the men about the change. Then, one could've set up the meeting," Bella observed.

"That makes sense," Newton said. "They likely wanted to steal valuables, not kill her."

"What about the note?" Jillian asked.

"I'm not discounting the possibility that someone else isn't responsible. Talking to Charley Ammers might help in that regard. We may need to interview Ophelia Upchurch after that," Jax said before looking at Richard and Jenny. "What did you two turn up?"

A rueful grin creased the older man's face. "Not nearly as much as the rest of you, but we spoke with the Geneves and the Coopers again. Both ladies described Mrs. Lackner as being reserved. All four had heard gossip about Mrs. Walling's penchant for spending, which you heard about, too."

"We stopped at the café during the slow time, so Sam Push sat with us," Jenny added. "He knew Mrs. Lackner in school, and he mentioned her stepping out with Brad Farber and them maybe having gotten married, which we now know happened."

Jax turned to Richard. "It's getting late, but if you'd place a call to your friend at army headquarters in Washington, he might find out what happened to Brad Farber. I know it'll take time to get an answer, and I've got him almost off my list."

"It seems unlikely that he's still alive and calling his wife," Bella said, "but I'm curious. And calling Washington reminds me of you contacting Mick O'Donnelly. There doesn't seem to be much chance that someone you arrested as a Prohibition agent is the killer."

Jax released a pent-up breath. "Thanks for bringing that up. I need to let him know we've probably got our suspects right here. I hope he hasn't spent too much time on my concern."

"You were right to check," Richard said. "Just like it's a good idea to see if we can find out about Brad Farber. Even if it takes a while, I'd like to know."

The others agreed with him.

"I'll put a call in to Agent O'Donnelly," Jillian said.

"I can take notes while you do," Bella told the clerk, who nodded her agreement and left the room.

"I'll make my call right after Jillian finishes, unless there's more to discuss," Richard said.

"We haven't tracked down Charley Ammers yet. Too many other avenues to take." Jax ran one hand over his face. "Nolen, will you go to the house? Newton, I'm going to have you head to Marion. We're already spread thin, so having the two of you in one place isn't workable. I don't want to lose sight of Abner or Charley."

"I talked to some of their friends," Nolen put in. "A couple were evasive, but they run with Charley and Abner."

Jax nodded. "Newton, head over to the Crater place. If you get any big news, contact the office. "As soon as the sisters are back, I want to talk to Mrs. Marren. I'll sit tight here for a time."

The deputy headed out before Richard got up and held the chair for his wife. "I'll call my buddy now."

Jenny nodded. "After that, I'll check with my mother and see when we should pick her up."

After the couple left the office, Jillian poked her head back in. "Cherry will try to get a connection as soon as possible. I'll stay late and type up the notes. I'd like to hear what Nolen finds out anyhow. For now, I'll be at my desk."

When Nolen followed her, Jax stopped him. "I'd like you to check the items we brought back for fingerprints. The bag handles, picture frames and glass, and so on. If they match the others you got, especially the ones on the design board, that could help us."

"Will do," the younger man said before stepping into the main office.

Jax turned to Bella. "It'll be dark soon. I'd rather you didn't drive back to Ballantyne alone. Richard and Jenny could follow you. She could even ride with you. You'd be able to try on your dress before they come back to town."

Bella frowned. "I appreciate the thought, but I want to stay and see what you discover. You're planning to go to Boxwood if the sisters get home, aren't you?"

"I am, but it'll be dark by then. Mr. Marren and his buddy may be there, too."

"Yes, and you shouldn't go alone." Annoyance and worry meshed themselves together inside Bella.

"I won't. Nolen and Richard will go along."

Annoyance surpassed worry. "You want to keep track of Abner and Charley, which will fall on Nolen. If Richard follows me home, he can't be here and go with you right away, if that neighbor calls. Which means he can't follow me home." Jax's nostrils flared with a sharp intake of breath, a sure sign that he was fighting not to fuss over her. "Isn't that right?"

"It is," he agreed in a grudging tone.

Bella couldn't hold back a giggle. "I'm right."

His lips quirked, and his eyes glittered. "You are right." When she opened her mouth, Jax held up one hand. "And you love when I say that."

The giggle became a guffaw. "Indeed, I do." It had become a joke between them, and Bella enjoyed Jax's light-heartedness. For a time after the war, his smiles had been few and fleeting. "Back to the subject at hand. I'll stay and see what happens. Maybe you won't be going to Boxwood tonight."

"If not, I hope we get another break."

The tension in his voice and expression had Bella laying her hand over his. "It hasn't even been forty-eight hours, and you've worked almost nonstop."

His fingers entwined with hers. "You have your dress to consider, but you've spent most of your time helping me."

"Mrs. Burtis needs time to alter both Ida's gown and mine. As far as everything else, I already told you it's well in hand." She bolstered the assertion with a grin.

"Then, having your company would be great. Maybe we should order from the café and eat here." The suggestion was barely out of Jax's mouth when Richard stuck his head in the doorway.

"I told Jenny the same thing. I'd like to wait for a call back. My friend at army headquarters usually works late. If he gets my message, he'll let me know he's seeking information about Farber."

"Great," Bella replied. "It'll be fun to eat together." She maintained an upbeat demeanor because, like Jax, she hoped they found the last pieces of the puzzle soon. And worried they wouldn't.

Nolen came back just as the group, including Jillian, was finishing supper. She patted the seat next to her. "We have plenty left, and you should eat something."

After grabbing a sandwich, Nolen reported his findings. "Before I looked for the boys, I checked the fingerprints." A grin curved his lips. "They're good matches for all the ones we found in the dressmaker's work area. Hers are likely among them, but the larger ones have to be from men, and there's two sets."

"Good work," Jax said before murmurs of assent went through the group. "What about Charley and Abner?"

Nolen's smile flattened. "Charley stopped at his home, but he and Abner said they were doing some odd jobs at the Crater place. I went over, and they weren't there, so I checked a few of their usual hangouts. No sign of them."

Jax slumped back in his chair. "It makes little sense that they'd be calling from Marion, although I suppose they could put someone else up to it."

After another swallow of coffee, Richard voiced his agreement. "That's a possibility."

"Both Cherry and Mrs. Ammers would recognize the boys' voices. If they're involved," Bella said.

"We still have a group of suspects." Jax shook his head. "I can't eliminate the mayor's niece, since her maid of honor confirmed the threat." The young woman had returned the call while the group waited for dinner to be delivered.

"If she hired Abner and Charley to ruin the dresses, would she be charged with murder?" Jillian asked.

"The local prosecutor would have to decide," Jax replied.

"I doubt if the charges for any of them would be murder," Richard added. "Manslaughter is more likely."

Before anyone had more chance to discuss the matter, the telephone rang in the main office. "I'll get it." Jax hurried out but returned in short order. He was pulling on his jacket as he addressed the group. "There's a vehicle at the Lackner place, and lights are in the house. Doc Smedlay was out that way and noticed both."

Richard got to his feet. "I'll go with you."

"Me, too." Nolen shoved one last bite of food into his mouth before standing up.

When both Bella and Jenny rose, Jax focused on his betrothed. "I'd like you to stay here. Please."

Bella wanted to argue, but what he asked was sensible. "Of course."

Jenny slipped an arm through Bella's. "The two of us will be waiting." Her blue gaze went to her husband. "Be careful, dear."

The senior constable brushed her forehead with a kiss. "Always."

Jax crossed to Bella and bent to press his lips to her cheek. "We won't be long."

Multiple feelings spread through Bella. In the past, she had envied the easy affection between the Jenkinses. Now, she and Jax could show—in small ways—their love for each other. "Good, and you take care, too." She had said those same words when they parted after the long weekend in Paris, the weekend when Jax and Matt had used their leave to be with Bella. Would Jax make the reply he had then and several times afterward?

"I absolutely will."

When he winked, Bella knew he remembered. Although she wanted to grab his arm and keep him from going, she managed a tremulous smile. "See you soon."

After the two men left, the women settled back at the table. "There's no reason to worry. It's unlikely that Mr. Marren and his buddy are at the house. If they robbed the place and killed Mrs. Lackner, they're probably long gone. Anyone with a shred of sense would be."

Bella nodded, but fear clawed at her insides. Killers often had no sense or any boundaries, either. And they could only go to the electric chair once.

At the Lackner house, Jax and Richard caught Mrs. Marren and Mrs. Tillis off-guard. The pair was sitting at the kitchen table, when Jax peeked in the window. Engaged in a heated conversation, neither sister heard the lawmen until the pair, guns drawn, entered the room.

"Stand up and put your hands in the air. Both of you," Jax ordered.

"We've done nothing wrong," Mrs. Marren shot back, but her sister immediately followed orders.

"Mrs. Marren, get up." Jax's voice rang with command. He didn't want to physically accost the woman, but she could be armed. Taking a chance would be foolish. Just when he thought he would need to manhandle her, she did as he asked.

"Keep your gun on them, Richard, and I'll cuff the pair." Jax didn't look at the man next to him. Instead, his attention remained on the women.

"Cuff us," Mrs. Marren screeched. "Why? We haven't done nothing wrong. I'm here to get the rest of my things."

"Sitting at the table? It looks more like you're waiting for someone. Your accomplices," Jax suggested. On their way to the house, he and Richard had discussed taking the women for questioning, as well as securing them in the vehicle. If Mrs. Marren wasn't involved in Elsie Walling Farber Lackner's death, Jax would be shocked. Her sister was an unknown, but he wasn't risking trouble with her, either.

"Let's do as they say," Mrs. Tillis urged. "We don't need no more problems. I don't anyhow."

"Be quiet," her sister said.

"Are you two waiting for anyone?" Jax glanced from one sister to the other.

Mrs. Marren was quick to answer. "Course not."

Jax narrowed his gaze at her sister. "What do you have to say, ma'am?

Mrs. Tillis licked her lips as if she was parched. "No one's coming here."

"Unless it's those boys who were stealing," Mrs. Marren put in.

"What boys?" Richard posed his question as if he had no idea of who she meant.

"The ones who worked out here for a while. Both was lazy," the woman replied. "Silver disappeared when that Crater kid were working. Probably had his friend's help."

Since Jax wasn't sure who took the missing items, he avoided a direct reply. "We can discuss all that in my office."

When the sisters were manacled, the lawmen led them to the automobile and put them in the back seat. Jax sat up front but kept his attention on the pair while Richard drove to town.

After parking in front of the constable's office, Jax led Mrs. Marren inside while Richard escorted Mrs. Tillis. The lawmen had caught the sisters off-guard, for which Jax was grateful. Although neither woman was armed, they might have put up a struggle and ended up hurt. His reluctance to be rough with female suspects was not something he considered in detail. After months in the trenches of France, Jax wanted to avoid harming anyone. Another reason being a constable was not his best job option. When he looked at Bella, who had been waiting in the outer office with Jillian and Jenny, he was glad he had other choices now. "We found them in the house," he said to the women.

The housekeeper emitted a harrumph. "I told you folks my sister and I would pick up the rest of my things."

"And I told you I wanted a deputy there when you did." Some of Jax's annoyance surfaced in his voice. Mrs. Marren had complained bitterly the entire way into town. Her sister had not issued a peep. "We need to get both cells ready." He ignored more complaints from the housekeeper.

"Nolen is back there making sure things are in order," Jillian replied.

Jax nodded. "When he comes back, I'd like him to be ready to take Mrs. Marren to one after we question her."

"I'll tell him," the young clerk replied.

Richard turned to Jax. "Do you want Jenny and me to stay out here with Mrs. Tillis while you and Bella talk to Mrs. Marren?"

"That'd be good," Jax replied. "Bella can take notes."

"Of course," Bella quickly agreed.

After Bella entered the inner office, Jax followed with the housekeeper. He gestured to the table. "Sit down, ma'am." Jax removed the cuffs but kept them close at hand.

"I don't see why you had to bring my sister and me in. You coulda asked your questions at the house." Despite her complaints, Mrs. Marren took the nearest chair, folded her arms across her bosom, and stared at Jax.

Jax ignored the comment. He held a chair for Bella and sat next to her so they both faced the housekeeper. "This shouldn't take long, if you cooperate," he advised the older woman.

Mrs. Marren made no reply, but Bella picked up her notepad and pencil. She flipped to a blank page and nodded at Jax.

"Ma'am, we've learned some information since we last spoke with you," Jax began, "and I'd like to go over some to get your view."

The housekeeper's expression went from dismissive to dismayed. "I hope you found the killer."

Her words and tones were at odds, but Jax pressed on. "We discovered you aren't a widow."

Mrs. Marren's sagging jaw dropped and, for a long moment, she stared at him. Then, she laid her clasped hands on the table and looked down at them. "We haven't divorced yet. Not enough money."

Jax turned to Bella and nodded toward the housekeeper to signal he wanted her to ask a question. She got the message. "You've worked for Mrs. Lackner since last summer. You told us about being well-paid, along with having room and board. That should've given you sufficient funds."

A shuddering breath left the older woman. When she looked up, her gaze was troubled—even fearful. She licked her lips. "I been saving."

The tentative tone and her nervous tics could be an in-road. Jax let a moment of silence develop before inserting a wedge. "So, you must know where your husband is."

Bella backed him up with another prong of attack. "Does he contact you at the Lackner house or at your sister's place?"

The older woman's bosom heaved as she breathed fast and shallow. Her gaze darted from Bella to Jax and back.

"Take your time," Bella said in a conciliatory tone.

"Yep, there's no rush." Jax wasn't sure the woman's reaction was real, but he didn't want her to have a heart attack.

Within moments, Mrs. Marren appeared to regroup. "Oscar, my husband, calls both places. Told him not to, but he don't listen."

"Did he want the divorce or money?" Jax asked.

Again, the older woman's attention moved from Jax to Bella and back. "Mostly, money." Her voice was barely audible. Gone was the blustering woman from earlier.

"I understand that he's been in trouble with the law. Lost his job for stealing from his boss," Jax said.

All color drained from the housekeeper's face. "I didn't countenance the stealing, but we was struggling to pay the rent. Partly cuz of him going to speakeasies. Booze ain't cheap there, or so Oscar says."

"Rotgut isn't expensive, but good bootlegged liquor can be." Jax knew as much from his time with the Prohibition Bureau.

"My man wants the best of everything." Bitterness surfaced in Mrs. Marren's voice. "For himself."

"Did you really want a divorce?" Bella asked. "Or did your husband threaten to leave you if you didn't help him get more money?"

The insightful questions didn't surprise Jax, but he hadn't thought of them himself. Repressing a smile proved hard. Not only did he love Bella, Jax respected and admired her.

Mrs. Marren closed her eyes and put her hands to her face. For several moments, she shook her head as if to clear her mind. When she finally spoke, her voice was rough and ragged."I didn't have nothing to do with the missus being killed."

Questions rose hard and fast in Jax's mind. But who had committed the murder? Did the housekeeper get Abner and Charley to steal for her? Since the last interview with Mrs. Baggeley, Jax knew Elsie Lackner had originally planned to be away on Monday morning. Had the boys been surprised when they found her at home? Surprised enough to kill? What about the telephone calls? Who had made them? Jax considered how to get honest answers. Finally, he decided on a simple query. "Who did?" When she did not immediately reply, Jax spoke again. "If you don't want to be charged in her death, you'd be smart to tell us all you know."

The housekeeper kept her head bowed as, for long moments, a heavy hush descended on the room. After what seemed like an eternity, Mrs. Marren looked at Jax. "Oscar and his buddy was only going to rob the place." She swallowed convulsively. "She shoulda been gone early Monday. She were supposed to be gone. I give my key to him, so they could get in and out while the missus was away."

The admissions added to the charged atmosphere. When Jax glanced at Bella, he saw she felt a range of emotions, much as he did. "Oscar is your husband's real name," Jax said, to confirm the supposition.

"Yep. Oscar Marren," the woman replied. "His partner is Leo Crossley. They used the other names when they went looking for work."

"Were those two really employed near Marion?" Jax asked.

The housekeeper's gaze darted around, as if she was seeking the answer. "They did some chores is all."

"And you didn't see them there?" Bella posed the question.

Mrs. Marren shook her head. "It were a story for the missus."

"Where was Mrs. Lackner planning to go?" Jax asked, although the answer had come out earlier with Mrs. Baggeley. The housekeeper had told a lot of lies, and he wanted to pin her down on each one.

Mrs. Marren's hands trembled. "To meet her first husband in a little restaurant near Marion. I never been there, but I heard the name. At least, she thought it was him." The housekeeper filled in with details, most of which the group already knew. "Oscar refused to telephone her himself."

"Your husband's pal was the one calling and pretending to be her first husband?" Jax asked.

"Yep. When I was helping the missus haul belongings to the lower attic, some frames fell out of a box. The paper wrapping was loose, and I seen her and her beau. She cried a bit, said they'd married, but she'd lost him in the war over in Cuba. Never knew what happened."

Surprise held Bella momentarily mute. When she found her voice, she said, "Mrs. Lackner was a private person. I'm surprised she'd say so much."

"Never did again, and she swore me to secrecy. Didn't want no townsfolk knowing, so I kept silent," the housekeeper said.

"Except for telling your husband and his friend, so they could plot to steal from her," Jax added.

The housekeeper shook her head. "It weren't my idea, but I wanted to get back with my man. Being a housekeeper ain't easy work at my age. Especially not with my rheumatism. The missus were a demanding one."

"So, you thought robbing from her was all right?" Jax asked. "We know sterling silver disappeared over the last few months. Not just Monday morning. And we know you tried to pin the blame on Abner Crater."

Mrs. Marren bowed her head. "It were wrong, but we was desperate. Oscar's been out of work for a while. That's why I took a job away from home. He moved in with his buddy, and I lived at the Lackner place. Saved us rent money. He was gonna look for work. Then, we'd get back together. But word of him stealing got around, so getting a job were hard."

"And he kept right on robbing folks. I'm guessing his boss and Mrs. Lackner weren't the only ones," Jax said.

"I didn't know," the older woman said in a plaintive tone. "And I didn't know Leo was coming with him. Not yesterday morning. I only know he called the house."

"Crossley pretended to be Bradley Farber for quite a while." Jax wanted explicit confirmation.

"Yep. I didn't like that," Mrs. Marren said. "It were wrong to keep her hopes up."

"Stealing is wrong," Bella put in. "Yet, you were part of that."

"I'm guessing you weren't just part of the robberies," Jax added. "I bet you took the sterling silver piece-by-piece and got it to your husband. When his roommate saw the stuff, he wanted in. Where is it? And the ruby pin, too."

"They sold the silver. Not sure they had time to get rid of her pin. I said not to bring his buddy in, but Oscar was afeared of Leo. After I met the man, I were, too."

The excuses exasperated Jax. "You claim to not know much, but you must've put your husband up to calling Mrs. Lackner and pretending to be Bradley Farber." At least Jax figured that was the case.

"That was not only deceitful, it was cruel," Bella added.

When the housekeeper turned to Bella, anguish lined her face. "It were wrong, but I only wanted to get her out for a while, so Oscar could steal jewelry and such. Usually, she went with a friend, but they didn't want to do it then, in case she came back. If I'd knowed she didn't go, I woulda stopped them. But I figured on her wanting to see her man."

"Which was impossible, since he's most likely been dead for over twenty years." Jax's jaw hardened.

"I dunno why she didn't go meet him." Mrs. Marren continued along the same lines with her excuses. "She shoulda gone."

Annoyance filled Jax. "You egged her on in thinking her husband might still be alive, didn't you? Even though, after two decades, it was hardly possible."

"Didn't think it was so bad at first," the housekeeper muttered.

Jax ran his fingers through his hair. "You must've known how upset she was about possibly committing bigamy."

"Her second man were dead," Mrs. Marren replied. "Ain't no bigamy involved."

"She wouldn't have been in legal trouble," Jax said, "but if Farber had really come back here, he could've revealed damaging information. Gossip might've ruined her business."

The housekeeper put her hands flat together, as if in prayer. "Why didn't she go to meet him? That's what I wonder."

Jax grudgingly revealed what they knew. "Her friend Mrs. Baggeley convinced her he had to be dead."

The housekeeper braced her elbows on the table and bowed her head. "I shoulda known that woman would interfere."

"Almost anyone would be leery of the claims." But Elsie Walling Farber Lackner had wanted to believe the lies, had wanted to believe she could make up for her harsh words before her husband went to war. That certainty sent sadness shooting through Jax's heart like an arrow. He and Bella were lucky. So very lucky.

"She didn't seem leery," the housekeeper protested.

"But she had to be shocked at first," Bella said.

"Yep," the housekeeper said. "He were her first love, and a woman don't get over that no matter what happens later."

Jax studied Mrs. Marren. "I'm sure you told her as much when she confided in you." Disgust underscored every word. "You took advantage of her being all alone, and in more than one way."

The woman made no reply.

"Where are your husband and his accomplice?" Jax asked. "We know one call was made from a boarding house near Marion. Are they still there?" His heart raced as he waited for her to answer. Newton was a skilled lawman, but he could be in danger if Marren and Crossley shot it out. Jax might need to place a call to the local constable, so his deputy had help.

After several moments, Mrs. Marren met Jax's gaze. "They was gonna meet us at the house later tonight."

Her answer sent Jax's pulse into overdrive. "What time?"

"Around midnight," she replied.

A twinge of relief touched Jax. Newton would be back by then, so all four lawmen could confront the killers. Confront, arrest, and jail them.

Chapter Ten

A fter Mrs. Marren was escorted to a cell, her sister sat at the old table across from Bella and Jax. "I weren't involved in the thieving, and I knew nothing about them killing that lady."

Her distraught tone and wide eyes telegraphed grave apprehension. Bella wasn't sure she believed Mrs. Tillis, so she posed a query. "Why were you there this evening? You must've known your brother-in-law and his partner were coming."

Mrs. Tillis shook her gray head. "No, miss, not until we got to the house. Sis told me then about her man and his buddy. I didn't like the idea and wanted to go home, but she insisted we stay. Said it'd all get straightened out tonight, and I weren't to worry about nothing. She planned to leave with Oscar, and I was glad of it. I moved to Boxwood cuz of her being in Moreley. Wanted to be close and get reacquainted, since we been living far apart for years. Houses are cheaper over that way, and I found a neat little cottage. When Sis came, she said she and that worthless man of hers was split up. But they wasn't." The woman prattled on in a staccato rhythm.

After jotting down some notes, Bella glanced at Jax, who looked uncertain. Again, she wondered if Mrs. Tillis was honest or good at lying. "They were all planning to leave tonight?"

"They was. I drove my vehicle. Sis said I could drive myself home after they took off. She planned to go with that worthless husband of hers in their old Packard," Mrs. Tillis said.

"With your own automobile, you could've left any time," Jax pointed out.

"I shoulda done that, but I knew Sis and me wasn't apt to cross paths again. Just wanted a bit more time with her, and the menfolk isn't coming for hours yet," the older woman replied.

"Did you take any of the jewelry or sterling?" Bella asked. "Is that why you two came early?"

"No, miss, absolutely not. Me and Sis was raised better than that. If she hadn't married Oscar..." Mrs. Tillis's voice trailed off as she shook her head.

"Can you give us any other information? Something you overheard or such? That would help your case," Jax suggested.

"My case? Am I going to jail?" Alarm weighted every word from Mrs. Tillis.

"Not right now, although I don't want you to leave town," Jax replied. "Do you know anything?"

She shook her head again. "I know the men got an old black Colonial Tourer, and they'll be out at the house around midnight. If I knew more, I'd say so."

"All right." Jax released a pent-up breath. "The only secure space I have is a cell, so you'll have to stay there until we catch them."

"Will I be near Sis?"

"You will," Jax said.

The woman agreed without demur.

After Jax led Mrs. Tillis out of his office, Bella finished her notes. When Jax—with the Jenkinses—came back, Bella studied his taut expression. "What are you planning to do?" Bella asked, although she could guess.

"Wait for Newton," Jax replied. "I want the four of us out there when they come."

"We put a call in to the restaurant. That way, we can find out if Marren and Crossley were there today," Richard added.

"Good. Newton is probably on his way back." Jax pulled his pocket watch out. "We've got some time, so we might as well sit down and try to relax."

The next thirty minutes passed slowly, except for a return call from the restaurant. The diner owner reported Marren and Crossley had eaten there and left. Soon afterward, Newton arrived with the same news.

"I didn't get any helpful information," Newton reported. "The diner owner told me where the two of them were staying right now. I headed to the boardinghouse. The landlady didn't like them and was glad they'd cleared out after lunchtime."

"I wonder where they spent the day?" Jenny asked.

"A good question," her husband replied. "Maybe scouting out their escape route."

"They won't be escaping," Jax put in.

His deputies and Richard nodded.

"Are we going in one vehicle?" Nolen asked. "There's a carriage house, but Mrs. Lackner's automobile is in it. We could fit another car in, but not two."

"That's a good point," Jax agreed. "I suppose we'll have to go together."

"With the two suspects, you won't all fit into any of your vehicles coming back." Bella allowed the observation to stand for a moment before continuing. "I could drive out and a couple of you could return with me."

"Great idea," Nolen said with unfeigned enthusiasm.

Newton quickly agreed, while Richard and Jenny, both grinning, looked on. Meanwhile, a frown furrowed Jax's forehead. "That's not necessary."

"How will all of you get back here?" Bella asked. "You could call, I suppose, and I'd come pick you up. But midnight is late for me to be on the road alone." She wanted to go along. Why wouldn't he agree? "The Ford has more room than your Chummy, and Newton's two-seater won't do at all."

Jenny put one hand to her mouth, but not before a smile bloomed. Next to his wife, Richard cleared his throat. "A good point, Arabella."

Jax's scowl deepened. Finally, he responded. "All right, but you need to park the Ford in the carriage house and stay there."

"Of course," Bella replied, not keeping a note of triumph from her voice.

"There's no reason for anyone to stay here," Richard said. "The two sisters are safely locked away, and we can secure the door to the cells along with the main door. Then, Jenny can ride along and stay with Bella."

"I'd be happy to do that," his wife said.

"What about me?" Jillian asked. "Can I go, too?"

Nolen, a grimace on his face, opened his mouth, but Bella cut him off. "Sure. Ride with Jenny and me." Laughter filled the room, although none came from the young deputy. Or from Jax.

Ninety minutes later, and an hour before midnight, the group headed to the Lackner house. Richard, Jenny, Jillian, Nolen, and Newton went together in the Jenkinses' spacious touring car. Jax rode with Bella.

As soon as she backed her Ford out of its parking place and headed out of town, Jax shifted to look at her. "Please stay in the automobile in the carriage house. We should get a jump on those two, but it's as likely as not that they'll resist arrest. I'd like to know you're not in harm's way."

"I will stay in this vehicle and use good sense," Bella agreed. "I know having me along goes against your judgment, but the building isn't close to the house."

He noticed she didn't say *better judgment,* but Jax let it slide. If he thought Bella would be in even minimal danger, he would have stood firm. Even with little risk, he might have held her off. But this would likely be their last case, and she deserved to be close-by. "You always use good sense." Almost always, but why quibble?

"Thank you. I try." Amusement softened her voice.

Jax chuckled. "I'm sure you do."

When they pulled into the Lackner drive, Bella continued to the carriage house, where the rest of the group waited. Before they climbed out, she turned to Jax. "Mrs. Marren's car being in the driveway should convince the men that the sisters are still here."

"I hope so. It's why we didn't take it to town," he replied. "We left lamps on at the back of the house for the same reason. Let's join the others."

As soon as Bella and Jax were with the group, Richard spoke. "I moved our vehicle behind the carriage house, since there was some space. It can't be seen unless someone goes back that way, and we'll nab them long before they wander."

"I bet that's where Marren and Crossley kept the old Colonial," Newton observed.

"You're most likely right," Nolen agreed.

"Yep," Jax replied. "As for tonight, they'll probably stop back here, since lights are on in the kitchen." He glanced around the dark yard. "It won't be hard for us to stay out of sight until they exit their vehicle, and we'll have the drop on them. As soon as I call out for them to put their hands in the air, I need all of you to turn on your flashlights. Once we have a good view of the pair, we should be able to arrest them. At least I hope we will."

"Mrs. Marren claimed it was Crossley who killed Mrs. Lackner," Bella pointed out. "He may give up quickly if he thinks he can avoid a murder charge. I know that's up to the prosecutor."

"It is," Richard agreed, "but mentioning the possibility might help."

"Then, I'll do it." Jax followed that statement with instructions on where each lawman should set up.

Nolen and Newton moved out first, and Richard hugged his wife before taking his place. Jenny nodded to Bella and Jax. "I'll wait completely out of sight."

When they were alone, Jax pressed a kiss to Bella's forehead. "And I'll be careful."

"I know," she murmured.

"Please stay in the carriage house until you get the all clear."

"Sure," she murmured.

"See you soon." Jax wanted to say more, but it would have to wait.

Bella returned to the Ford and took the driver's seat. Heavy shadows filled the carriage house interior, which gave the place an eerie feel. To dispel her uneasiness, Bella turned to Jenny. "Thanks for coming along. I didn't want to wait at the station."

The older woman laid a hand on Bella's arm. "I understand. I've never gotten used to waiting and worrying when I knew Richard was going to make an arrest."

"You two have been married for many years," Bella observed.

"Almost thirty, and he's been a lawman all that time. When he retired, I thought we were in the clear. Then, the war came along, and he pitched in at small departments."

"Since then, he's helped here a lot," Bella said.

"He enjoys it, and so do I. Not that I don't worry at times like this, but they have a sound plan," Jenny said, "and they're all good lawmen."

"Yes, they are," Jillian agreed, "so there's no reason to worry."

Since Bella sensed the girl might try to quell her own fears, she shifted to look at Jillian. "They are, so we shouldn't fret."

"But some anxiety is natural," Jenny put in as she also faced the youngest of the trio. "If you're considering marriage to a lawman, you need to be prepared for him to be in danger. The main thing is not to let your fear distract him."

"That seems important," Jillian replied. "Are you two a little scared?"

Since denying the obvious was foolish, Bella agreed. "I am. You both know Jax was wounded twice in France, and again last spring, during one of our investigations."

"I've heard about his injuries from Nolen," Jillian said.

"I know, too," Jenny said. "Richard was only shot once while on duty, but it scared me for months and months. Every time he walked out the door, I feared never seeing him again."

Bella leaned against the steering wheel and stared into the darkness. For a time, she forgot about the young clerk in the backseat. "I've wanted Jax to be a golf pro again, but his war wounds make that impossible. At least in his mind. He thinks he should play well, and he's hardly played at all. Mac and I agree he could work at Ballantyne as the co-pro with Griff, since we don't care about how Jax plays."

"But Jax does." Jenny made the statement.

"He does, and I understand." Bella released a pent-up breath. "I hoped the surgery would make a major difference."

"Give it time, and maybe it will," Jenny said.

"Maybe." Bella wasn't convinced, but she had no chance to ponder the idea because the sound of an automobile interrupted. As anxiety overcame her, she put a hand to her mouth. Remaining still and silent was crucial.

Outside, Jax crouched behind the front bumper of Mrs. Tillis's vehicle. Richard was at the other end, while the deputies were strategically placed near the back door and out of sight. Jax pulled his service revolver out of his pocket and waited until the two men—Marren and Crossley—moved toward the house. As far as he could tell, neither had a weapon in his hand. While Mrs. Marren insisted her husband had no guns, she might lie for him. Or not know. It was fairly certain the woman wasn't aware if Crossley did. Everything considered, Jax wasn't risking lives on uncertainty.

He let the suspects get halfway to the house before rising slightly and calling out. "Put your hands high in the air, both of you. If you've got weapons, toss them away. All four of us are armed, and we won't hesitate to shoot."

As soon as the orders were out, Nolen and Newton flipped on their flashlights and trained the beams on the two men standing stock-still in the middle of the backyard. Several moments of silence ensued, while Marren and Crossley exchanged a long look. Finally, the shorter man stuck his hands up.

The other one, tall and thin, chastised him. "I ain't giving myself up, and you'd better not, either, Marren. You're close enough for me to knife."

The stockier man stepped away. "You're the one who killed that woman. That weren't necessary, and I ain't taking the blame for you. My wife knows it was you, too, so you're on the hook. And you're stayin' there."

Clearly, the last speaker was Marren, so Jax took advantage of the man's demeanor. "You'd be wise to listen to your friend, Mr. Crossley. Killing him will only make matters worse for you. Throw the knife down and move a few feet away. Then, get your hands up. I don't want to shoot you, but you need to follow orders, or I will." For an endless period, Jax thought Crossley would test him. A breath of relief left him when the man did as he was told.

Within a few minutes, both Marren and Crossley were hand-cuffed, with rope securing their ankles, and in the Jenkinses' vehicle. Nolen and Newton, their weapons still drawn, sat with them in the backseat. Richard turned to Jax. "You riding with us or with the women?"

"With you. Let me tell Bella to go ahead of us," Jax replied. The suspects were not likely to cause trouble now, but he wanted to take every precaution. He quickly crossed to where she, Jillian, and Jenny stood just inside the carriage house door. "I suppose you heard everything."

Bella nodded. "I'm glad Mr. Marren gave up right away."

"So am I," Jax agreed. "If he hadn't, Crossley might've tried to fight us off. This way is better for everyone. I'm riding with the men, but we'd like the three of you to go ahead of us. Wait in the Ford until we get them settled inside the constable's office."

"Fine," Bella said.

After she and the other women climbed into the vehicle and headed out, Jax returned to the other automobile, got in, and sat back for the ride to town.

Within a short time, the lawmen had their suspects inside. "Where do you want to put them?" Richard asked Jax.

Jax ran a hand over his face. Weariness was overtaking him, but he still had work to do. "We should get the women out of the two cells, so the men are secure. I'll call the county sheriff and see if they have space in their jail. If so, we can transfer Mrs. Marren and the men tonight, since the sister seems like an innocent bystander."

"She does," Richard agreed. "Do you want to put her up at the hotel overnight? It's late, and her vehicle is out at the Lackner place, too."

"Good idea," Jax replied. "Let's question the men separately and go from there."

After the Marrens and Crossley were fingerprinted, Newton did more comparisons while the rest of the team watched in silence. After a few minutes, he looked up. "There's still a set that probably belonged to Mrs. Lackner, and Mrs. Marren's prints don't show up. But the men's prints match both other sets I took."

"That's great," Jax said.

"It is," Bella agreed.

Richard concurred, as did Jillian and Jenny. The fingerprints were strong evidence.

"Nolen, will you bring Mr. Marren in?" Jax asked. "Jillian, would you wait at your desk?"

"Of course," she replied.

The pair left, and Jax turned to Bella and Richard. "From what the housekeeper said, her husband got roped into thievery by Crossley. I don't know that we can believe her, but I want to start with Marren and see if he'll give us information. We can interview Crossley after him."

"I agree with you," Richard said. "With luck, one of them will tell the truth. We already have a lot of evidence, and fingerprints don't lie. Even so, a confession would ice the cake."

Newton escorted Oscar Marren, a wiry man of middle years, into the room and to the table.

"Sit down," Jax said to the suspect.

Marren took a chair and laid his manacled wrists on the table. "I ain't done nothing wrong. If my woman said different, she's lying. Nothing new there." A greasy lock of dark hair fell over one eye, but the other eye burned with resentment.

"Is there a good reason your fingerprints would be found in Mrs. Lackner's work space?" Jax maintained a calm expression and tone.

As the prisoner clasped his hands together, the handcuffs clattered against the tabletop. Bella stared in dismay. Imagining those fingers using her bridal veil as a weapon sent chills through her. Mrs. Marren claimed Crossley was the culprit, but—like Jax—Bella wasn't ready to swallow the story. To banish the disturbing image, she put pencil to paper and waited.

"My wife were her housekeeper. Of course, I visited," the man replied. "Nothin' odd about that."

Jax set his jaw before speaking again. "You went to the dressing and sewing rooms when you saw Mrs. Marren?"

"Sure, the wife always had to clean, pick up, and such," the man replied. "I helped her."

Bella made a notation before letting her gaze slide to Jax. His features were schooled, even though they both knew one of the Marrens was lying. From the start, the housekeeper had said she was not allowed in the dressmaker's work area. Others had confirmed the information, which levied suspicion on the woman's spouse.

"Very interesting." Jax leaned back and folded his arms across his chest.

In the comment's wake, silence built. Bella joined Jax and Richard in eyeing Marren, who shifted restlessly in his chair. The suspect's dark gaze darted to each figure watching him. Finally, he replied. "Nothing so interesting about it."

Another silent interlude passed before Jax responded. "Your wife never cleaned in those rooms. She never went into them at all. We've got a few people who will testify to that fact."

The color leached from Marren's ruddy complexion. "They're lying."

"Someone isn't telling the truth," Richard put in.

"Liars don't get any breaks," Jax said, "especially when they're also murderers."

Marren bowed his head. After several moments passed, he mumbled a response. "I didn't kill her. Crossley did it."

Bella glanced from Richard to Jax. Both lawmen were focused on their prisoner. While she found the man's assertions to be forthright, Bella wondered what the others thought. To her, the statements indicated the first crack in Marren's defenses. After investigating several murders, Bella knew more fissures were apt to develop.

"I'm guessing he'll say the exact opposite." Jax made the observation in the same cool, controlled voice. Nothing in his demeanor indicated an urge to close the case quickly. Only the stiff set of his shoulders gave a clue to his tension.

The same tension assailed Bella. The killers could be held in jail on the current evidence, but discovering which one murdered Mrs. Lackner was important. She had no doubt about the ultimate outcome, but Bella did not want uncertainty shadowing their double wedding ceremony. Or keeping them from traveling to Niagara Falls.

A sharp exhalation left Marren. "He will, but he'll be lying." He looked straight at Jax. "I only planned to steal from her. Ever since I hurt my back in a fall, I been without work. It ain't been easy."

"Your wife told us," Richard said. "I don't countenance theft, but I understand needing a job and not finding one. It's happened to a lot of folks these last couple of years."

"But most didn't become thieves," Jax added with a twinge of asperity.

"It were wrong," Marren admitted. "I know it were. But Mrs. Lackner had plenty. That big house, jewelry, silver. She didn't even miss the trays and bowls that my woman took. Later, I always come when she were away. Like she shoulda been that morning."

"Once you knew she was home, why didn't you leave and try another time?" Bella asked.

"That's just it. We didn't know 'til we got in the house and up the stairs. She heard us and come to the door of her showroom. Recognized us right off. When she asked what we was doing there, Cross jumped her. She fought like heck." Marren swallowed convulsively. "But he pushed her back into the room. She'd grabbed a pair of scissors before coming to see about the noise we made. They struggled for them."

"Which is how Mrs. Lackner's palms got cut up," Jax said.

"Yep," Marren agreed. "His hands didn't get no wounds, which surprised me, but he's strong. I told him we oughta tie her up, grab the jewelry, and get away as far and fast as we could. Cross said he'd bind her in the workroom, and I should slash the dresses and leave a note about canceling a wedding. That way, it'd look like someone wanted to get even with her or one bride. My missus had already told me about three weddings coming up, so it seemed like a good way to confuse things." The man glanced from Jax to Bella. "Said you two was among them. Made her nervous about doing more stealing, cuz she knew about your past cases and worried you might get on to us. Mrs. Lackner coulda told you about missing items. That's why I didn't wanna take her jewelry." Marren put his manacled hands to his face. "We were all gonna leave the area after we got that stuff, and it woulda worked if Cross hadn't been stupid. He didn't tell me about killing her until we got in the automobile."

"You took the datebook?" Jax asked.

"Yep. It were in plain sight, and Lackner noted her meeting with her husband in it," Marren replied.

"And the valuables? Where are they?" Jax's expression remained impassive, but his voice held an edge.

"All but the pin were sold," the man said.

Bella wasn't sure if she believed him, but another question arose from the recesses of her mind. "Why was mud on two of the gowns?"

"Cross did that. He hoped it'd confuse things. Plus, he's plain mean," Marren replied.

The ploy had only partially worked. "Why call and pretend to be Mrs. Lackner's first husband?" Bella asked.

"To upset her," he replied, "and to make her wonder if he was the one stealing, if she ever noticed missing items. She woulda been less likely to go to the law if she'd feared bigamy would come up. She told my missus about her man going off to war and never being found. Said he had to be dead, or so she figured when she got married again. Her not knowing for sure give us a way to keep her quiet about the telephone calls. She weren't too sure at first, but my wife give me details that most folks wouldn't have known. That helped."

Clever plotting and perfidious actions had put Mrs. Lackner at a distinct disadvantage. Little wonder the dressmaker had said marriage was not for her. Even though her second husband was undisputedly dead, the humiliation of marrying while her first spouse was alive would have been a burden. Sadness for the woman filled Bella's heart. Mrs. Lackner had suffered great losses in her life, only to have it end in murder.

"So, she might've realized someone was stealing from her," Jax said, "and been too worried about what might come out to let me know."

A half-shrug lifted one of Marren's shoulders. "Could be."

As she considered the dressmaker's anxiety over the previous few weeks, Bella figured Mrs. Lackner had become increasingly anxious about the calls and the thefts. Anxious enough to confide in her housekeeper. Despite her protestations, Mrs. Marren had known exactly how to manipulate and rob her employer. Maybe the woman did not countenance the killing, but she hadn't been honest about what happened, either.

Jax wrapped up with a few questions about the actual murder and its immediate aftermath before sending Marren back to his cell. Richard escorted the prisoner, leaving Bella and Jax alone.

"You look pale," he said to her. "I know hearing the details has to upset you."

"It's not much different from our previous cases, as far as information. But thinking about Mrs. Lackner realizing she was being robbed, wondering if Brad Farber was involved, and fearing what would happen if he revealed himself...it's awful."

"It is," Jax agreed.

"She must've thought Farber wanted to get even with her for sending him off to war without a word. We know she regretted it later, especially after she got word of his probable death. Then, to discover he might be alive..." Her voice trailed off as emotion overtook Bella.

Jax lightly clasped her hand. "I know. It's terrible. Even worse, she confided in Mrs. Marren, who used the knowledge to further the theft ring."

"The housekeeper acts like the murder upset her, but I'm not sure if it's Mrs. Lackner's death or them getting caught." Bella grimaced. "That sounds awful."

"But valid," he replied.

Regret flickered through Bella like a flame, refusing to be doused. "I never looked beneath her surface, so she had me convinced about being a loyal employee."

"Mrs. Marren didn't want anyone to suspect her of guile, let alone robbery. Remember how she acted when we first interviewed her? Tears in her eyes. Hardly able to speak." Jax huffed out a quick breath. "It wasn't until we dug deeper that some cracks showed. Even then, she kept up a decent front. Finding the letters was a boon."

Richard's return interrupted the conversation, and Jax released Bella's hand. The older man grinned. "A betrothed couple can hold hands."

Whatever Bella or Jax might have said was cut off when Nolen led Crossley into the room. The man, tall and lean, stood still until Jax gestured to the chair recently vacated by Marren. "Take a seat."

After he sat down, Crossley stared straight at Jax. "I suppose Marren and his woman told a pack of lies about me. She never liked me, and he ain't able to stand up for himself. Tied to her apron strings."

"I'm not revealing what either said, but we want to ask you some questions," Jax replied.

Crossley slumped back in the chair. "Go ahead."

"What were you doing at the Lackner house tonight?" Jax voiced the query in the same measured voice he had used with his questions to Marren.

"Marren wanted to visit with his wife," the prisoner replied. "I rode along."

"We heard he called her sister's place and found out she was staying there," Jax said.

"He lied," Crossley shot back.

"We didn't hear it from him," Bella put in.

The man turned his pale gaze on her as his lips formed a sneer. "Another female sticking her nose into men's business. Oughta be at home, where a woman belongs."

"The world is changing, Mr. Crossley," Bella shot back. "Women can do a lot of different jobs now."

"They certainly can," Jax added, "and you'd best keep a civil tongue when you address Miss Stewart."

Crossley returned his focus to Jax. Before the man could reply, Richard spoke.

"Miss Stewart is an excellent detective and an important part of our team. Treat her as such, son." Richard kept his gaze on the prisoner.

When Crossley spoke again, he failed to comment on the warnings from Jax and Richard. "I dunno who told you that, but I thought he was going to see his wife."

"Doubtful," Jax said, "but a more pertinent question is, why were your fingerprints found in Mrs. Lackner's house?"

Every trace of arrogance left Crossley's expression. He swallowed convulsively before clearing his throat. "Coulda been planted."

Bella stared at Crossley. Surely, the man knew better. But maybe he didn't realize playing dumb would not help.

"Impossible to do." Jax drummed his fingers on the tabletop. "We already know you and Marren stole things when Mrs. Lackner was out of the house."

When Crossley laid his hands on the table, the jangle of his handcuffs drew Bella's attention. Although thin, the man had heavily muscled forearms and beefy hands. Both indicated enough strength to wield the veil as a weapon. Her gaze traveled to his long fingers, where a few slight cuts were visible. "I'd like to see your palms," she said.

The prisoner sent her an angry glare. Before he could open his mouth, Jax jumped in.

"Do as Miss Stewart wants." Authority undergirded Jax's words.

Slowly, Crossley agreed to the edict. When he did, more minute slashes were evident.

"How did you get injured?" Jax turned back to the man.

As Crossley's breathing became fast and shallow, his gaze fell to his upturned hands. He stared at them as if an answer would appear. Long moments passed before he found his voice. "Doing odd jobs."

"Those are fresh. Where have you been working this week?" Richard asked.

The prisoner sneered. "Over near Marion."

"Exactly where, and who hired you?" Jax tried this time.

Crossley shrugged. "I don't pay no attention to names. Work a day or two, get paid, and move on."

"You know where you were," Bella observed.

"Don't much care, since I won't be going back." A chortle left him.

217

Jax rested his elbows on the table. "Maybe you can answer this question: how would your fingerprints get in Mrs. Lackner's lower attic?"

"Marren and I remodeled those two rooms for her work area," the suspect shot back.

"You went into the closet and up to the attic during that time?" Jax asked. "Why?"

Crossley glared at Jax. "To see if there was usable materials for remodeling."

"While you were up there, you also handled framed photographs?" Bella inquired.

The man's bearded jaw dropped before he regained his composure. "She had some laying out."

"These were packed away, but the surrounding paper was disturbed. Deputy Rogers could get good prints. Prints that match the ones we took of you tonight." Jax stared straight at the man, who bowed his head. "Nothing to say, Crossley?"

Bella held her breath. The fingerprints had been compared quickly and, although they looked quite similar, further work would need to be done for them to be powerful evidence in court. Jax had been careful not to disseminate details, but he'd dangled enough information to, with luck, trap Crossley.

"All right. We was both up there, cuz Marren's woman said some valuables was stored in that area. We went through the boxes in front first," Crossley replied.

"Before or after you killed her?" Jax asked.

Crossley slumped forward and hung his head. "We was gonna grab more silver and some jewelry. Lackner shoulda been out of the house. But she were in her bedroom on the other side of the wall. She heard us and come over."

"And you killed her." Bella made the assertion.

"She got nasty. Said she'd see both Marren, and me put away for good. I been in the slammer a couple times already, and I ain't going back. I didn't plan to kill her, but she fought hard. Real hard." When he pushed his hand forward so that his shirt sleeves bunched up a bit, scratches were obvious. "She used her nails on me. That's what set me off. That and her caterwauling. I told Marren to grab something to shut her up, and he handed me that long veil."

"Then, the two of you finished robbing her, destroyed the dresses, wrote the note to make it look like some disgruntled person was involved—an unhappy customer, a spurned suitor, or someone like that." Jax made the assertions with obvious abhorrence.

"Weren't nothing else for us to do," Crossley said. "If the woman had gone to the meeting place, she wouldn't have been in our way. Foolish of her."

The man's lack of remorse was appalling. Once she regained her equilibrium, Bella analyzed the statements. If Mrs. Lackner had struggled and screamed, Mr. Marren would have heard her. If so, how could he not have suspected what was going on? Not that she had sympathy for him or his wife. Both were criminals.

While Jax and Richard interrogated Crossley in greater depth, Bella took notes. When the senior constable finally led the killer out, she felt the tension seep away.

Jax laid one hand over hers. "I didn't think he'd admit to the murder, but I'm glad he did. Although with the fingerprints and other evidence we have him dead to rights, a confession will make the process quicker."

"Will Mr. Marren be charged as an accessory to murder?"

"That's up to the prosecutor, but I'd say it's likely. As far as Mrs. Marren, she definitely merits robbery charges, and she helped conceal the crime," Jax said. "Since Richard and I both believed Mrs. Tillis saying she knew nothing until this evening, I imagine she's in the clear." Jax's green gaze narrowed on Bella. "You said little in that regard."

"She seemed genuinely shocked and upset, so I agree. How long will you keep her at the hotel?"

"Newton can follow her home in the morning, but I wanted to keep her here until we talked to the men."

Richard's return interrupted their conversation. "Crossley is in a cell."

"I'd like to get the men and Mrs. Marren to the county jail yet this evening," Jax said. "We'll need to wrap up, which I'd also like to do tonight."

"A good plan," Richard said.

An hour later, the Moreley deputies returned from their task. "You didn't have any trouble getting the Marrens and Crossley to the county lockup?" Jax asked Nolen and Newton.

Both shook their heads, and Newton replied, "Mrs. Marren complained at the start, but getting them settled wasn't an issue."

"There's plenty of space over there, with a separate area for women," Nolen added, "and guards all night."

"It's the best place for them," Newton put in. "More security than any local jail can offer."

"Agreed," Jax said. Keeping the inmates in Moreley was not feasible, since only two cells existed. In previous cases, space had not been a concern. He hoped it wouldn't be in the future, either.

"The sheriff scanned the report," Nolen said, "and it's in excellent order."

Jax glanced from Jillian, who sat at her desk, to Bella, who stood beside him. "That's due to outstanding work from the two of you. Putting all the details together was an onerous task."

"Not so bad for me," Bella replied. "Jillian typed everything up, and we went over it together. She added everything from Nolen's and Newton's work at the scene."

"You'd already done a lot, going on interviews and sorting through the trunks and crates," the young clerk replied. "And you organized the information very well."

"Everything is in good order," Richard agreed.

"We only have a few loose ends to tie up. Let's get word out first thing tomorrow about Charley and Abner no longer being under suspicion." Jax turned to his deputies. "How about the two of you talking to them after they surface? It'd be good if you mention how their past behavior put them under scrutiny. Maybe that, and some serious discussion about doing the right things, will keep them both on the straight and narrow."

The deputies agreed on all counts.

"Thanks," Jax replied. "You've both done wonderful work on this case."

"The sheriff mentioned how much Nolen's photographs will help. The fingerprints are big, too," Newton added.

As Jax listened to the exchange, pride swelled his heart. His team was proficient, professional, and collegial. No one hogged the credit, and they worked together beautifully—even as exhausted as they all had to be.

"It seems like everything is wrapped up, for now at least," Bella observed.

"Yep," Jax agreed. "We won't have more to do until the three suspects go to trial, which won't be right away."

"Thank goodness," Jillian said with a grin. "Your wedding is in a few days."

"Yes, it is." Jax turned to Bella. "You ought to go home and rest."

"Everyone should," she replied.

"Since my mother is spending the night at Ballantyne, Richard and I will head to your house, Jax," Jenny said.

After the Jenkinses left, Nolen turned to Jillian. "I'll take you to your place."

"Good. I called my aunt a while back to say I was working late, but she may wait up," the young clerk replied.

"All three of you should get going," Jax said to his staff. After they said their goodbyes, he turned to Bella. "I'll follow you to Ballantyne."

"You'll be out tomorrow?" she asked. "We can have the supper we planned for last night. It'll be one of the last evenings of quiet, since some of our guests arrive on Thursday."

"I'll be there," he assured her. Jax needed some quiet time alone with her. Time to discuss their future.

Chapter Eleven

Wednesday morning, Jax called Bella with news about Bradley Farber. Richard's friend had dug deep into the Spanish-American War files and found several informal reports that Farber had succumbed to yellow fever. Since he had been nursed by locals, the information had never been marked as official, or shared with his widow.

That evening, Bella and Jax, along with Ida and Griff, joined family, a few friends, and staff at dinner in the inn's expansive dining room. Although the setting was formal, the atmosphere was relaxed. Warmth filled Bella as she observed the gathering. How fortunate she was to have wonderful people join in the celebration of her marriage to Jax. They were missing out on supper alone, but they would make up for that soon.

Following the meal, Mac and Ida's father ushered the gentlemen into the library, while the ladies adjourned to the family quarters. After a half-hour, the men joined them. More casual conversation ensued.

When the grandfather clock in the lobby struck ten o'clock, Mrs. Byington suggested they all seek their beds. She smiled at the brides. "Perhaps you two will see your fiancés out."

Gratitude filled Bella, who wanted a few moments with Jax before he left for town. Ida and Griff chose the loveseat facing the lobby hearth, so Bella suggested she and Jax stay in the family suite.

"Do you want me to build up the fire?" he asked.

"No, we should both get rest, so I won't keep you long." She patted the place beside her on the sofa. "Tomorrow will be busy getting ready for more guests arriving. We're having a big dinner in the evening, and I want to check all the details beforehand."

With one hand, he stroked her cheek. "You have help. Mr. and Mrs. Byington, Mrs. Rogers, and Mac can handle any last-minute issues, along with the rest of your staff. Let them do most of the work."

A soft sigh escaped her. "You're right. I'm so used to double-checking all events here. It's what I do the last thing at night and first thing in the morning. I'm so glad we aren't having other weddings here soon."

"It's a lovely setting," Jax said, "but the mayor is happy with his niece marrying at his home."

"And he never needs to know she was a suspect." Bella chuckled.

"No, he doesn't," Jax replied. "I doubt if Vera Placette will say any more. I ran into her father this afternoon, and he apologized for her behavior."

"Did he say what they're doing about Vera's dress?"

"She'll be wearing her mother's gown, and Mrs. Placette is wearing her Christmas dance attire."

"It was lovely, as I recall. But what about the attendants?"

"One of Vera's cousins married last year. Her sisters and Vera were in the wedding, so those outfits are also being modified for the bridesmaids. Mr. Placette shared Vera isn't happy, but he's willing to give the young couple a down payment for a house, if she stops grousing."

"A smart man." The conversation reminded Bella of their living arrangements. "Are you sure about living here instead of at your house?"

Jax moved his hand to grasp hers. "I have something I want to tell you related to our future and my work."

The solemnity in his tone and expression sent anxiety prickling along Bella's nerves. He had promised not to go back to the Prohibition Bureau. Had he changed his mind? Wouldn't he have discussed it with her before now? Would yet another obstacle stand between them? "What?"

"Something good. At least I think you'll like the idea. Maybe I should've asked you before talking to Mac."

Her pulse sped up. "What did you talk about with Mac?"

He exhaled sharply. "You know, I saw the surgeon in Toledo last week."

She nodded. "And you got an excellent report, didn't you?"

"I did, and you know Griff and I were gone a few times since then. Up until the murder."

She nodded. "You two weren't clear on exactly where or why." The excuses about them being absent had not been clear, but Bella had so much else on her mind that seeking details hadn't been a priority. Besides, she and Ida had wondered if their fiancés were planning surprises for them. "It wasn't for more follow-up with the surgeon, was it?" Anxiety crept into her voice. Was something else wrong?

"No. The surgeon is pleased, and so am I. It turned out that the original diagnosis wasn't right as far as my bicep trouble. I can give you the anatomical details, but it turns out the problem was easily fixed. Anyhow, since Griff went along with me, and the weather was pleasant, we made a stop on the way back that day we went to Toledo."

Confusion clouded Bella's mind. "I know. To talk with a friend."

"It was my old boss at Crystal Lakes."

"Why didn't you say so? I know him."

A moment's hesitation preceded his reply. "Because we didn't just talk, we played golf." A slight smile played across his lips. "I need a lot of practice, but I got some last week, when Griff and I played again. Several times. We agreed my game can be salvaged, although I'll probably never be a dominant player again. That being said, I won't embarrass myself or, more importantly, you."

With her heart pounding in her ears, Bella tightened her hold on his hand. "What are you saying?"

"I'm saying I can play decently enough to be a golf pro again, if you'll hire me."

Bella threw her arms around his shoulders. When he held her close, she relaxed against him. "Oh, Jax, is that what you and Mac discussed?"

"It is, because I wanted his opinion. Are you upset I didn't come to you first?" He pulled back and narrowed his gaze. "I wanted to surprise you."

She gazed at his beloved face. "I'm not upset. I'm surprised and excited. But are you sure you want to give up being a law-man?"

"Very sure. It hasn't been terrible, but I don't love it. Not like I love golf." He ran his fingers through her glossy brunette bob. "And not nearly as much as I love you."

Her tummy did funny flip-flops. "I love you, too, but I don't want you to take the job here because it's what I want. You need to want that."

"Believe me, I do." His hand cupped her chin. "What about you? My return to golf as a career will mean an end to our sleuthing."

"I suppose it will," Bella replied. "I enjoyed detective work, but I won't mind focusing on the resort. And having you here as a golf pro is a dream come true for both of us."

"It's not quite the dream I had as a boy, because I'll be working with Griff instead of Matt." His voice was rough with suppressed emotion.

As bittersweet memories swept through Bella, she glanced at the mantel where a photo of her brother, Jax, and herself held a prominent place. When Jax's gaze followed hers, she felt him release her and turn toward the hearth. "This picture wasn't here before."

"I moved it from my suite. You said yours got battered from going to war with you."

"It did."

For a while, Jax stared at the picture. "That was a happy day, and I thought many more would follow."

The image had been captured after Jax and Matt won their first Ballantyne four-ball tournament, when the pair was eighteen. "The two of you won again, more than once."

"We did, and I thought that would continue indefinitely." A wistful note entered his voice.

A shuddering breath left Bella. "All of us did."

"I miss him." Jax shifted to face her. "I know you do, too. And your parents. Especially with our wedding on Saturday."

When he put an arm around her shoulders, Bella laid her head on his chest. "I keep thinking about all of them and your parents, too. I wish they were here, but I'm lucky Mac will give me away and even luckier you and I will be together for the rest of our lives." She didn't keep her emotion out of her voice.

Her girlhood dream was coming true, although not as she'd imagined years ago.

"We will be, and it's my goal to make sure you're happy all those years."

"And vice versa."

For several moments, silence filled the room. Finally, Jax broke it. "It's good we didn't move many of your things to my house, since we'd be moving them back after our honeymoon."

A sudden realization hit her. "What will you do with your place? You mentioned renting or selling."

"I don't think Nolen will mind if I reveal he and Jillian are betrothed." Jax grinned. "They told me earlier today. They're waiting until after our wedding to announce it. Since neither of them have much family, the ceremony will be small and maybe as soon as next month."

"How wonderful," Bella replied. "I'm so happy for them. Are they going to buy your house?"

"If Nolen gets the constable's job, which he should. If not, I'll rent it to them."

"Everything is falling into place for all of us." Pleasure and gratitude rippled through Bella.

"It is. Now, we only need to decide what rooms you and I will share. Your suite or the family quarters?"

Bella looked around the room. The quarters had a parlor, a lavatory, and three bedrooms. Two were small, since she and Matt had used them as children. Later, they had both taken suites on the third-floor. But this area had been the family hub. Although the kitchen next door had served the inn and the Stewarts, there was a table for private dining, along with the cozy grouping of furniture near the hearth. While her personal accommodation provided ample space for one, it might not suit a couple, which she and Jax would be by this time on Saturday. "Down here is probably better. It'll need some sprucing up, since no one has lived in it since my parents died." She shifted to face him. "What about the furniture in your house? What do you want to bring?"

"Only a few personal items. Nolen and Jillian will need furniture. If they rent or buy my house, I'll leave most of it for them."

"I'm sure they'd appreciate it." When the chiming of the grandfather clock in the lobby interrupted, Bella shifted to sit straight up. "It's getting late, and we have big days ahead."

Jax stood before reaching out and pulling Bella up. "I can hardly believe we're finally getting married. For a long time, I didn't think we'd ever overcome the gap between us. I didn't even dare to hope."

Bella laid her free hand on his chest and felt the steady, strong beat of his heart. "No gap now, and there never will be again." She lifted her head and brushed a feather-soft kiss across his lips. "Until tomorrow." Bella stepped away and reluctantly watched him leave the room.

On Saturday morning, Bella and Ida took turns in each other's suites. Mrs. Byington, Mrs. Rogers, Jenny Jenkins, and Jillian joined them to help. As the time of the ceremonies grew closer and closer, Bella's excitement escalated. Soon, she and Jax would be husband and wife.

Thirty minutes before the wedding, the other women left. Bella studied her reflection in the tall mirror. Although deeply sorry about Mrs. Lackner's murder, she loved her mother's dress. The shimmering white gown had a lacy flounce at the bodice and matching cuffs on the long sleeves. Bella loved the way they flowed over her hands.

The dress worn by Ida's mother was similar. Their headwear was alike, too. After seeing her veil used as a weapon, Bella had not wanted another one. Briefly, she considered a hat but quickly finding a dressy one to match the gown proved difficult. Before Ida's parents had left to pick up flowers, Bella had suggested crowns of the blooms and received enthusiastic agreement from both Byington women. When she and Ida opened the boxes to find red and white roses, they were enchanted. Now, looking at her reflection, Bella thought the entire ensemble was perfect, and her parents would approve. So would her brother. Bella still wished they could be with her, but none of them were ever far from her mind, and they were always in her heart. They always would be.

A knock at the door interrupted her, and she opened it to see Mac, resplendent in his best suit, standing in the hall. His wizened face lit with a broad smile.

"Ye look lovely, lass," he said, in a thick voice barely cloaking his own emotions.

"You look quite dapper yourself," she replied.

His grin widened. "I dinna spruce up often, but today be most special." He took her hand and tucked it into the crook of his arm. "Be ye ready to wed Jackson?"

Her heart fluttered. "I am ready. I hope he is, too."

Mac's gray gaze sparkled. "He, Griff, and their best man be downstairs in my suite. They all be ready, particularly ye groom." His expression became serious. "Ye two have waited a long time for this day."

"We have, but nothing will part us now." She chewed on her lower lip. "Thank you for giving me away, Mac. I can't explain how much it means to me."

He patted her hand where it lay on his arm. "'Tis my honor and privilege to escort ye down the aisle, lass."

Moisture pricked at Bella's eyes, and she blinked hard to keep it at bay. The appearance of Ida and Mr. Byington got Bella back on track.

Mr. Byington, tall and stately in his well-tailored attire, smiled. "You girls look beautiful."

Ida squeezed her father's arm. "I already told Dad how handsome he looks. You're very spiffy, too, Mac."

The Scotsman winked. "Thank ye, lass."

After clearing his throat, Ida's father spoke again. "It's almost time, so we best head to the top of the staircase. Your little cousins and Jillian should be there already."

The quartet made their way to the second-floor landing. Lilly, Ida's seven-year-old cousin, held a basket of roses, greens, and ribbon, while her twin brother carried a pillow with the rings loosely attached. Jillian, resplendent in her dress, stood next to the children. "We're ready," she said. "The twins' mother asked me to signal when you two are. She'll give the high sign for music to Mrs. Smedlay."

The best friends looked at one another. In unison, they replied, "We are."

Although she was eager to marry Jax, Bella felt a flutter of nerves as she watched the others descend the long, wide stairway. When Ida and her father got to the end of the staircase, they turned toward the large parlor where guests had gathered. Strains of Mendelssohn's wedding march reached Bella as she watched her friend disappear into the doorway.

"It be time, lass," Mac said.

Bella nodded and moved down the flight of stairs. When they reached the archway, she looked at the end of the parlor, where the minister stood in front of the fireplace. On the left, Ida—her face aglow—waited while on the right, Griff, his attention on his bride-to-be, stood with the best man, but Bella's attention riveted on Jax, who looked more handsome than ever in his dark suit, crisp white shirt, and maroon tie. She realized the moment he caught sight of her, because his eyes grew wide and his lips curved into a smile. When the music again sounded, this time for her, Bella gripped Mac's arm tighter and moved forward. The closer she got to Jax, the less nervous she felt. For what seemed like an eternity, Bella simply gazed at his beloved face. She barely noted when her friend and Griff exchanged vows but experienced a surge of elation when it was her turn. Their turns. Every word was etched on her heart and soul and, when Jax slipped the gold band on her finger, Bella experienced an outpouring of joy—joy that was reflected in his grass green eyes.

After the minister said, "You may now kiss your brides," Jax leaned down to feather his lips across hers.

He lifted his head a fraction. "I love you, Bella Stewart Hastings, and I'll spend the rest of my life showing you."

"We'll spend the rest of our lives showing each other," she promised.

As the music again filled the room, Bella slipped her hand into the crook of Jax's arm. He lightly clasped her fingers with his and, together, they walked up the aisle and into their future.

About the Author

D.S. Lang started making up stories to entertain herself as an only child, and she is still making them up. Now, she puts them in writing. Her mysteries are set after the Great War in smalltown America. The female amateur sleuths are dedicated to cracking cases and catching the bad guys and gals.

After earning Bachelor's and Master's degrees in education, D.S. worked as a golf shop manager, teacher (junior high, high school, and college), program manager, tutor, and mentor. She has a lifelong love of history and often gets sidetracked on research when she should be writing.

When she is away from the computer, D.S. enjoys reading, swimming, spending time with family and friends, and walking her dog Izzy.

D.S. LANG

Thank You!

Thank you for reading <u>An Uncertain Ceremony!</u> I hope you enjoyed the story. If you have time, please rate or review it. Comments from readers are helpful and appreciated. I am on Goodreads and BookBub. Most retailers also accept reviews.

https://www.goodreads.com/author/show/21325652.D_S_Lang

For more information, please go to my website, Facebook, and/or Instagram pages.

https://www.dslangbooks.com

https://www.facebook.com/profile.php?id=100064024056297

https://www.instagram.com/dslangbooks/

You can sign up for my newsletter on my website, and you will receive access to free short story prequels. In my monthly newsletter, I share links to other authors' work, news about my books, a peek into the writing life, historical tidbits, and more. Your email will never be shared, and you unsubscribe at time!

Books in the Arabella Stewart Historical Mystery Series

For more information on the series, please visit https://www.
dslangbooks.com